# SECRETS OF A HIDDEN TRAIL

## Bridgett Jackson

Bridgett Jackson 4/13/07

PUBLISH AMERICA

PublishAmerica
Baltimore

First printing

At the specific preference of the author, PublishAmerica allowed this work to remain exactly as the author intended, verbatim, without editorial input.

ISBN: 1-4137-8290-6
PUBLISHED BY PUBLISHAMERICA, LLLP
www.publishamerica.com
Baltimore

Printed in the United States of America

# DEDICATIONS

This book is especially dedicated to my two wonderful children who have inspired me and encouraged me throughout their entire lives. You make life an exciting adventure and fill every day with love. Thank you for sharing your lives with me.

In addition, dedicated to my husband and partner in life, whose love and unwavering faith makes everything impossible seem reachable. Thank you for believing in the possibilities.

Many thanks also, to my parents for giving me the opportunity to live in such a wonderful corner of the world and for providing love and support through the years.

# ACKNOWLEDGEMENTS

Many thanks to the people of Monroe County, especially the Tellico Plains and Coker Creek area who carry on the rich traditions of the mountains in East Tennessee.

Special thanks to the many friends and relatives who contributed to the development of the book by contributing stories, information and reading the manuscript many times during the editing process.

My deepest appreciation goes to Kat Dalton for her contributions to the cover design for this book. Her creative work as an artist and love for the mountains are evident in everything she does.

Also, many thanks to the Tellico Plains Press for writing the many current and historical articles provided in their publication on the Southern Appalachian region.

# CONTENTS

# Cabin in the Woods

She smiled and snuggled a little deeper under several layers of quilts as the morning sun began to creep into her eyes. The sweet fragrance of spring flowers drifted through the window left ajar during the night and filled the cabin with the promise that spring had arrived. This was Maggie's favorite time of day although she dearly loved everything about her life on the mountain. The beautiful sunrise that made the mountains seem to rise out of the misty clouds started her days. Rich colorful sunsets basked the mountains around her with deep hues of red and purple and seemed to make the mountains glow with mystery. At night, she loved the moon and stars. It was easy to feel as if a person could touch the stars with no city lights anywhere on the mountain to hide their glow. This was her little corner of paradise, a place where she felt safer than any place on earth.

After a 20-year career with the social work agency, Maggie finally decided to hang up her career and return to the place she always dreamed of living. For years she joked with coworkers and the little flock of children she worked with that, she would some day move to the last mountain from nowhere. So, when she finally had her fill of work with the agency and all of the needy people she served, she returned to the one place where she felt she could disappear from the world. Here, she felt she could erase some of the painful images she saw through the years and spend time renewing her soul.

Maggie lived in a very remote section of the highest portion of the Appalachian Mountains most of her life with her grandmother in a small ancient log cabin. After the death of her grandmother, Maggie lived and worked in the city until she could save enough money to move back home and live on the mountain she cherished in her grandmother's log homestead.

Maggie grew up watching her grandmother tend to the sick and needy people on the mountain whenever they needed help. Everyone seemed to know they could come to her grandmother when they were sick for an herbal cure, help with a problem or even if they needed food or clothing. Her grandmother seemed to know just what to do in every situation. Her grandmother inspired Maggie as she grew up. Watching her work with people was the driving inspiration that helped Maggie through graduate school and into work with the social work agency. Maggie wanted to continue her grandmother's work in her own life.

Yet, work and life in the city was completely different from life on the mountain. It became more and more difficult for Maggie to renew her spirit in the city and there always seemed to be a never-ending stream of people who needed help. The intense work with people in crisis continued for almost twenty years until Maggie decided to sell everything she owned and return to the sanctuary of the mountains where she could enjoy being alone. The stress of working with people who were under extreme duress and often in fragile situations left her tired and emotionally drained. In the city, she never seemed to be able to find the time or appropriate place to nurture herself and rebuild her inner strength.

Maggie's goal to return to the mountains she loved was a beacon of light that guided almost everything she did during her career. With the completion of the Cherohala Skyway between Tennessee and North Carolina, the area where she lived with her grandmother was finally a little more accessible. When Maggie was able to save enough money for the minimal living expenses, she returned to her grandmother's homestead and finally accomplished her lifelong dream.

Maggie rolled over and smiled when suddenly, a great commotion outside the cabin roused her from a dreamy half-sleep. The sound of Max's deep bark echoed through the crisp morning air. Maggie slowly stretched, then shuffled to the front porch in her cotton gown. She opened the door to see Max thrash around the woods in hot pursuit of a groundhog. Max was all dog. He reveled in the chase. It never seemed to matter what he was chasing, he simply loved the pursuit and was very good at it.

Maggie watched the commotion as each time Max discovered the groundhog's hiding place, the groundhog boldly stood up to face him, bared its teeth and hissed loudly in defiance. At times, he even lunged at Max, gnashed his teeth and slashed his front paws towards his attacker. He did everything within his powers to protect himself and his den. Max seemed to smile at the ferocious, yet feeble efforts of the groundhog.

*They remind me of people,* Maggie thought, *the aggressors and the defenders of the world. Guess there is not much difference in the animal and the human worlds after all. They are each doing what comes naturally. Kind of puts some of the human animals I've known in perspective.* Maggie watched the battle continue.

The groundhog was huge. From the porch, he looked like he must weigh twenty-five pounds or more. His soft brown fur seemed to ripple and shine as he waddled through the field undaunted by Max's advances. Halfway across the field, he must have sensed the need for urgency as Max circled closer and closer with each attack. Suddenly, the groundhog abandoned his hope for a successful battle, made a mad dash for his den and disappeared down a hole in the ground.

Maggie watched as Max attempted to plunge in after him and began to dig deeply into the den. Dirt flew all around him as he used his size and strength to pry the hole to the ground hog's den open. His massive body quivered as his head and shoulders disappeared into the ground. His enormous tail made huge clockwise sweeps that seemed to propel him as he dug deeper and deeper into the ground.

Max, short for Maximum Canine, was a tiny ball of fur when he was a puppy, yet, he continued to grow until he became the largest dog Maggie had ever seen. The pup of a Newfoundland and a Great Pyrenees, Max was solid muscle, weighing in at 135 pounds.

An old mountain man who had been a friend of Maggie's since she was a child gave Max to her when she moved back home to her grandmother's cabin a few years ago. Max was only six weeks old when Digger left him on the doorstep with a big red ribbon tied around his neck. Maggie tried to refuse the gift at the time; the last thing she wanted was more responsibilities. Yet, despite Maggie's protests, Digger seemed to know just what Maggie needed even before she did and left Max anyway. They quickly became devoted companions and now were almost inseparable.

When Maggie first came home to the mountains, she just wanted to be alone. She did not intend to have contact with another living soul. Maggie spent so many years dealing with the pain and suffering of humanity she simply wanted to seek solace and comfort in the sanctuary of her beloved mountains and be - alone! Digger knew this would not be good for Maggie.

He gave Max to her partially to keep her company, and partially as a way of making sure she was safe when she was alone on the mountain. Over the years, Max proved to be a constant companion and loyal defender. She had no doubt he would sacrifice his life defending her if anyone tried to hurt her. One of his favorite activities was to accompany her on her many treks through the woods when she hiked the trails that wound up and down the mountain ridges in the National Forrest near her home. His role as guardian and protector was evident with every move he made on their hikes.

For most people, Max looked ferocious because of his enormous size and solid black color. Even more intimidating than his size, was his deep baritone bark, which resounded through their little mountain paradise sending chills through anyone who did not know him. Maggie did not make it common knowledge that he was a teddy bear at heart. He loved to give sloppy wet kisses to all her friends and often tried to crawl into the lap of anyone who did not mind an awkward 135-pound bundle of fur on them.

Maggie stepped gingerly down the dirt path to the sparkling stream that gurgled in the woods along the side of the cabin. Here by the water, the rich aromas of the earth filled her senses. The moist ground, damp leaves and fresh spring grass all filled her with the essence of spring. She tried to define each fragrance as she breathed in slowly. The musky smell of damp maple and oak leaves hung under the trees. Delicate wisps of honeysuckle and jasmine floated through the air from new spring blossoms that grew on the fence near the stream. Even the smell of sunshine on the damp stones by the stream brought wonderful memories and sensations to her mind. She breathed in deeply to draw the renewal of the year into her soul. Each breath seemed to recharge her spirit.

She watched as the sun shone on the sparkling water and realized again, how much she loved this place. She felt as though her very soul belonged here on this mountain. The temptation of the water as it gurgled and danced over the stones was too inviting to pass by. Maggie gathered up the end of her gown and tiptoed across the stones in the water until she was in the middle of the stream. The water was so cold. A fine mist rose off the water as Maggie stood on a moss-covered stone. Closing her eyes, she lifted her arms to the sky, took in a deep breath and whispered her morning blessings as she began her meditations.

She did not hear Max charge toward the stream. When he suddenly realized Maggie came down from the cabin to the stream, he forgot all about his pursuit of the ground hog. He immediately leaped and bounded through the woods to greet her. He plowed through the middle of the stream and created huge wakes of water that splashed over everything in his path.

The shock of the cold water upon Max's sudden arrival startled Maggie and caused her to suddenly loose her balance and plunge into the stream. Icy hot needles of pain seared through her body as the frigid waters rushed over her. The water was so cold it burned. She let out a startled scream and gulped for air.

"Maaxxx!!!" she yelled.

She tried to get back up as quickly as she could, irritated with the cold water and the disruption of her peaceful morning meditations. The crisp morning air felt freezing now that she was so wet. She gasped for a breath as the water swirled and splashed around her. Max decided the new game was wonderful and had a delightful time as he splashed and bounced all around her. She laughed and splashed him back until finally; he calmed down enough for her to make it out of the water.

Maggie ran quickly towards the cabin. Her thin cotton gown clung to her skin as she ran. She slipped and fell just as she came out of the woods, tumbled onto the soft path in front of the cabin and covered her gown with dirt and leaves.

*Good grief, what a way to start the morning,* she told herself as she pulled the wet gown over her head while she ran. Max leaped and bounced along the path beside her, thrilled that Maggie came out to play so early in the day. Maggie could not help but laugh at him and his playfulness.

"You'd better be glad we live in the mountains instead of in town, Max. I'm sure we would raise a few eyebrows if we started a commotion like this in town." Max seemed perfectly content as he followed along beside her and wagged his tail.

By the time Maggie reached the house her whole body shivered uncontrollably. She jumped into a steamy, hot shower and tried to recover from the shock caused by the frigid water. Her skin tingled from the warmth of the shower. Her fingers still felt as though a million tiny hot needles were pricking them. Maggie stayed in the shower until her skin did not look quite so blue and she was able to regain a warm feeling in her body again.

She put on her favorite sweatshirt and jeans and sat down to enjoy a pot of hot tea. It felt good to be warm again. She smiled as she watched Max basking in the early spring sun. Exhausted from his morning adventures, his shiny black coat glistened in the sun as he lay in the new spring grass. In the distance, the groundhog looked as though he was re-arranging his den. He seemed to be chattering to himself as he made frequent trips into his den and back out again.

Maggie smiled as she watched them. "You and I have a lot in common, little ground hog. We both had to face some formidable forces in our lives, but we both do what we have to do no matter what the odds are. Then, we usually have to clean up the mess when the big guys are gone."

After the morning's brisk plunge in the stream and the hot shower, Maggie was finally ready to begin her day. She walked over to the fireplace, stooped and pulled the kindling box away from the stonework around the fireplace. She then tugged at a loose stone near the bottom of the stonework.

As the stone pulled free of the fireplace, Maggie reached into a small crevice behind the mortar and stone and brought out an old green Mason jar filled with change. She shook the jar and viewed the contents as she tried to judge the amount of money inside. This was her rainy day jar, filled with change to use only for special occasions or for emergencies. Today she decided she was going to use the change to purchase something special.

Quickly, she gathered the rest of her things together and headed for the jeep. As much fun as she had when she played with Max, she was ready to get going. She planned a little adventure of her own today. First, she needed supplies from the little town at the bottom of the mountain and then she planned to stop by an herb farm on the way home. Maggie spent a lot of time cultivating the herbs in her garden and was always on the lookout for more.

Max thumped his tail and rolled over in the grass when she walked past him. She scratched him behind the ears and ruffled his thick fur. "You rascal," she said as she smiled. He rewarded her with a huge swipe of his dripping tongue right across her face.

"Max! Gross!" she said as she tried to wipe the sticky kiss off her face with the back of her sleeve. "I was so clean!" she laughed. "You stay here and have fun. I'll be back soon," she said as she opened the door to her jeep.

Max thumped his tail against the ground as he flopped over on his back and rolled his eyes in reply. He looked like he had a huge grin on his face as he lay in the cool grass.

Maggie climbed into her ancient jeep. It had at least 200,000 miles on it and showed no signs of stopping any time soon. The exterior had many bumps and scratches from her explorations throughout the mountains. It even had one place that looked like a bullet hole, but she was not sure. At any rate, it was perfect for her simple needs. She did not have a vehicle when she first moved to the mountains and needed something durable to help her get around on the rugged roads during bad weather. When she heard of the forest service auctions, she purchased an old used jeep that was perfect for her needs.

*Not much to look at*, she thought, *but just right for me, and a real deal, too*. Maggie proudly paid $600 dollars for the jeep after she made the winning bid at the auction and drove off the lot that very day. She was more than happy with the jeep's performance over the years. A durable, functional vehicle, it would go over or through almost anything on the mountain. She cranked up the engine and headed into town.

The road from her cabin was only a dirt service road for several miles until it came out onto a main road that curved and wound through the National Forrest and finally emerged near the small town at the bottom of the mountain. The views of mountain ranges around her home were visible on some of the curves and lookout sites the forest service provided along the road for visitors to the area. Maggie grimaced when she reached the main road and saw a number of advertisement signs stuck into the ground and posters tacked to trees that heralded the upcoming city elections.

*It is a shame someone had to ruin the scenery with trash like that,* she thought to herself. *Ought to be against the law to ruin a tree by tacking signs to them anyway, they didn't do anything to deserve having trash stuck on them.*

She chuckled when she saw the mustache someone had drawn on one of the contestants who ran for a seat on the city counsel.

*He looks like he could be a stand in for the man that played 'Boss Hogg' on the 'Dukes of Hazard' with his potbelly and clean white suit.* She told herself, *I don't know what it is about politicians, but they all seem to think wearing white clothes puts them in the category of honest and trustworthy. They must not realize it is easier to get dirty when you wear white.*

"You had best stay squeaky clean if you want people to trust you." She absently shook her finger at the sign.

"That fella has something up his sleeve anyway," she said as she continued to drive down the mountain. "I don't know why, but I just don't trust him, something about him doesn't feel right. It just feels like he is up to no good or has a hidden agenda with everything he does. One of these days, I will figure out what it is, but for now, I am just going to have to go on my gut feelings. Guess I need to hear one of his speeches before I make up my mind, I'm being judgmental again."

Maggie learned some harsh lessons after leaving the shelter of her grandmother's home and entering the world outside their mountain. They were lessons that taught her that not everyone placed other people's needs ahead of their own personal needs. Although, her belief in the resilience and good of human nature never faltered, she learned she must be wary of people whose dark side motivated their behaviors. At times, she felt repulsed by the evil she knew existed in the world. At other times, she wanted desperately to fix the problems even though she knew that was not possible. She knew she could use her experiences in a positive way if she tried hard enough. It was a skill she admired and continually tried to develop.

# The Crooked Old Woman

Maggie pulled under a shade tree alongside the road and reopened the newspaper before she drove into town. The ad in the paper read, "Old fashioned herbs for sale, dozens of varieties not seen in years." The long ad listed many herbs, plants and flowers for sale. Since Maggie was interested in growing herbs for natural remedies, she immediately called the number to see what new types of herbs the grower had to offer that she did not have at home as soon as she saw it.

The elderly woman who answered the phone seemed bright, alert and filled with knowledge as she described her wares. After talking to her for some time, Maggie was convinced the things the woman sold would soon have her in touch with ancient varieties of healing herbs similar to the ones her grandmother taught her to use years ago. She was eager to find the farm and make some additional purchases to add to her herb garden at home.

Maggie brought her "rainy day jar" from the secret hiding place in her cabin and eagerly began to follow the directions the elderly woman gave her over the phone. No matter how closely she followed the directions, she could not find the place anywhere. She searched for the herb farm all morning long. Maggie felt her own anxiety and frustration grow as the time for her appointment passed and the herb garden was still nowhere in sight. She thought she knew every place in town but could not seem to find the herb farm.

After she passed the correct driveway two or three times, she was surprised when she discovered the address was not in the country at all, but right in the middle of town. Maggie was a little skeptical, but continued on her journey. After all, she thought she may have written the address down wrong or misunderstood the woman.

As Maggie turned into the drive, she noticed a faded plank painted with the correct house number in the grass. It was the only indication she drove in the right direction. A dirt driveway filled with ruts and pools of water curved and disappeared between two buildings before it turned out of sight. The jeep groaned and creaked as she made her way down the drive, careful to avoid as many of the deepest holes as possible.

Massive old trees hung their branches low and scraped the top and sides of the jeep as she slowly made her way to the end of the drive. There she saw an ancient brick house nestled under the trees that was crumbling and falling down. The house seemed dark and forlorn, as if no life stirred within its walls for many years. A broken window, a fallen wall, a shingle from the roof ready to fall, all led her to believe she had made a wrong turn after all. Yet, there on the porch, right on the wall was the house number she looked for all morning long.

Curious, Maggie decided to investigate the house while she was there in case someone was inside waiting for her visit. Carefully, she approached the front of the house and watched her step for fear she might fall through. The rotten planks on the ancient porch appeared to be over a hundred years old.

"Hello...is anyone there?" Maggie gingerly rapped on the door.

When she heard no response, she knocked a little louder and more strongly to make sure her knocks were loud enough for anyone inside to hear. Still no one came, so she knocked louder and more strongly time and again until the pounds on the door echoed within the house. When no one answered her call, Maggie stepped to the window and tried to peer through.

The house was so dark and dreary it was difficult to see inside. She rubbed a dirty window pane near the front door with the sleeve of her coat as she tried to clear as much of the dirt and smudges from the windowpanes as she could. When her eyes finally adjusted, she could see stacks of papers and books strewn across the floor and a thick layer of dust that lay undisturbed for what looked like a century or more. Believing the house abandoned; Maggie retreated across the treacherous porch and back to the jeep to review her directions once more.

Suddenly, just as she reached the jeep, a motion fluttered in the corner of her eye, a quick, fleeting movement that caught her by surprise. Quickly she turned just in time to see a glimpse of a shadow dart around the corner of the house!

*Were my eyes deceiving me?* she asked herself. *Was anyone there?*

She watched what seemed to be a tiny, hunched figure that scurried and hurried about. She watched as it disappeared to the back of the house somewhere. Maggie laughed a nervous laugh. She looked to the left and to the right to see if anyone else might have seen the hunched figure scurry around the corner of the house. No one else appeared to be anywhere near the ancient old house.

She wondered if someone was really there, or if she had seen a vision of sorts. Maggie pinched herself to make sure she was awake and listened to the sound of traffic as it continued at the end of the drive. Maggie rubbed her eyes and looked around the yard a little more carefully. She knew she was awake. It appeared to be the same day and time. Yet what she saw did not seem right.

Curiosity had a magnetic hold on her now, an invisible force that pulled her along. She could not force herself to get into the jeep without knowing for sure what she had seen. Ever so cautiously, Maggie walked around the edge of the house. She pried the brushes and shrubs apart. As she squeezed through the small opening, brambles tore at her coat and pulled her hair. Once free from the briars and brambles, she began to shake leaves from her hair as she hesitantly stepped through the gate.

"Hello," she called faintly at first. "Is anyone there?"

A small, hunched figure darted ahead of her and scurried over another porch on the back of the house. The creature looked like a very old woman, but Maggie could not be sure. To her, it looked as though it perhaps might be some kind of gnome or creature of sorts. Maggie could see from the distance the woman's spine was curved. She looked as if it bent at the waist and was unable to stand up straight.

She wore three cotton dresses, one over the other with a sweater and a jacket that did not match each other on top of the dresses. Old stockings filled with runs drooped down her legs and fell into a pool around her ankles. Several pieces of bailing twine wrapped around her legs. They looked as if someone tied them just right to hold old plastic bread bags on her feet.

Maggie's mouth was agape as she took in the sight.

*I cannot believe it!* she thought to herself. *This does not seem right. Could this unusual creature be someone who lives all alone, someone whom time and friends have long since forgotten. Is she truly and urchin or a gnome? Grandmother always told me there were creatures like this living in the forest.*

The old woman rushed past without a glance, muttering as she scurried into a gnarl of shrubs in the back.

"Ummm...hellooo," Maggie said. She wondered if the hunched figure did not see or hear her when she spoke because the woman continued to scurry away. She wasn't sure what to do. *Should I follow this creature or run to the jeep as fast as I can?*

A sense of fear and anxiety gnawed inside, yet, her curiosity was stronger than her desire to retreat to the jeep, so she took a deep breath and followed the crooked old woman into the jumble of weeds.

*This is so strange,* she thought. Confused, Maggie wondered, *Is this the woman I spoke to on the phone? It does not seem it could possibly be true. That woman was bright and alert on the phone, she even promised to be home. This woman seems disheveled and confused at best.*

Maggie watched as the old woman scurried around the clearing near the edge of the woods unaware of a guest. Maggie began to talk to the old woman as soon as she stepped through the thicket, but was amazed to arrive just in time to see the woman disappear again! She wondered where the woman went this time. Suddenly, the hunched figure returned from the brush again, scurried right under Maggie's nose and then was gone once more!

She came barely to Maggie's waist as she hustled about. She talked in a gibber that barely made sense; fast confusing talk to someone Maggie looked for, but just could not see. Maggie could hardly understand a thing the she said. A word here, a phrase there, disjointed speech that made no sense. She followed her in and out among the trees as she tried to explain the ad she saw in the newspaper.

"Hello," she called. "I'm searching for 'natural things'. Do you have any herbs?" She held up the newspaper clipping about herbs.

The old woman abruptly stopped in her tracks, which caused Maggie to stumble and almost fall over her. The woman then cocked her head and looked up with a piercing bird like eye.

"Hummm, herbs you say," she said in a crackly voice. "I have only the old fashioned kind - heh, heh, heh. Cure you they will." Then off she scurried again!

"Wait! That's what I was looking for!" Maggie said as she thumped her head. "Gosh, just when I thought she was making some sense!"

She followed the hunched figure more quickly now to a hidden clearing she did not see before. Although Maggie's skills as an herbalist were fairly new, it did not take a veteran to see it was many years since herbs and flowers had grown anywhere near. The old woman disappeared in a patch of weeds as high as her head and emerged with a clump of something she handed over to Maggie as she very clearly spoke.

"These special plants I only share with a few. Listen close and I'll share them with you."

In her crackly old voice, she told Maggie a confusing, rambling tale of her days as a child when she played among flowers and trees in her yard. She told of plants brought here from distant shores by relatives no one remembered anymore. There was something about a pirate or a prince and a bad man or two. Maggie was not sure which one was true. They seemed to be stories from the old woman's past that somehow jumbled with a fairy tale or two.

*One thing is sure*, Maggie told herself as the day wore on, *this woman's memories of love live in each thing she grows, whatever they are.* The weeds or herbs she handed Maggie were treasures of a vaguely remembered past.

"Too many here, not enough there."

She divided and portioned some of everything she had. Then, she handed Maggie an unusual plant that looked like a weed filled with tiny seeds as she said, "This one will help with the fog in here." She laid a crooked, gnarled finger on Maggie's forehead and began to trace the lines across her head. Maggie jumped back with surprise and wondered how the old woman knew she sometimes felt there was a fog in her head.

"And this one will help free what's stopped up in there," she said as she pointed at the center of Maggie's chest then grinned. A sly grin crossed her lips as she laughed and said, "You know what you have to do."

Shocked at her words, Maggie looked quickly at her chest. *Stopped up? What does she mean by that? Does she mean I have some kind of blockage or something - a heart problem perhaps?* Frightened, Maggie held the plants the old woman handed her and watched her a little more closely. *Does this old crone think I'm sick or something? How would she know something like that?* Maggie wondered as she felt the temperature of her face and placed one hand on her heart.

"Whatever do you mean?" Maggie asked the old woman in an alarmed voice as her temperature began to rise and her heart began to beat faster in her chest. "What makes you think I'm muddled?" Maggie had not used that term since her grandmother used it years ago. It seemed to erupt from her mouth naturally.

"Your words not mine," the woman said as she chuckled and looked at Maggie from the corner of her eye. "Time will tell, time will tell..." the old lady croaked in a sing song tone as she continued to give Maggie handfuls of plants and started to talk gibberish again.

With her arms so filled with bundles of plants and weeds she could hardly hold more, Maggie made her way past the rickety old gate to the front of the house again. After she plopped her treasures in the back of the jeep, she reached inside and pulled out her "rainy day jar".

The old woman smiled a wry smile and her eye began to twinkle as she spied the Mason jar full of quarters and nickels. She reached for it and with gnarled old hands shook it, then hid it somewhere inside a layer of her dress.

"This will do just fine my dear," she said with a chuckle as she scurried away. Then, without a backward glance she disappeared through the gate behind the house again!

Maggie stood with her mouth open wide as the hunched little figure scampered away with her special jar! She started to yell, "Hey wait! That's all I have", but shook her head in disbelief and crawled in the jeep instead. The jeep creaked and groaned as she slowly made her way back to the street and reality again.

"At least I'm still in the same time and place," she told herself. "The traffic's still here, the school and the bank."

She drove slowly away and wondered about the morning she spent in the old woman's yard, the unusual herbs she now had and the cryptic words the old woman said. This morning did not seem real, yet it must have been so. Her jeep was filled to the brim with plants, herbs, or - who knows what kind of mysterious things. Something felt familiar about this morning's experience, but she was not sure what it was.

*Must be the muddled part of my brain confusing things*, she thought.

She shrugged her shoulders and smiled as she thought about the bundles of gems she would plant - whatever they were, and decided to find out more about the crooked old woman with the old-fashioned herb farm.

After leaving the herb farm, Maggie drove through the town square in Tellico Plains to look for her old friend, Digger. He was famous around town as the "Original Mountain Man" since he was one of the few remaining genuine gold miners from the "old days". Always clad in a pair of faded overalls, dusty boots and a felt hat; Digger spent as many days as possible in the mountains surrounding town in search of gold.

When he was not on one of his gold treks, he spent many days on the bench in town square with several local mountain men as they chewed and spat tobacco juice, told tall tales and whittled the day away. They were a treasure trove of knowledge and a reminder of the pioneers who settled this area in the not to long ago past.

One of their favorite pass-times was to tell tall tales to anyone who would listen. Of course, you could not believe half of the things they said. Most of their stories were filled with half-truths and exaggerations passed down from generation to generation. It did not matter whether the stories were accurate or not to most of the people in the community. Everyone loved to hear them talk and enjoyed the traditional flavor they added to the community. These men were the eyes and ears of the town and usually knew just about anything that happened with everyone in the community.

A few years back, a new developer came into town and tried to turn the town into a future economic bonanza for him and others. He bought a great deal of property in the area and tried to pass laws to force storeowners in the town square to redesign their shops so they would look like a Swiss village, which was comical. As rich in history and culture as the area was, the one thing it did not have was history related to Swiss alpine villages.

One could mention the logging industry, iron works factory, vegetable canning company, bushwhackers, the War Between the States, the Indian War, gold miners, pioneers, or any number of other things and somebody in town always knew somebody who was associated with one of those things. With all the knowledge available, none of the old timers knew anything about Swiss villages. This area was the original Wild West when pioneers came across the mountains. There wasn't much around that was refined or civilized at all when the area was first settled.

Another thing the developers did during their redevelopment plan was remove all the old park benches in town square because they felt it was undesirable to have old men in overalls sit on them all day as they chewed tobacco and told tall tales. With no place to sit and talk in town square, the men had to move to another area. Therefore, in the name of progress, the development committee evicted the old mountain men. They eventually moved to a local diner for their gatherings. Maggie shook her head as she drove through the square and thought of the changes.

*Progress! Progress and politics! What a terrible combination, that's too bad. The town is at risk of loosing its unique flavor now. We can learn so much from those old timers. They have lived history and seen things we will never again see in our lifetimes. All we have to do is listen to them as the talk about their experiences and learn from them.*

She headed to the local hangout for the old timers, the Tellico Pride, to see if she could find Digger there. The Pride was now the hot spot in town, located across from the high school and the grocery store; it was the main fuel station around. Gas, food, newspapers, gossip - you name it, you could find it at the Pride. Most of the old timers spent their free time there now.

When first built, the BP was the clean crisp green and white color of many modern gas stations. In just a short time, it had taken on the flavor of the area. Shelves stocked with camping supplies, hiking gear and items of local interest filled the shelves. Fantastic local country cooks made food that was prepared in the small dining area. Every newcomer to the area was encouraged to stop by the station for a visit as part of his or her welcome to the area.

After Maggie bought gasoline, she told Sharon, the clerk, about her unusual morning experiences and asked her if she knew anything about the old woman with the herb farm. Sharon knew just about everyone in the small community and didn't hesitate to pass on the information. She just laughed when Maggie asked.

"You mean old lady Cates?" She said with a smirk. "She's the old maid, retired school teacher here in town. She is nuttier than a fruitcake Maggie! What in the world were you doing over at her place?"

"Well, I saw an ad in the paper about someone selling some herbs and went by to check it out," Maggie replied. "She didn't seem like the same person I talked to on the phone, though."

"That's old lady Cates, alright. She's got Ole' Timer's disease. Some days she is just as clear as the rest of us. On other days, she is 'off the wall' crazy! Sometimes we catch her running around the building here or looking through the trash cans and have to call her nephew to come get her and take her home."

"I was a little concerned about her. She didn't look like she had enough to eat or wear," Maggie commented.

"Honey, let me tell you, that woman's richer than half the people in town and smarter, too. She keeps her money squirreled away and won't spend it. Don't you go worrying your head about her, girl. She has a nephew that looks out for her."

Maggie nodded. It was hard to believe anyone would choose to live in such poverty if they had a choice and had the means to have anything they wanted.

*There must be some reason Ms. Cates enjoys her life the way it is or she would change. Maybe she feels she needs to save her money for something, or maybe it's a way to keep her nephew coming over for visits, or maybe she's just plain ole' crazy. Whatever it is, she sure had me roped in, I was ready to jump right in and save the day for her and she didn't need me at all!*

Maggie began to ask around the store for Digger while she was there. Busy ringing up another customer on the cash register, Sharon pointed towards the booths in the eating area where several of the older men Digger's age sat as they talked and drank coffee. A heated debate seemed to be going on about the pending election in town.

Current topics for the election kept most local voters hotly divided. There were the "traditionalists" who wanted to keep things the way they were now and always were, and there were the younger voters and business leaders who wanted to see new industry and career opportunities in the area for people their age. Maggie stood by their booth as the men discussed recent changes in the area and lamented the differences in lifestyles that were sure to come should voters ok new industry.

"Maggie, you're one of the younger ones, what do you think about the petition to turn some of the protected areas into business districts and open them up to new industry?" George asked intently.

"Hey, you guys know me. I'm a die hard naturalist. I want to keep everything related to nature as protected as possible. There are plenty of places for industry somewhere else, not in the middle of the forest," Maggie said as she looked at the trio. "We've got to protect nature as long as we can."

About that time, a short, portly fellow came up to the group and handed out business cards to the men. Maggie recognized him as the man on the campaign poster she saw earlier stuck to one of the trees by the road with the funny mustache drawn on his face. She watched the reactions of the older men as the politician started to shake hands with them as he talked.

"Now, men, I'm here to tell you that there's a way to make everyone happy in this little valley. We can make this whole area grow into, a virtual Bonanza for those of us who get in on it from the start. It's a way for us all to get rich! A vote for me will be a vote for the things you want to see happen in your neck of the woods." He spun the words right out of his mouth like an orator in a performance as he paused to slick back his hair. He intentionally ignored Maggie when she held out her hand for a business card.

*Slick tongued devil!* Maggie thought to herself as she turned to him.

"Exactly what is your campaign platform Mr.? I don't believe I caught your name."

"Hubert T. Brown, missy, that's my name. It's on my card." He said as he showed her a business card then flicked it away and stuffed it in his pocket. "Now, don't you go worry your pretty little head about things like platforms and politics, I'm sure you women have better things to do," he said as he broadly smiled, turned his back to her and attempted to block her from the conversation at the table among the group of men.

*Pompous jerk!* Maggie thought as she sweetly smiled, moved around him and then slid into the booth beside Bob.

"Actually, I'm very interested in your platform, Mr. Hubert T. Brown," she said as she crossed her arms and stared directly at him. "Exactly what IS it that you feel you can do for this community that will benefit EVERYONE - men, women, and children alike without taking advantage of anybody in the process?"

A deep red flush rushed over Hubert T. Brown's face as he avoided looking at Maggie and shuffled his feet.

"My, my, my, looks like we've got us a little wildcat here don't we, boys," he said stiffly with a tense forced laugh. He attempted to shift the focus of Maggie's attention away from himself. "This one seems like she's a real women's libber!" He continued to speak only to the men as he wore a sneer on his face.

Maggie could see she was getting under his skin and irritating him when she saw little beads of perspiration pop out on his forehead. Heedless of his discomfort, Maggie continued to pepper him with questions that made him obviously more uncomfortable.

"What is your stance on industry in town, or your feelings about the preservation of the wilderness areas? How do you plan to keep this area as it is for our grandchildren and great grandchildren? Do you plan to sell their inheritance before they are even born?"

Bob, Neil and George all grinned and exchanged knowing looks. Their eyes twinkled with merriment as they watched the politician squirm in his shoes. They had seen Maggie in action before and were counting their blessings they were on her side of the table. Known as a formidable opponent when on one of her crusades for justice, Maggie was often in the middle of a debate. They watched and waited for the sparks to fly as Maggie continued to grill the politician about his political platform.

Ignoring her, Mr. Brown slipped his thumbs in the waistband of his trousers and began to speak in a loud voice. He almost seemed to inflate as he began to speak.

"Men, I'm sure you would all agree that if women stayed in the home where God meant for them to be and if every woman in this area listened to her husband like God laid out for us in the Holy Bible, then we wouldn't have all the problems in the world that we have right now. We all know that the origin of sin started in the Bible when the WOMAN tempted man with the apple. That's where it all began!"

You could have heard a pin drop on the floor as the three men looked up at Herbert T. Brown with their mouths open.

"Ohh, Lordie, better hold on to yer seats, this is gonna be a rough ride!" George whispered to Bob as he softly blew out a whistle and slid a little further away from where the politician stood at the end of the table.

Maggie felt the anger boil within her and opened her mouth to speak. "Say what you want. Just remember Mister Hubert T. Brown, if what you say is true - it only took the power of a mere woman to tempt and bring down the fall of man, but it took all the powers of Satan to tempt a woman."

Enraged, the politician looked as if his entire head was going to burst. His face turned blood red and a large purple vein began to throb on the side of his head.

Before she could utter another word, Neil started to get up from his seat and move away from the booth. He motioned for her to follow him outside. She glanced at him but remained locked in place, unable to move a muscle.

"Wait just a minute here, Neil. I'm not finished yet!"

Neil grabbed her arm as he walked towards the door and guided her outside as he whispered, "Maggie, I know he's got yer dander up, but he ain't worth arguing with a'tall. He's jest speaking out of both sides of his mouth 'n ye know it."

Maggie shrugged her shoulders and tried to shake off the anger that rose so quickly inside her. *I thought I had better control of myself than that*, she thought angrily to herself as they walked outside of the Pride.

"Thanks Neil, I'm sorry, didn't mean to get so worked up. He is so arrogant! I didn't realize my anger was still so quick to rise, and so transparent. Guess I still have a lot of work left to do."

"Life's always about growing and improving ourselves, Maggie," Neil said as he patted her on the back. "Say yer lookin' fer Digger?"

"Yes, if you see him, tell him I'm headed back to my cabin, he can find me there, thanks, Neil," she said as she gave him a hug and turned to leave. She was tired of being in town and ready to go home. Maggie asked everyone who might have a clue as to Digger's whereabouts while she was in town, but no one had seen him in a day or two. Puzzled, Maggie looked around outside the store once more and did not see his truck in any of the places he usually parked.

*That's not like him*, she said to herself as she walked to the jeep. *He usually isn't home during this time of day; this is about the only other place he might be. He told me he needed me to go with him somewhere, but I don't know where else to look right now.*

She sat in the jeep and tried to decide if she needed to go to his cabin when she saw, and heard, him pull up in his old, faded green truck. The sound of the engine would give him away long before she actually saw the dilapidated old Ford truck or smelled the huge plume of exhaust smoke that followed him everywhere he drove.

*He'd have a hard time sneaking up on anyone in that thing,* Maggie thought to herself and smiled as he pulled in beside her.

"Hey Digger! Where have you been? I was a little worried about you, haven't seen you in a few days," Maggie spoke eagerly.

"Maggie, Shhhhh!" Digger stepped up to her window and leaned his head inside. "Ye've got to go with me tomorreee. Ah've found it Maggie, ah've really found it this time!"

"Are you serious! You've really found gold in your new mine!"

"Shhh! ah told ye, jest meet me tomorree at the trail to Whipperwill Mountain and ah'll take ye thar," he whispered, "And don't tell NOBODY! Jest make sure ye pack for two or three days."

"Ok, I promise." She held up her hand in a solemn promise.

"Tomorree then." Digger nodded and turned to walk away.

Maggie smiled and waved. *I love these treks with Digger.*

Then it dawned on her, "He said two or three days!" Maggie loved to hike and camp, but a two or three-day trek with Digger would be exhausting. For someone as old as he was, Digger was in amazing shape and could keep up with any hiker. As she headed home to pack for the trip, she smiled.

*I don't know how I get myself into these things.*

Digger was one of her Grandmother's best friends for as long as she could remember. He often stopped by her Grandmother's cabin during the time she lived there. Sometimes he stopped simply to visit and other times to check on them or to make sure they had enough to eat. He always seemed to keep a watchful eye on them no matter what season it was.

Some of Maggie's fondest memories were of her grandmother and Digger as they sat around the fireplace after dinner, talked and told stories of the old days. Maggie learned of the mysteries of the forest and of the mountains that surrounded her home while she sat on the braided rug by the fire.

Often, her grandmother, who was called Wani'nahi' which is a name for a beloved woman used by the Cherokee, would tell her stories about their Native American heritage. Those stories in particular were fascinating to

Maggie. She felt a special connection, a kinship with each person in the stories.

Maggie's great grandmother was a full-blooded Cherokee medicine woman who passed her skills on to her daughter, Maggie's grandmother. Grandmother, or Wani'nahi' as Maggie called her, taught her the skills of a medicine woman when Maggie first came to live with Wani'nahi' in her cabin in the woods.

Through the years, Maggie learned of healing and spiritual matters through Wani'nahi's Native American eyes and through Digger's mountain man eyes. Digger was a mountain man through and through. Maggie gave him the nickname Yan-e'gwa which meant Big Bear in the Cherokee language. She loved his visits to their cabin as a child.

Sometimes in the winter, Digger would play his harmonica when he came to her Grandmother's cabin to sit by the fire. Grandmother would pull out her corncob pipe and fill it with rabbit grass, which was a poor man's tobacco. There was nothing very special about rabbit grass, it did not even taste very good, but nothing enhanced a good folk tale like a crackling fire and a corncob pipe.

During those moments, the people she loved the most in her life transformed into mystical creatures. They ceased to be Grandmother and Digger and became Wani'nahi' and Yan-e'gwa as they told tales of ancient spirits that lived in the forest and of days long ago.

Often her grandmother took her Dulcimer down from the mantle and played beautiful bluegrass music. Maggie never saw sheet music or music books in their cabin. Her grandmother played everything by ear. The music came from her grandmother's heart.

Digger loved the music, too and often got so caught up in the rhythm and melody of the songs he could not keep still. He sometimes even began to break into the ancient form of clogging. His body looked as though it could move on its own accord. First, his feet would begin to shuffle, and then his legs would move in time. Before she knew it, Digger was in the middle of the floor as he danced and clogged in time with the song. Sometimes, his body looked like a ribbon in the breeze - liquid and rhythmic, every part of his body a graceful movement in time with the music.

At other times, he became so wound up with the beat of the song; it looked like every part of his body had a mind of its own. His arms could swing in circles at the shoulders in one direction while it looked like they could swing in a different direction at the elbows. His legs moved the same way. He danced and clogged around the room until he did not have an ounce of energy left. As a child, Maggie sat on the floor spellbound as she watched and listened. She clapped her hands and tried to keep time with the music of the heart and soul of Appalachia.

# The McCutchen Gang

After purchasing a few much needed supplies, Maggie turned onto the single-track forest service road that would take her home. Exhausted after her day's adventures, she was ready to get back to her private little cabin and become a recluse again. The road home was barely passable during this time of year. Filled with ruts, stones and limbs that fell during the winter, this track was rarely used by anyone other than herself and the owners of two other homes situated off the same dirt road. It was often lonely and desolate.

After she drove about two miles, she came to the curve before McCutchen's home. The McCutchen's ancestors lived in the area since the first settlers moved in several centuries ago. Their house was snuggled in a pristine setting deep in the woods on a plat of land cleared by some of their own ancestors years ago.

The remote location of many of the houses in this area kept people who lived here from access to many modern conveniences such as electricity and television. As a result, many residents still lived their lives in a manner similar to the way their ancestors lived many years ago when the first homesteaders settled the area.

The current house on the McCutchen property was a small three room shanty hurriedly made of rough cut timber years ago when the loggers and iron workers first needed homes for their families. At one time, it was most likely a very attractive home, but due to financial difficulties and lack of desire for a larger home, no one ever replaced it with a larger home.

Now, the boards were weathered and worn in many places. They were a dull shade of gray, as most of the paint had long since worn off. Some of the boards were warped and pulled away from the edge of the house. The tin roof was a dark shade of orange and brown where it rusted through leaving holes of various sizes. The roof seemed to have holes in more places than not and looked as if it has a dozen patches.

In front of the house, the ground was barren and worn down to the clay from the many footprints of children and adults through the years. An old barn on a hill behind the house looked as though a strong wind could blow it down. A corncrib, pigsty and outhouse filled the rest of the yard.

Maggie asked Digger once why no one planted grass between the buildings near their house, or why they did not make a path to the stream so the grass in the yard would grow. Digger reminded her that old timers kept guineas in their yards because they acted like watch dogs even though they were large birds. Guineas were great to have around because they were loud and warned folks of intruders. They also killed snakes that tried to come around the house. Digger taught her it was easier for guineas to see snakes in the yard if there was no grass, so, few people planted grass around their house.

Maggie slowed the jeep down as she neared the McCutchen house. Anticipating an ambush, she kept her eyes open as she scanned the bushes and ditches beside the road.

*It's only fitting there should be bandits on this road*, Maggie thought, *After all, this area was famous for bushwhackers for centuries and the McCutchen boys are not doing anything new. They are just following a family tradition.*

It was several days since Maggie made a trip off the mountain so she needed to be cautious as she neared this place. Sometimes, when she drove up the mountain the McCutchen boys tried to prevent her from reaching home or going up the mountain any further without stopping in front of their house.

On one return trip home, someone pulled a fallen tree across the road in front of the home. She was then forced to stop and drag it out of the way before she could continue. Another time, someone placed large stones across the road in such a way it was impossible to drive around them. Disturbances did not happen every time she drove by, but they did happen often enough to force her to be cautious each time the passed the house.

*I think I'm going to make it through here free and clear this time*, she thought as she entered the narrow passage in front of their house. *I never know when I am going to be able to pass this place and go straight home and when someone is going to try to trap me!*

Cautiously, she looked to the left and to the right side of the road as she drove. She made certain to look behind the rocks and in the shadow of the tree. Nothing out of order seemed to move. Then, suddenly, about the time she arrived in front of the house, a huge pile of leaves and hay fell from the tree above her. It landed right on top of the jeep and covered it with debris!

"Dang!" she said as she laughed. "I forgot to look up!" She stopped the jeep and waited for the banshee call. She counted as she waited for the McCutchen boys to appear.

"Five, four, three, two, one...," she whispered.

"Yyyieee!!! Yip! Yip! Yip!" The sound of the battle cry came through the air as two sets of little bare feet dangled down from the tree, legs wiggling and flapping in the air. Then, two little boys, their overalls and white undershirts covered in dirt and grime, dropped from the trees and landed on the ground in front of her. They immediately began to jump up and down, as they yelled and circled the jeep.

Maggie tried to refrain from laughing at the two little boys as they celebrated their victory and danced around the jeep while they whooped and yelled. *These guys are just like the street urchins I used to work with in the city*, Maggie thought. *The only difference is the setting. People are similar anywhere you go.*

She smiled as she remembered her work with children for so many years. For her, nothing was as rewarding as working with people, especially when they were unable to help themselves.

As a family therapist, Maggie specialized in the cases no one else wanted, the ones no one thought could improve, those who were too difficult to bear. She loved having those on her caseload. She could always see something, some spark that needed just a little boost to fan it into a flame. She could always find some glimmer of hope in everyone waiting for the right person to nurture it. Maggie spent most of her time working in crisis intervention as she helped families learn to find their strengths and make it through even the worst crisis.

When finally exhausted from their victory dance, both of the boys folded their arms across their chests and solemnly walked to her door, then waited for her to get out of the jeep.

"Looks like I'm a hostage!" Maggie said with a look of exaggerated fear on her face. A huge pile of leaves and hay fell on her head as she opened the door and climbed out.

Zack and Jonah broke into hysterical laughter, held their stomachs and shoved each other as they celebrated their victory.

"Jonah, it looks like you're feeling much better," Maggie said. She grinned as she tussled his hair. Jonah reminded her of what she thought a four-year-old Scottish immigrant boy might look like. His bright red, unruly hair was as noticeable as the freckles that covered his body from head to toe everywhere

31

Maggie could see. He was painfully thin and small for his age.

"I'm doing fine. Lookie here, Maggie." Jonah rolled up his shirtsleeve to show Maggie a budding muscle.

"Wow! You certainly are!" Maggie gasped. "Before you know it, you're going to be a grown up man!" Jonah grinned, blushed and shoved his brother before he dashed off to the front porch of the house. His four-year-old body was so small and thin for his age that Maggie often wondered if he had enough to eat.

His older brother still giggled so hard his stomach began to hurt from watching Maggie shake hay out of her hair.

"Zack, it looks like you're in fine spirits today." She smiled.

Zack was two years older than his brother. He was only slightly taller than Jonah and just as thin. Zack seemed to have received the Irish genes in the family. He had beautiful, creamy skin, dark hair and thick black eyelashes that fluttered over his steel blue eyes.

Maggie thought Zack was probably an "old soul" as his deep, intense eyes seemed wise much beyond their years. He was often serious and quiet when visitors were around the house. At six years old, he felt as though he was the head of the household and acted that way most of the time. Zack lingered behind to walk with Maggie. He was the oldest, and felt as though walking her to the house was something a man should do.

"I've been taking care of mamma just like you said, Maggie," he told her earnestly. "I brought in the wood for the stove, carried out the ashes, and carried up fresh water from the springhouse so Mamma can take good care of the baby."

"That's wonderful Zack. I am sure your mother appreciates it very much. She needs all the help you can give her. It's hard to do everything yourself, especially when you have a baby and little ones in the house."

Maggie thought of Zack as a little warrior. She often thought of the time a few months ago when Zack appeared on her doorstep in the middle of a terrible winter storm. He was soaking wet, trembling from the cold and barely able to catch his breath.

"Mamma sent me to fetch you Maggie," he stammered.

As soon as she saw him shivering on her doorstep, she brought him inside, wrapped a quilt around him and moved him closer to the fire to warm up.

"Did you run all the way from your house in this storm, Zack?" Maggie asked as she wrapped a towel around his head and tried to dry the snow off him as it melted.

"Yyyyesss," he stammered. His teeth chatted and his lips were blue from his long trek through the cold stormy night.

"No wonder you're so cold, that's over four miles!" Maggie exclaimed as she dried his hair a little quicker and bundled the quilt around him more securely. "What's going on Zack is everything Ok?" Maggie asked, genuinely concerned.

"It's Mamma," he said, his teeth still chattering. "She says the baby's 'bout to come. She says she's hurting real bad."

Maggie could see the fear in his eyes. Maggie quickly bundled Zack into the jeep and drove a wild, bumpy ride through the rain and sleet to make it to Doc's cabin before she took Zack back to his home. She and Doc then spent the rest of the stormy night at the McCutchen's home delivering Rena's beautiful baby girl.

As they struggled to help Rena give birth, they worked together side by side towards a common goal. During that storm, Maggie and Doc had connected on a level beyond anything she had ever known before. It felt as though they had known each other in another time and place, each somehow being able to know the other's needs without asking.

Exhausted after the difficult delivery; they sat by Rena's wood stove and drank hot coffee while they rested and listened to the sounds of the storm. In the next room, they could hear the little kitten like mews of the newborn as she learned to nurse. A peaceful feeling seemed to surround the cabin like the calm after a storm.

She and Doc found themselves speaking of things deep in their souls. Maggie listened as Doc told her of places he traveled and things he experienced. She found herself speaking of beliefs and experiences that she never felt comfortable speaking with anyone about before. Maggie's face flushed as she remembered the warm feeling she had from being around another kindred spirit. She felt an unsettling flutter inside as she remembered being around Doc.

The sound of a flock of guineas brought Maggie back to the present. As Maggie and Zack approached the house, the guineas scattered across the yard. They squawked loudly and warned everyone inside that an intruder was near. The small black and white birds were a little larger than a chicken and ten times as noisy. A large calico cat named Gertrude McFuzz lay on the porch basking in the sun, apparently undisturbed by the guinea's racket.

Zack's mother came to the porch and wiped her hands on a dishrag tied around her waist. She smiled and quickly looked away when she saw Maggie.

"Hi, Maggie, I see the boys rounded you up again," she said with a bashful giggle. Rena loved Maggie's visits almost as much as the boys did, but was too shy to admit it.

"Come on in, I'm makin' some tea," she said. She hung her head down and wiggled her toes as she looked at her feet. She blushed as she waited to see if Maggie was going to come in and stay for tea or not.

Maggie noticed that many mountain folks were reluctant to make eye-to-eye contact with people other than family. It may have been a custom, or a superstition or just plain old shyness. She made a mental note to research it a little and find out more about the custom or habit whichever it might be.

Rena was extremely bashful and rarely saw anyone other than her own family members. It was a big step for her to invite Maggie for tea. It took quite a while for her to gather up the courage to begin inviting Maggie inside. She rarely left her little mountain cabin and never visited a city larger than Tellico Plains. It was such a small town that less than eight hundred people lived in the whole community, valley and surrounding mountains included.

Sometimes, Maggie wondered if Rena did not encourage the boys to find ways to stop her on her way back up the mountain, because she was too shy to ask on her own. Either way, Maggie often stopped to visit on her own. She did love to have tea at Rena's house and she loved to see the boys and the baby.

Rena's husband was an extremely conservative man. He believed a woman should stay home and conduct herself as a wife should according to his own interpretation of the *Bible*. According to his beliefs, she should be meek and obedient to his wishes. Maggie felt he probably reinforced Rena's shyness in order to keep her at home.

Since the logging accident last year that took her husband's life, Rena made do with the things she had without the benefit of his income. Her husband was always a good provider, but worked irregularly and never thought about providing for his family if something happened to him and he was unable to work. Finances were difficult since his death, but Rena always seemed to be able to make ends meet by weaving baskets for the local crafts stores and gathering herbs and berries that grew wild in the mountains during the spring and summer.

Maggie smiled as she entered the little house. Checkered red curtains fluttered in the open windows allowing a fresh breeze to flow into the main room. A warm comfortable feeling surrounded every corner in the little home. A hand crocheted afghan neatly placed across the back of the couch added a

34

cheerful splash of color to the room. Hand made pillows adorned the couch and chairs giving the room a comfortable, homey feeling. Anyone could see someone cleaned and shined the bare wooden floors with care. The house seemed to be spotlessly clean.

The spicy fragrance of sassafras tea filled the room. Rena usually made tea from some herb or root she found while foraging in the woods. Sassafras was one of Maggie's favorites. The smell of sassafras always reminded her of her grandmother and times they spent together around her fire talking and drinking tea. While Rena poured the tea, Maggie peeped in on little Abigail who was soundly asleep in her crib.

"She's adorable, Rena. I think she must have gained two or three pounds since I saw her last! Do you think she'd wake up if I tickle her?"

Rena giggled, "You always say that, Maggie. Pick her up if you want to, I don't mind and she'd love it."

"Oh, no, I'm just teasing, Rena. She needs her beauty rest. I just wanted to peek in on her. She looks great! Are you getting any rest for yourself?"

"Only when they're all asleep." Rena smiled.

They spent the afternoon talking about the baby and herbs that grew in the surrounding woods. Rena promised to take Maggie with her when she went into the mountains to forage for herbs and ramps. Although Maggie never tasted ramps, she knew that Digger loved them and wanted to get some for him when they were ready. She also wanted to see native Ginseng as it grew in the mountains.

After her second cup of tea, Maggie stood up to leave. As she headed out the door, she called the boys, "Hey guys, I have a strawberry patch that will be ripe soon. Want to make a bargain?"

"Strawberries! Sure, Maggie, we love strawberries."

"If you guys will help me pick them and weed the patch, I'll trade half of my strawberries for your work."

"Yippee! We get to go to Maggie's house!" they both cried in unison as they pranced around the yard.

"You have to help me work," Maggie reminded them sternly.

"We will, we will!" they eagerly agreed as they began to wrestle with each other in the yard. Rena smiled and nodded, pleased with the agreement.

"Ok, then, that sounds like a bargain to me! I'll look for you in a couple of days!"

Maggie knew better than to offer Rena a handout. She would have immediately offended Rena and damaged their friendship if she tried to give

Rena something free. Many of the families who lived in the Appalachian Mountains were poverty stricken, but very proud of the things they did have and resented the thought of someone giving them something free.

The implication in a handout was that what they owned was not good enough and someone else felt obligated to help them out financially. No one wanted to feel as though they owed another person for anything, even a favor. Maggie tried to be sensitive about these feelings and usually tried to negotiate a trade or a swap of skills or crafts for things when she could. Rena often traded wild herbs or plants she found in the woods for the milk and treats Maggie brought for the boys when she made trips to town.

As Maggie said her goodbyes, the boys ran down to the creek to play in the water before supper. Maggie smiled as she watched them splash fearlessly into the water in spite of the icy cold temperature. She climbed into the jeep and headed home to her little cabin in the woods. She was eager to plant her herbs before sunset and fix some much needed dinner. In the excitement of the day, she forgot to eat anything and was ready to eat and curl up with a good book for the evening.

# Home Again

Max was busy waging another battle with the groundhog when Maggie arrived home. Over the past few weeks, the two critters seemed to have made a daily event of harassing each other. It was comical to watch. When Max was not looking, the groundhog often tried to sneak up and eat his dog food. This invariably resulted in a wild chase through the woods or field where each seemed to relish tormenting the other with a game of hide and seek.

Max often retaliated by attempting to destroy the groundhog's den when he noticed the critter was depleting his food stash. He tried as hard as he could to pry his body inside and catch the scoundrel that ate his food. The groundhog was able to find numerous places to hide or disappear just at the moment his persecutor was on his tail. Max ended up tired and exhausted; the poor critter usually had to build a new den elsewhere in the field. In spite of the numerous battles, neither Max nor the groundhog seemed ready for a truce with each other.

After much thought, Maggie decided to name the groundhog Basil due to his preference for that herb in her garden, although she almost named him after the Greek god, Sisyphus in honor of the most notorious trickster on earth. Reportedly, Sisyphus cheated death, stole the god's secrets, scorned the gods continually and spent his life trying to trick them and rebel against them.

He did this even though the gods had tremendous powers over him. Sisyphus' passions for life filled him even in the most hopeless circumstances. The gods sentenced him to a life of mindless manual labor that accomplished nothing, yet he continued to snub his nose at the powers that tried to control him.

*You remind me of myself, Basil.*

Maggie felt a strange kinship with both the mythical Sisyphus and the groundhog. She was fascinated with anyone who had a zest for life despite the odds against them. Their continual effort to test the powers that tried to control them in their everyday life amazed her. They each loved their role in life. No matter how many times Max tried to destroy the ground hog's den, or catch him and have him for dinner, the groundhog never seemed to give up his determination to test the dog's patience.

Right now, it looked as though Basil was winning the current battle. It all started when Max, who was basking in the sun after an exhausting morning of pursuits of varmints and critters in the yard, noticed a familiar movement from the tall grasses in the field. His senses alerted, he sat up and began to watch the slow, steady movement in the grass as the critter made its way across the field.

Maggie watched Max train his eyes on the movement, his body tense in readiness. She knew from watching him in the past, he tuned out all distractions at this point. His whole body seemed geared for the chase to begin. As Max slowly rose, he never lost sight of his prey. He looked very much like a runner on the starting line. He lowered his head and shoulders, stared straight ahead, body poised, ready for the challenge to begin.

Just at that moment, the movement in the grass stopped. Basil's head and shoulders appeared above the grass. He stood up on his haunches, sniffed and scouted around for danger. His stillness was amazing as he sniffed the air. He almost looked like the stump of a tree or a carving of a groundhog instead of the real thing.

The instant Basil was completely still, Max exploded from his stance. His paws sounded like the hooves of a runaway horse as he sped toward his prey. Surprised, the groundhog leapt straight up in the air when he saw the huge dog barreling down the field toward him.

The groundhog made a mad dash for his den with Max in hot pursuit. He was a blur of fur as he dove inside the tunnel just as Max came to a screeching halt right above him. His hot breath followed Basil into the den. Max was frenzied now, as he tried to get his head deep into the den. Furious that Basil had beaten him once again, he suddenly stopped.

Maggie thought he was stuck because he was not moving. She stood on the porch so she could see the shenanigans better. She had to hold her hand over her mouth to keep from laughing when she saw Basil's head and shoulders pop up out of the earth in a new den about 15 feet away from where Max dug. Max's rear end was high in the air, his tail straight up as he slowly pulled his head out of the entrance to the den. Dirt and mud covered his head and snout. Awareness suddenly dawned on him.

Basil stood on his haunches and whistled a long, "thzzzzzth," then disappeared into the new den again.

Wildly, Max dove for the new opening and began his frenzied digging once more. Each time Max dug in one place, Basil popped up in another opening, whistled loudly toward Max and the chase continued. This commotion went on for twenty minutes or more until Max was so exhausted and frustrated he finally plopped down in the middle of the field, too tired to move. He rolled his eyes in Maggie's direction as she walked to the jeep.

"I think you enjoy that game as much as Basil does, Max." Maggie laughed as she began to bring in the supplies she purchased for the cabin. "You guys are going to have to call a truce or I'm going to have a yard full of holes," she told Max as he slowly thumped his tail in the grass.

Maggie carried the supplies into the cabin then placed the bundles of herbs at the edge of the woods where she watered them with water from the stream to keep them moist until she could return and plant them in the garden. Enormous oak logs that were hand hewn many years ago provided the main structure of the ancient cabin Maggie owned. It had a large front porch supported by many flat fieldstones underneath. River stones that were stacked and wedged together with clay from the river formed the stone fireplace at the end of the cabin.

Maggie felt as though she became a part of the earth when she entered the cabin. The floor was made of natural slate cut from a mountain nearby. The slate helped keep the cabin cool in the summer and collected warmth from the fireplace in the winter to help cut down on her heating expenses. Her favorite place to sit was in a rocking chair near the large front window on the porch that spanned the length of the cabin. This special spot overlooked the mountains and forest around her home. From here, she could see into the field and the edge of the woods where she often saw wildlife grazing in the fields or drinking in the stream at dusk.

The house was solid, although it needed few repairs when she moved in a few years ago. The only major work was on the tin roof, which she replaced a few years ago when she discovered she did not have enough pots and pans to place under the leaks during a storm. She loved the sound of rain on the tin roof and could not bear to have anything else in its place.

Inside the cabin, a large great room with a huge fireplace made of stones from the stream covered the left end of the room, while an open kitchen and eating area filled the right end of the room. A loft above the main room contained shelves filled with painting supplies, pottery and unfinished projects. Walking through a door in the center of the cabin, Maggie could enter the second room that adjoined the cabin on the back of the house. The bedroom and bathroom added long after construction of the original house provided the only modernization in the cabin.

When Maggie came to live with her grandmother, Digger helped her grandmother make the new addition so there would be room enough for her to have her own space. He also helped build the bathroom and install the first plumbing the cabin had ever known.

Maggie filled her cabin with the things she loved the most. She donated most of her possessions to charity groups when she returned to the mountains and kept only the things that were most dear to her. She kept her great grandmother's iron bed in her bedroom. She filled it with quilts made by her grandmother. In her den, she kept a comfortable leather couch, a braided rug and a rocking chair.

Treasures given to her in the past adorned the walls and shelves of her cabin. There were paintings, carvings and hand crafted items made by people she met or worked with through the years. A hand woven basket made by Rena filled with dried flowers sat on the table by the fireplace. Two god's eyes made of carved willow branches and yarn made by Jonah and Zack during crafts class at school dangled in the corner of the room. Pottery, carvings, and paintings each with a special place, each with a special memory, decorated the room and made it feel like home.

She used to think it strange that so many people made her things related to bears. She always knew bears were her totem animal and finally concluded that on some unspoken level it must be apparent to others as well. On occasion, when she told people she felt grizzly bears were her totem animal, she was surprised when heads nodded in agreement.

Her grandmother taught her each one of us could feel close to all of nature when we meditate and listen. She said, "For every person there is an animal guide to help them through life. Listen, girl. Listen to the sounds of nature when you're out in the woods and you'll know which animal spirit can give you strength to deal with the things you have to face in life."

She walked to the window and touched the prism that dangled in front of the glass. A colorful rainbow bounced around the room with the movement. A warm feeling flooded through her as she remembered again the night she helped Doc deliver Rena's baby.

The sound of the teapot whistling brought a halt to Maggie's reminiscing for the moment. Suddenly, when she realized how hungry she was, Maggie quickly decided to make supper with her tea. She re-heated a pot of vegetable soup she made the day before as the sun began to set. Brilliant rays of red and gold seemed to cling to the trees and ridges as if they were reluctant to let go of the day.

Max slowly made his way to the porch ready to sleep through the night. After a long yawn, he placed his front paws in front of him, stretched his entire body then groaned as he plopped down to sleep. He thumped his tail slowly when he saw Maggie.

"You almost got him today, didn't you, Max." She teased him as she scratched him behind his ears. He rolled his eyes up at her and thumped his tail a little louder. She laughed and went inside to curl up by the fire and read. The warmth of the fire and crackle of the wood quickly put Maggie into a sound sleep.

...she was alone, surrounded by darkness, as she tried
to find her way. In the distance, she could see a small
light. She could hear the sound of footsteps behind her,
heavy footsteps. The sound of leather shoes as a man
walked on pavement and followed her - she turned to run....

The sound of Max's deep growl woke Maggie from her sleep and the unsettling dream. It started as a deep guttural sound, faint at first, then stronger and louder until Max was on his feet. He blocked the top of the front porch stairs in a defensive stance. His fur seemed to bristle and stand out which made him look much larger than normal.

Maggie was familiar with the tones of Max's barks. He had a playful bark he used when he and Maggie played, one he used when he tried to roust varmints out of the woods and one that he used when he was chased Basil. This sound was different from the rest. It was more menacing, threatening to something she could not see. Maggie rarely heard this tone before. She knew there was some type of danger and Max was ready to protect her. She rose from the couch and walked to the window to see what was happening.

It was difficult to see anything from inside the cabin. She started to turn the lights on, but decided against it, as that would only allow anyone outside the cabin to see her and prevent her from seeing anything outside in the dark. Quietly, she slipped outside onto the porch. Max stood at the top of the steps, his body rigid, hackles raised. Maggie could see his snout crinkle slightly as he bared his teeth when he growled. Maggie looked in the direction Max stared. It took a few moments for her eyes to adjust to the night sky.

She could sense his presence before she could see his silhouette among the trees. She shuddered as goose bumps rose on her skin and the hair on the back of her neck stood up. She felt the pressure of Max's body as he leaned against her leg. She looked down and let her fingers rest on his back. When she looked up again, the figure was gone! A chill of fear ran through her as she quickly scanned the woods for some sign of the stranger who lurked in the shadows near the cabin.

At first, she thought maybe Digger decided to come by the cabin for a visit, but Digger would not come in the middle of the night and Max knew Digger. He would not feel threatened by Digger or try to protect Maggie from him. It was after midnight, no one would come for a visit at that time of the night, only some stranger. It had to be someone Max didn't know, someone he felt he needed to protect her from danger.

*Besides*, Maggie thought to herself, *Digger wouldn't stand in the woods like that. He would come up to the porch.*

Maggie watched the woods for a few more minutes before she decided the visitor had gone. Max seemed to relax a little. He began to wag his tail and gently lick Maggie's arm while he continued to watch the woods where the mysterious visitor disappeared.

"It's ok, boy, I think he's gone." Maggie slipped back inside the cabin and bolted the door behind her.

Maggie tried to think of who the stranger might be. She remembered she heard talk of strangers in town - drifters they said, folks that just hung around. Some of the mountain folks were pretty superstitious and wary of strangers.

Then, there were the folk tales of the mysterious man who walked the ridges at night. Stories of Dynamite Dan, who some say died in a mining accident so long ago that no one remembered for sure how long it was. Also, it was tourist season, and hikers on the trails and kayakers on the river filled the trails and streams with people until the first sign of winter.

If she had time, she decided to do a little scouting in the morning before she met Digger and see if she could discover anything. If nothing else, she could get rid of a little of the anxiety she felt after seeing the stranger in the woods.

Maggie packed her backpack for the trek with Digger before she attempted to get any more sleep. Water for the hike, dried vegetables to make the vegetable stew Digger loved so much, oatmeal, energy bars, dried fruit and her water filter all fit neatly into her bag along with a small teapot and mess kit. She stuffed an extra pair of socks, pants and tee shirt into the bottom of her sleeping bag, then tightly rolled the whole bundle up and tied it to the bottom of her pack. A knife and a first aid kit were the last things to go in the pack.

"Travel light, that's what I always say," Maggie said to herself. "Take no more than twenty pounds." She stood her pack by the front door and tied her old, dented goldpan on the outside of the pack.

She smiled as she touched the old, worn pan. She learned to pan for gold as a young child when she came to live with her grandmother. One early spring morning, Digger brought her one of the shiny metal pans that looked so beautiful. Maggie wanted to keep it in perfect condition when she first got it. She shined it daily in an effort to keep it from rusting or getting any dents on the beautiful reflective surface.

At the time, Digger gleefully laughed at her. He told her she was a green horn, but he would help her recover from it. Thinking she had some new kind of malady, Maggie eagerly wanted to see how Digger was going to cure her "green horn" disease. At the time, she did not realize that the cure had nothing to do with curing her, but meant Digger was actually going to cure the pan.

First, Digger built a smoky campfire after he bought her the pan and then waited until the smoke was billowing from the fire just right. Then he held her shinny new pan over the smoke, tilted it and passed it back and forth over the smoke until he had covered the entire thing with black soot. Maggie was ready to cry when she saw the condition of her shinny new pan until Digger explained the reason for what he had done.

"Ye kin leave it shiny if ye want to, Maggie, but ye ain't gonner find ye narry a drap of gold if ye do. Gold's shiny 'n if yer pan is shinier than the gold, ye ain't gonner see it. Ye gots ta have a black pan so ye kin see the gold."

He then took her to the creek and showed her how to muck a pan of mud and silt down to the gold to show her what he meant. Reluctantly, she watched him as the muddy water swirled around in the pan until he worked it down to the last little strain of black sand and the thin little stream of gold particles that sparkled and glistened so brightly they seemed to jump out of the pan. She blackened her gold pans ever since that day.

Before going to bed, Maggie looked outside at Max who was still on the porch and seemed to be alert and on guard. His ears were pricked and sharply tuned to noises. His eyes frequently scanned the woods as he slowly turned his head one direction and then the other to listen for unfamiliar sounds. His nose constantly sniffed the air.

As much as she needed the rest, it took quite a while before Maggie was able to drift off again. This time her sleep was restless and fitful. She kept having dreams of shadowy strangers and dark places, of someone who followed her into the night.

Maggie woke up the next morning feeling tense and a little unsettled. She did not sleep well after the appearance of the stranger last night. Something kept nagging at her, some unconscious thought or memory. She was not sure exactly what bothered her. There seemed to be something familiar about the stranger.

*Who would lurk in the shadows in the dark of the night?* She asked herself. She felt a chill and shivered again, then shook her head in an effort to shake all of the frightening thoughts away.

After a pot of hot tea and a bowl of oatmeal, she dressed for her journey. Today, it did not take her long to prepare something to eat because she was so hungry. Being a dedicated vegetarian, she refrained from eating meat for over ten years. She loved to cook with the fresh vegetables and fruits from her garden and often made exquisite dishes using her herbs as seasonings. Today, however, she was eager to get going and did not have time to cook.

When she was loaded and ready to leave, she turned to Max, "You'd better stay here boy." Max wagged his tail eager to come with her on the hike. "I don't want to leave the cabin unattended with a stranger lurking in the woods. So, until we know who it is, we will have to take turns staying home. This time it's you!" she laughed. "I'm going to meet Digger, you stay here!" Max wagged his tail and obediently sat down on the porch as he watched Maggie head down the trail to meet Digger.

The trail from the cabin led through a dense thicket of brush and trees that covered the rugged mountainside. Maggie ducked under tree branches and crawled over rocks as she made her way over the steep ridge to the main trail where she and Digger arranged to meet.

Maggie tried to stick to the faint trail she and Digger made earlier to avoid any unnecessary slips or falls. The forest was densely filled with huge ancient oak trees, massive pines, firs and maples that shed their leaves each fall and covered the ground with thick layers of leaves and pine needles that made walking off-trail treacherous on the steep mountain ridges. Often the smaller shrubs that covered the forest floor were filled with vines and razor sharp saw briars that easily tangled or tripped up unaware hikers.

Maggie made her way to the meeting place and waited for Digger to arrive. It was not long before she could see his old felt hat and hear the clang of his backpack as he arrived over the ridge. Maggie smiled, picked up her pack and their journey began.

# Digger

"C'mon, Maggie. Ye're gonna have to keep up if we's gonna make it 'afore dark," Digger called over his shoulder.

"I'm going as fast as I can," she replied as she plopped down on a large flat rock beside the trail and allowed her heavy backpack to slide to the ground. She winced as she adjusted her socks and retied the laces on her heavy hiking boots.

"Hiking isn't as easy as it used to be, you know," she grumbled. She watched Digger effortlessly crawl over a tree that had fallen across the trail, his backpack snug against his back, gold pan and canteen swinging as he walked.

"Gggrrhhh...that man!" she muttered to herself as she watched him lumber up the trail and whistle cheerfully as he walked.

Digger and Maggie were friends for as long as she could remember. She kept reminding herself he was "the original mountain man, as old as the hills and as young as the spring". She had no idea exactly how old he was, all she knew was that he seemed really old the first time she saw him, and that was over forty years ago when she was only five years old.

The first time she met Digger, Maggie stood beside the stream near her grandmother's home. She was busy that afternoon collecting beautiful stones from the water. She loved to stack the stones and arrange them so water could cascade over the tops and form sparkling miniature waterfalls.

That afternoon, Maggie spent a lot of time arranging the rocks into little pools to hold the salamanders she caught in the stream. When a shadow fell over her while she played, she looked up and noticed the old mountain man standing by the water. He wore a tattered, old brown felt hat, faded overalls and worn out leather boots. This outfit did not seem to change with Digger over the forty years since then.

Maggie could barely see his face through the stubble of gray beard. Through the years, Maggie always remembered his eyes more than anything else about him. His eyes were the color of the summer sky, so blue they seemed to jump right out of his face. His eyes never changed, they were always a beautiful color of blue. For that matter, Maggie thought, his clothes did not seem to change either, even after forty years.

He laughed that day so long ago, while he watched her as she diligently worked to place her salamanders in the pools she made in the stream. "Better be careful thar, lil' girl. Them's baby alligators," he said with a straight face. "What ye gonner do when the momma comes out?"

She returned his stare with a steady gaze. In each hand, she held a slippery, squirmy salamander while mud and creek water dripped down her elbows and covered the front of her dress.

"Reckon I'll have to make a bigger place," she said solemnly.

Surprised by her solemn response, Digger lost control of his straight face and burst out in laughter. He never encountered a child so young who could keep up with his tall tales. He decided that very day to teach her how to spin a tall tale and how to pan for gold. They were fast friends ever since.

Throughout her entire life, Digger taught her the "mountain ways". He taught her how to find food in the woods, how to find her way out again if she was ever lost and how to use the land to her advantage. With his help, Maggie learned to revere and respect the wild, lonely places and knew how to survive alone in them.

Often when she hiked with Digger through the rugged terrain in the mountains, they found relics and artifacts that were centuries old. No matter what they found, they never removed any of their ancient finds from the mountains. Digger said it wouldn't be right.

"When something is in its final restin' place, that's sacred - like holy ground," he would say. They always lingered a few moments when they discovered something special, then tried to imagine what transpired so many years ago to bring the relic to its final resting place. They often came up with many theories between them.

Maggie loved their treks together because she knew each one had a purpose, something Digger wanted to share with her, or something he thought she should know. This time, Digger was taking Maggie to one of his hidden gold mines she had not seen before.

She spent time inside mines with him before and did not care for them as much as she enjoyed panning for gold in the creek. The mines Digger inhabited frequently were dark and scary. Often they were filled with spiders, sometimes bats and snakes. Some of the caves were often even structurally unsafe for entry. She preferred to be outside where she at least had a chance to escape if she needed to do so.

Digger turned and grinned when he reached the top of the ridge. "Ye comin' or ain't ye?"

"Alright already," Maggie mumbled as she got up and headed on the trail again. "I'm not as young as I used to be you know." Each step of the trail pulled at the muscles on the back of her thighs and legs as she struggled up the rugged mountain path.

"Ye're as young as you think," Digger quipped as he turned and disappeared over the top of the ridge.

Maggie grinned as she rolled her eyes and shook her head.

"I wish I was close enough to smack you on the head!" she said as she struggled to make it up the steepest part of the trail.

Suddenly, Max appeared through the trees.

"HEY! I thought I told you to stay home!" Maggie scolded.

Max trotted right past her without a glance and followed Digger over the top of the ridge then disappeared down the other side. Max loved going on adventures with Digger. As much as he wanted to mind Maggie and do what she told him to do, nothing could keep him from a trek with Digger and Maggie. The thought of staying behind was more than he could bear.

"Geezzee!" Maggie struggled over the fallen tree as she made her way to the top of the ridge. "If you guys think you can gang up on me, you've got another...think...ohhh, WOW!!!" she gasped, "This is incredible!"

Maggie stepped out onto a narrow ledge around the rim of a crevice that was no more than two feet wide. It felt as though the whole earth opened up into one the most breathtaking views anyone could ever see. There were mountains, valleys and ridges of every shade of blue and green imaginable. A bright blue sky spanned as far as the eye could see beyond the tops of the mountains. Wispy white clouds floated high in the sky, while a trail of misty clouds seemed to hover over the crest of the mountain ridges in the distance.

The view almost took her breath away. Maggie gasped in disbelief. Mesmerized by the beauty of the scene, she unconsciously stepped forward to get a better look. Digger immediately grabbed her arm.

"Better watch it there, Maggie. That first step's a doozey."

Maggie looked down and for the first time saw the sheer drop that fell 300 feet from the rim toward the valley below. A rush of nausea and dizziness almost overcame her when she saw the sides of the ridge and the jumbled rocks and undergrowth of brush that tumbled down the side of the mountain to the valley floor.

She began to sway, as the whole world seemed to whirl in front of her for a moment. Her heart pounded, she broke out into a sweat and felt as though she was going to get sick and loose her breakfast.

Maggie immediately closed her eyes and grabbed the safety of the rock wall until she was able to regain her balance and step back to the safety of the trail. She took several deep breaths as she tried to control the panic that swept over her until she could slowly open her eyes again. When she finally was able to squeeze open her eyes just a little bit, the first thing she saw was Digger's face right in front of her. There he was with his funny, little crooked grin, his blue eyes sparkled and twinkled with glee. Maggie screamed with surprise.

"DIGGER!"

"See thar, Maggie, ah knew ye wuz gonna like it! Hee, heeee, ah always did like it whin ah could surprise ye, and ah did it too, didn't ah? Ah surprised ye! Got ye all flustered, too, didn't ah?"

"Ohhooo, boy!" Maggie gasped. "That's the truth!"

"Now that ye got yer breath back, come over here and let me show ye whur we're going." He held Maggie's arm as they stood a little closer to the edge on the rim of the mountain.

Digger and Maggie stood on a portion of a trail, which branched off from a trail now called the Unicoi Turnpike, a big name for a trail that was now only barely visible. The Turnpike trail at one time was one of the main routes of transportation when early pioneers first settled the area, although, by the 19th century the trail was rarely used anymore. It practically disappeared from view and was almost forgotten by the public. Finally, in June of 1999 when the National Millennium committee declared it one of 16 National Millennium Trails it began to receive the recognition it deserved. This declaration acknowledged its role in American history along with other famous trails such as the Louis and Clarke Trail.

"Maggie, they say this here trail yer standn' on comes down from the Unicoi Trail. That trail could be the oldest road on this continent. Sum folks say its 1,000 years old, mebbe older, even as old as the prehistoric days."

Digger began to tell Maggie about the ancient trail that ran along the ridge tops of the southern Appalachian Mountains from Canada to Florida. At one time, some of the passes in the mountains were the main crossroads connecting the Carolina coast to eastern Tennessee and the west. Digger turned away from the edge of the overlook to continue their journey.

"The Unicoi trail is known in history as 68 miles of bloodshed 'n misery. It may have one of the bloodiest histories of any trail in the country," Digger continued speaking as he started to walk down the treacherous path.

As she looked out over the breathtaking view, it was hard for Maggie to imagine the trail having a bloody history. Beautiful pink rhododendron bushes lined the sides of the trail and filled the air with the sweet aroma of spring. Birds whistled and chirped as they passed. The forest was alive with signs of life and beauty. A sense of peace and tranquility was everywhere.

"What happened through the years to give the trail such a bloody history?" Maggie asked as she followed, eager to hear more.

"This here's the 'lost highway', probly made centuries ago - long 'afore the Cherokee or the Creek Indians ever lived here. Thar wuz always wars, Maggie. Since time began, thar wuz always wars, raids, folks wantin' what somebody else gots. It's the way folks are, the way it's always been."

Digger turned to make sure Maggie was not having too much trouble as she followed him. They slowly and carefully worked their way down the steep side of the ridge. Max ran ahead of the pair, scouting for something to chase or roust out of a hiding place.

"Keep talking," Maggie called. "I'm listening." She maneuvered around a boulder and crawled under a low hanging tree.

"Anyways, one group of Indians wud com 'ere 'n see the beauty o' the place. It wuz a paradise. They'd end up farmin', 'n raisin' thar young'uns 'n such. They'd build villages and settle into comfortable livin'. Then, a'fore ye knew it, another tribe wud sneak across this very trail and go down the mountain and wipe 'em out."

"It's like ah wuz tellin' ye, Maggie, folks is always wantin' what someone else gots. Sumeone passin' on the trail wud see what a purty place this wuz and they'd go home and tell their folks. It wud go on and on from thar. One group wipin' out another 'till the Cherokee showed up."

"Fer a long time, this whole area used to be part of the Cherokee Nation. When the first settlers came here from the coast, they accepted 'em as one of thair own and helped 'em larn to survive. They worked and fought alongside the white folks and even tried to larn their ways. Then, in the 1830's, they had the first gold strike in North America, right here, purty close to this trail ye'r standin' on right now."

"What happened?" Maggie eagerly wanted to know more. She heard about the gold rush in the Coker Creek and Hot Branch area, but wanted to know how it related to the Unicoi Trail. The areas were so close to each other, only a few miles apart; it was hard for her to believe she lived in this area almost all her life and never heard the entire story of the trail.

"Well, at first the gove'ment built a fort up 'ere to keep the white folks outta Cherokee land, kind o' protect 'em 'n all." Digger stopped to rest on a large moss covered stone by the trail. A trickle of water bubbled out from the side of the bank beside the rock and ran over the stone. Digger dipped his bandana into the spring and mopped his face with the cool, clear water.

Maggie sat across from him on the remains of an ancient tree stump covered with soft green moss on the top and gray lichens on the sides. She began to sip water from her canteen.

"I've heard about the gold strike all of my life, but I've never heard about the fort."

"That's 'cause of what happened after that, Maggie. 'Bout the same time, they built that fort, thar wuz a gold rush up here. Well, when that happened, the gov'ment decided all injuns in the eastern part of the country wud be happier if they wuz livin' out west. So, they rounded up all the injuns they could find 'n made 'em leave so's the white folks cud move into this here little paradise." Digger began to tell Maggie the story of the "Trail of Tears". It was a sad story Maggie heard many times in her life, but never tired of hearing again.

"More than five tribes of Native Americans wuz forced to leave thar land and belongin's in the eastern United States and walk the 1,100 mile trek to Oklahomee, most of 'em wuz Cherokee. They had to walk across this very trail ye're walkin' on right now."

"But this was their land first!" Maggie protested.

"It's like ah was tellin' ye Maggie, this 'ere turnpike is full of bloodshed and tears, one group wantin' what another group had. They call the path the Cherokee took on the way west the "Trail of Tears". The fort the gov'ment built up here to keep the settlers protected from raids 'n ta keep' em safe durin' the gold rush wuz used as a holdin' pen to gather the Cherokee up 'an keep 'em till thar wuz enough gathered up to start a trip out west."

Digger was grim as he told of the many men, women and children who died on the journey, and the numerous graves left along the side of the trail as a result. "The thang is thar was lots of folks up here who grew up with the Cherokee 'n considered 'em friends. They didn't want 'em to leave. So, some folks hid 'em out 'n helped 'em try ta git away."

The sound of Max barking in the distance interrupted their conversation. "Sounds like he's ready for us to get going again," Maggie said as she slung her backpack over her shoulders. Digger wrapped his bandana around his neck and picked up his pack.

Digger led the way as they zigzagged their way down the steep ridge to the valley below. This trail was most likely an old game trail originally, then used by hunters to follow the game into the woods before it became a well-known path for travelers. Although the trail did not look as though anyone used it for hiking for many years, it appeared someone used it for hunting during the recent past. There was a continual problem in this area with poachers who hunted and trapped game illegally. This angered Maggie and as a result, she made efforts to expose illegal hunters and others who abused the land whenever she could.

Practically hidden from view below the rim, the small valley lay at the base of the ridge. The lush undergrowth of the forest filled the valley floor. Bright green ferns grew along the banks and under the trees. Thick rows of Rhododendron bushes lined the path, their branches bent almost to the ground with the large lavender flowers. Maggie breathed in deeply and filled her lungs with the sweet fragrance.

Across the small glade, Maggie could see an enormous oak tree whose branches were ready to burst into leaves. Around the roots of the tree dozens and dozens of bright yellow daffodils, nodded their heads in the sun. A gentle breeze blew across the tall grass and caused it to ripple and flow like gentle waves on the ocean. Maggie was delighted. She closed her eyes and imagined a pioneer homestead here, or an Indian home many years ago.

*There must have been someone here,* she thought. *Someone had to plant those yellow daffodils years ago; they are not native to this area and would not be here unless someone brought them here.*

Digger followed Max to the far side of the clearing where a small stream rushed and flowed along the edge of the field. Max immediately splashed to the middle of the stream, lay down and rolled around in the water until he submerged himself up to his nose in the pool. He looked as if he was in ecstasy as he slithered around in the water and rolled in the stream.

*Must be like Doggie Heaven to him,* Maggie thought. Max noticed her as she watched him. He almost seemed to grin as he squirmed a little deeper in the pool.

"Com' on, Maggie. We's gonna set up rite here." Digger waved her toward a small clearing near the stream. A small grove of trees and bushes protected it from view from the field or trail above.

"This is great, Digger!" Maggie dropped her backpack and gear on a rock. She laughed as she watched Max play in the water. "You sure picked out the perfect place for him. We may never get him out of the water."

"Let's set up camp an' then pan fer a while 'afore it gits dark." Digger tried to hurry Maggie along.

"Ohh boy, I haven't done this in a while." Maggie laughed as she and Digger hurriedly gathered up enough wood for the night and prepared a campfire to light for the evening meal. She changed into a pair of shoes she brought specifically to wear in the creek, rolled up her sleeves and waded into the creek near one of the banks.

Maggie used to plunge right into the creek without shoes, but learned one time too many that the quartz rock in the creeks was often very sharp and could inflict serious cuts and scratches. Now, she wore shoes designed for wear in water to protect the soles of her feet.

Digger was already busy as he shoveled mud and muck from the bottom of the stream into his pan. Soon, his pan was full to the brim. Digger sat down on a rock beside the edge of the creek and began to move his pan with the slow swishing, swirling movement that helped the gold particles settle in the bottom of the pan.

Maggie watched him as she had so many times before. There was a rhythm and music to his movements... *shhuu, chu, chu, shhuu, chu, chu, shhuu...*as he swirled the pan and dipped it in and out of the stream to clear the silt away.

With one hand, he kneaded the silt and sand then loosened it as he scooped away debris. As he dipped fresh water to clear the muddy water from the pan, he continued to work the contents of the pan with his hand until the pile of muck and silt reduced to a small band of black sand. Maggie watched Digger work as the black sand and water swirled in the pan until it revealed a thin band of gold particles that glistened and sparkled in the sun.

Digger looked up and grinned with his crooked, silly grin. "Ye gonna join me or ain't ye? Looks like ah'm doing all the work 'round here."

"Just admiring the work of a pro," she quipped as she filled her pan and began to work it down to the sand.

They worked the creek through the afternoon, as they panned and sifted through the sand and mud. Digger saved the gold they found in a small vial he kept in his pocket. Some of the gold was small and granular, other pieces were a pretty good size, flaky and rough. After a few hours, Digger stood up and stretched.

"What's wrong there, old man? Getting a crick in your back?" Maggie teased. "You're starting to look pretty stiff there by the creek. Don't tell me you're going to quit before I am."

"Hee, Hee, watch it thar, girl. When ye stay in the crik as many years as ah have, ye'll have as many stiff bones as me, too. Ah count mahself lucky if ah kin git all mah bones to crik in harmony."

Maggie laughed. "Hey, we've been in the creek all afternoon. I thought you were taking me to a gold MINE."

"Take a look at that gold in yer pan and tell me what ye see."

"Well, there's lots of black sand, pretty good band of gold, most of it seems to be in long flakes or slivers, not too much of the ground particles," Maggie replied as she studied the contents of her pan.

"What does that tell ye?" Digger asked.

"Just that the gold in this creek hasn't traveled too far in the stream, it has flaked or broken off from something fairly recently."

"Exactly!" Digger looked pleased with her response. As he looked up from his pan, his bright blue eyes twinkled.

Slowly, Maggie became aware that there was more to this little expedition than she realized. "Does this mean the source is close by?"

"Yer settin' rite by it!" Digger grinned. His eyes sparkled with delight.

"Where?!" Maggie exclaimed as she jumped up and began to look around. Brushes and trees filled the streambanks everywhere she looked. Nowhere could she see a cave or mine.

Digger laughed with glee at her inability to discover his secret. She finally conceded that she had no clue where she could find the entrance of the hidden mine. Digger finally decided to let her in on the secret.

"Turn around, look upstream towards that big boulder over yonder, then jest to the right of the stream under the big holly bush."

Following his directions, she stared into the darkness around the boulder and under the holly. The darkness started to take shape. A small opening, not quite round hid in the shadows.

"That's it!" Maggie exclaimed. "How in the world did you ever find it?" She gasped as she started to walk closer to the opening.

"Jest kind 'o fell into it," he laughed. "Ah com up 'ere wild turkey huntin' one day and fergot mah bullits. So ah thought ah'd dip a pan or two 'n see how this stream panned. It had been a long time since ah seen such fresh flakes. Spent every chance ah culd get lookin' fer the source of the gold," Digger continued. "Passed that place by a hundret times 'afore ah found it."

"Let's go see!" Maggie said as she eagerly started to wade through the creek to get to the opening.

"Hold yer horses, there." Digger stopped her. "We ain't goin' nowheres tonight."

"Are you serious?" Maggie could not believe her ears. "You mean you finally show me where the secret place is, and you aren't going to let me go inside!"

"It'll keep till mornin'. We's gotta build the campfar and fix some dinner." Digger started to get out of the creek. "We don't need to be tryin' to git dry after the sun goes down."

As they sat around the crackling fire and waited for their dinner to cook over the coals, Maggie told Digger of the strange visitor who came to the cabin in the middle of the night. Maggie laughed nervously as she told Digger of the visit.

"I was beginning to believe it was Dynamite Dan or worse!"

Digger laughed. "Well, ye know, 'ole Dynamite Dan might still be hauntin' these here woods."

Maggie rolled her eyes. She could hear a tall tale brewing. "Digger I was being serious, I was a little frightened. I really don't have a clue as to who it might have been."

"Now, Dynamite Dan," Digger continued, heedless of Maggie's protests. "He wuz a wiley ole' character. Born in the saddle, he wuz. Yess, sirrreee, his mamma gave birth to him while she was ridin' into battle fightin' the injuns off his pappa."

"He culd 'restle a grizzly bear, climb a tree as tall as a redwood tree or swim the length of the Mississippi River, weren't nothin' that could stop 'ole Dan - 'cept fer maybe the dynamite," he paused. "Then agin, maybe it didn't stop him!" Digger raised his eyebrows and nodded his head as he lit his pipe and slowly began to puff away.

"Oh, Digger!" Exasperated, Maggie shook her head and stirred the stew. Her stomach began to growl as the aroma of the vegetables bubbling over the campfire filled the campsite with the promise of a satisfying dinner. "I suppose you are gong to tell me it could be him."

"Ah ain't sayin' it 'twas, 'n ain't sayin' it weren't."

"So, tell me then, how did this man supposedly die?" Maggie heard the tale of Dynamite Dan many times before, but loved to hear it again every chance she could.

"Well, sum folk say he thought he found the mother lode of all mother lodes sumwheres back here in the hills of east Tennessee. They think he found a vein so rich 'n so pure it wuz gonna make him wealthy beyond belief." Digger paused as he took a few bites of stew and tucked his bandana in the front of his shirt.

"Supposedly he found this vein in a cave back here in these mountains and it was rich. Ah mean it was really rich. But he couldn't git to it 'cause it was headed right under a boulder in a cave, runnin' right under the cave wall. So, he debated 'bout what he shuld do. Shuld he take what he had and run, or go fer the mother lode."

"I imagine he couldn't pass up the chance to be the richest man of all time," Maggie commented sarcastically as she handed Digger a piece of a dried apple pie she brought from home and warmed up in a skillet over the coals.

"Nope, couldn't pass that up for a minute. So, he rigged the dynamite to blast jest one section of the cave. He jest knew it wud git him exactly what he wanted, but somethin' went wrong. When he set the dynamite to blow, he didn't make it out of the cave. The whole thang fell in on him and the mother lode, too." Digger propped his feet out in front of him and puffed on his pipe.

"Nobody ever found a trace of him after that blast, narry a hair. His kinfolks looked fer him fer months, some even fer years. They say his ghost still haunts these here hills at night. He's always jest a walkin', lookin' fer the mother lode he found then lost forever."

Maggie shivered involuntarily. "I suppose you want me to believe the stranger at my cabin the other night was Dynamite Dan," Maggie commented. "He would be over a hundred years old by now!"

Digger leaned back against a rock and crossed his feet out in front of him, again. "Stranger thangs have happened, Maggie."

"I think I'd rather take my chances with a hiker or a nosy neighbor than a 100 year old ghost," she laughed.

They pulled out their bedrolls and watched the embers of the fire die down. Somewhere in the distance, a night owl hooted as Maggie closed her eyes and tried to sleep. Max lay in the shadows at the edge of the clearing. He appeared to be sleeping, but Maggie knew he was alert, ready to be up at any hint of danger.

# Yan-e'gwa

I became a bear when I was just a little child,
never wanted to be anything else.
All my friends were kittens and puppies
and doves and things.
But inside,
I was all filled up,
every inch
not a speck to spare
with bear.
Wasn't just any 'ole kind of bear.
Always knew I was a grizzly bear.
I was HUGE,
golden brown,
soft and furry all over.
I could burry myself deep inside where
no one else could find me,
cause I wasn't there,
only the Bear.
He'd wrap his big arms around me,
surround me and
keep me safe and sound
in his arms.
Sometimes, when
my heart began to beat very hard,
when I became frightened,
or angry,
a ferocious growl burst from his mouth.
His body trembled with rage
as he shook his head in defiance,
but nobody heard.
only me.
'Cause he was the only one there,
only the Bear.

# Forbidden Secrets

Morning came with the first light of day as it peeked through the leaves of the trees. The fresh smell of the new day filled her senses. Maggie groaned and stretched as she turned over in her sleeping bag. The morning air was crisp and cold. A light frost settled on them during the night. Maggie snuggled deeper into her sleeping bag.

*To rise or not to rise...that is the question*, she thought to herself. *Should one remain within the warmth of one's cocoon, or rise and face the cold of day?*

"Ha! I made a funny!" she mused. She heard Digger as he came around the edge of the campfire with an armful of wood. He tossed the wood on the fire then called to wake her up.

"Com' on Maggie, time's a 'waistin'," he said as he threw another armload of wood on the fire. "Got ye some coffee goin', so git off yer keyster. We got us some tracks 'ta make today."

After coffee and breakfast bars, Digger and Maggie prepared to enter the cave. She gathered her flashlight, candles, matches, canvas gloves and baseball hat.

*Sure would be nice to have a hard hat to wear*, Maggie thought as she gathered her gear.

Maggie froze in her steps. Suddenly, a cold chill ran through her body as she realized what was nagging at her subconscious for so long. *The hard hat! The silhouette of the man in the woods by the cabin was wearing a hard hat!*

"Digger!" she shouted frantically, "I know what it is!" she called to him as he disappeared inside the opening of the cave.

Maggie shuddered. *I'll tell him later*, she thought.

She turned around and glared toward Max.

"Hey, this time you listen to me! Stay here!" She sternly shook her finger at him.

Max sat down and looked at her expectantly with his huge brown eyes.

58

He wiggled his body and wagged his tail in response.

"I'll be back soon," she told him as she turned and headed toward the cave.

The opening of the cave remained completely hidden from view unless a person knew exactly where to look to find it.

*Digger was right,* she thought. *You could pass this place a hundred times and never see it unless you just fell into the opening.*

Just to the right of a huge boulder that rose out of the stream, the entrance was nestled against a wall of stone that rose fifty feet or more. The dense undergrowth of holly and laurel grew in front of the opening and blocked it from view even a few feet away.

Hesitantly, Maggie stepped forward and peered inside. She slipped the canvas gloves on her hands and made sure she placed the hems of her overalls securely inside her heavy hiking boots. Sometimes razor sharp quartz rocks covered the walls inside caves. She did not want to risk an accidental cut so she wore canvas gloves. The gloves also protected her hands and fingernails from the stain red clay leaves that often lined the inside of caves in Tennessee. Maggie knew that sometimes there were critters in caves and she wanted as much protection as possible against snakebites, or from bites from any other critters for that matter.

She brushed aside a cobweb and crawled inside. She lay on her stomach and waited just inside the cave opening to allow her eyes to adjust to the darkness. It was so dark inside the cave she could see nothing beyond her feeble flashlight. Without her flashlight, she was unable to see even her hand in front of her face.

The cave was cool and damp. It smelled of musk and wet clay. Maggie blinked when something dripped down her neck. "Yuck! I hope that was water," she whispered to herself as she wiped it off with the back of her sleeve.

Digger called to her from the darkness ahead. She began to crawl toward his voice. "Where are you? I don't see your light," she called back.

"Jest keep 'a goin' the way ye are fer about twenty yards, 'n ye'll be able to stand up."

Maggie turned on her flashlight and began to crawl forward slowly. As she inched her way along the tunnel, she noticed the floor of the cave became sandy and filled with small round pebbles as it neared the main chamber. Rough, jagged edges from the quartz rocks lined the irregularly shaped walls of the cave. The narrow tunnel crooked and twisted its way for about twenty to twenty five yards. Finally, she saw Digger's light ahead of her. It looked small and insignificant in the darkness.

Digger stood in a room that appeared to be about twelve feet across, no larger. It was difficult to determine just how high the ceiling was inside the chamber. In some places, Maggie could touch the ceiling, in other places; she could not see the top of the room at all because it disappeared into the darkness. Sand covered the floor of the chamber. There seemed to be watermarks on the walls of the cave that indicated water was present in the chamber sometime in the past.

"Digger, is this place safe? It looks like it fills up with water at times. Look at all the sand on the cave floor. This place looks like a streambed."

"Listen!" Digger said emphatically. "Don't ye NEVER com' 'ere without me! It ain't safe 'ere most of the time. 'Specially when it rains! This whole dang chamber fills up with water from the stream."

"OK, Digger, I promise." She looked at him curiously.

"Now, come 'ere. Ah gots to show ye somethn' ye ain't gonna believe, then we need to git outta here." Digger moved to the back of the chamber where the smell of damp earth and musk was much heavier.

Maggie followed Digger to the opposite side of the chamber. Their flashlights seemed like tiny pin lights in the vast blackness of the chamber. As they approached the far wall, Maggie could tell there was a difference in the feel of the floor.

Instead of the sand she felt in the entrance of the cave, mud and larger chunks of stone, mostly quartz littered this side of the chamber. She looked up as Digger stopped. A ribbon of white quartz streaked throughout the gray stone walls of the cave and grew wider until it disappeared into the floor of the cave.

Throughout the white ribbon of quartz, Maggie could see soft golden streaks that seemed to glimmer even in the dim glow of her meager light. She could see the quartz was filled with dozens of veins of gold that zigzagged throughout the wall of the cave like jagged lightening bolts across the sky. Maggie gasped as she fell to the ground.

"Digger! This is the most fantastic thing I've ever seen!" She ran her finger along one of the veins and watched as tiny flakes of gold easily fell to the floor of the cave. "This is IT Digger! You really found it!"

"Yep, sure did. Only problem is, ah'd be a fool to ever take it out," Digger said as he admired the veins of gold.

"What in the world are you talking about?"

"Watch this." Digger took his pick and chipped away at one of the quartz rocks. A chunk of quartz the size of a softball came loose and fell to the floor of the cavern. Then, moments later, a whole section on the side of the cavern where they stood crumbled and tumbled loose to the floor. Stones and sand tumbled down after that.

Maggie jumped up as the stones and sand cascaded around her feet. "Digger!" She coughed from the dust that followed the crash of stones as fear raced through her veins.

"It's the mother lode, Maggie. The one ah've looked fer all mah life, 'n now that ah've found it, ah know ah can't have it. The mountain wants to keep it fer its own. It's like discoverin' the pot of gold at the end o' the rainbow and findin' out there's no way ye can carry it home with ye."

Maggie carefully walked over the pile of rubble to get closer to the quartz wall. The stones were loose and rough making them difficult to walk across in the dim light of the cave. She took off her glove and placed her hand on the band of quartz. She ran her fingers across the coolness of the bright white stone band. Streaks of black threaded through some parts of it; other parts contained tiny threads of gold.

Her fingers ran along one of the tiny streaks of gold that broadened as it ran through the stone becoming almost an eighth of an inch wide in some places. She gingerly pried a small flake out of the vein and watched as it fell to the floor of the cavern. Fascinated, she tried to dig out a small portion of the gold with her fingernail. Another chunk fell out and onto the floor of the cave.

Overcome with the purity and beauty of gold in its natural setting, Maggie took a few steps closer to the vein and reached into her pocket for a knife so she could dig deeper. She wet her lips, her hands trembled she started to work the vein.

"Digger, this is beyond words," she gasped, almost breathless. She stepped closer again and dug a little more fervently.

"Better be careful, Maggie. Ye'll get the fever and ah won't never git ye outta here," Digger warned. "They's been men stronger than you and me both that's been taken over by the fever. They lost their families, their homes and even their lives to it. It'd be best if'n ye didn't even take a drop."

"But, Digger! There's so much here! It's what you've searched for all your life. How can you just walk away from something like this?" Maggie was incredulous as she feverishly continued to dig away at the golden streak in the quartz. "How can you say there's no way? We will FIND a way! Come on, now. Help me, Digger! Hurry!"

"Maggie, look at yerself. Yer already gettin' the fever. Yer hands are shakin' and yer eyes are all glazed over. This ain't somethin' we kin play around with a'tall. Ah jest wanted to show ye the place. You 'n me are alike. We love these mountains and don't want 'em to change. Jest think about what would happen to this little valley if'n sumebody found this 'ere gold," Digger warned.

"Why, there'd be folks comin' in tearin' up the land, buildin' roads, runnin' off all the animals! They'd put up buildin's and all the stuff folks want that goes with the buildin's. Ye know it as well as ah do. Ah bought the mountain here so nobody will ever bother it, but the gold don't belong to nobody but the mountain."

Another section of the cavern crumbled and fell to the floor of the cave as they talked. Maggie shuddered. She knew he was right. She looked down at the pocketknife in her hand. Her fingers still trembled and her heart continued to race. She remembered the feeling that had overcome her only moments ago as she touched the gold. Embarrassed with her frenzied actions and sudden loss of control, she shook her head.

"Oh, gosh Digger, I'm so sorry," she gasped. "I don't know what came over me. It was like I was a different person!"

"That's the way it happens, girl, that's the fever. It jest takes over ye. But, you 'n me, we know thar's somethin' more important than the gold and that's the paradise that's already here. We gots to protect this area as long as we can."

"Com' on now, girl, we gotta git goin' or we won't be needn' one 'o them marble markers on a grave, 'cause we'll be 'ere fer all eternity," he said as he headed towards the entrance of the cave.

One last look at the beautiful streaks of golden lightening before she turned to go and Maggie was on Digger's heels. They crawled and clawed their way through the tunnel and out to the stream that ran through the little hidden valley. Maggie was ready to be out in the sunshine again. She always felt a little claustrophobic inside a building and a cave was about ten times worse.

Maggie breathed in a deep breath of fresh air as she emerged from the cave and counted her blessings to be out in the open again. The beautiful streaks of gold in the cave vaporized from her thoughts as if they were a dream when she gazed around the beautiful valley and thanked the gods of the daytime for the gift of sunshine. Maggie knew she preferred to be outdoors any time of the year. She shook off a shudder as a vague premonition enveloped her.

*The strange feeling I'm getting must relate to being in this place and the cave for so long. It feels as though I have been here before, but I don't remember ever being here in the past.* She shook her head in an effort to ward off the uncomfortable thoughts. *Maybe it's just because Digger was so determined to get the point across that the cave is dangerous.* She pondered these thoughts as she and Digger prepared their campsite for the last night on the trail.

Max was glad to see Digger and Maggie emerge from the cave, too. He leaped across the field and bounded through the water as soon as he first sensed they were on their way out of the cave. Maggie greeted him, then made her way to the stream where she washed off as much of the dirt and clay from the cave as she could.

Digger built a campfire while Maggie made a hasty dinner for them from some of the leftover stew they had the night before. They both were silent in thought as they ate their dinner. Both were completely engrossed in their own thoughts of the amazing things they saw in the cave and the need to keep the treasure a secret.

# Rendezvous with Danger

It took most of the next day for Digger and Maggie to make their way home. Max was ready to head for home when they finally packed up camp and started the return trip back up the ridge. Maggie was almost as happy as Max to find herself on the outside of the cave in the bright spring sun and headed for home again.

The cabin was a welcome sight as soon as it came into view when they came off the trail near her home. As soon as Digger left, Maggie dropped her backpack on the porch and sat down to pull her boots off, rubbing her sore feet in the process.

*Traveling back up the ridge was a whole lot harder than going downhill,* she thought as she massaged her stiff, sore muscles.

She knew she would sleep soundly through the night when she returned home to her own bed. Now, she was ready for a long hot soak in the bathtub. As she soaked, Maggie began to relax. Heat from the tub formed little wisps of steam that rose and seemed to melt into the air. Maggie closed her eyes and thought about her past two days with Digger. The enormity of his discovery and the tragedy of its secret were almost overwhelming.

"That gold mine is exactly the kind of thing we're going to have to keep secret or the whole valley will fill up with out-of-towners and we'll end up with another tourist trap like Gatlinburg or Pigeon Forge. They just thought there was a gold rush in the 1800's, if it happened today, there wouldn't be an ounce of natural land left. Even the animals would suffer," she said to herself as she soaked in the tub. "I certainly hope Mr. Hubert T. Brown never finds out. He'd try to find a way to make a fortune and steal it away from folks if he could." Maggie shook her head. She was not sure how, but intuitively she knew he had some inappropriate motive for running for office in the elections.

She finished her bath and slept soundly through the night. For the first time in as long as she could remember, she slept without dreaming. Physical exhaustion and the comfort of being home helped her to relax completely. She did not even lay in bed awake long enough to remember the stranger who was around the cabin recently.

After a well-deserved sleep, Maggie awoke refreshed and feeling renewed. She made a hot breakfast of oatmeal filled with dried dates and walnuts then sprinkled with brown sugar and cinnamon. She had several things she needed to do today. First on her agenda, were the boot prints. She wanted to examine the woods by the house and see if she could find some clue that might tell her the identity of the midnight visitor.

Several days passed since she saw the man's silhouette in the woods by her house. She knew the chances were slim a trail of the unknown man's footprints were still in traceable condition, but she still wanted to check it out just to be sure.

Maggie tied the laces on her hiking boots, grabbed her jacket and small backpack then headed out the door. She only planned to hike for a short distance, but learned long ago to always go into the woods prepared. Parts of the trails on the Skyway rose higher than 5,000 feet and the weather could change very quickly. Being prepared could sometimes mean the difference between life and death, so she tried to be prepared when she hiked.

"Max, where are you?" she called for him as she opened the door of the cabin and looked for Max. He was taking a morning swim in the creek. He came bounding up the path ready to go when he saw her. Maggie held up her hand as he approached.

"Nooo way!" She tried to look sternly at him. "I don't need a shower yet!" Max hesitated briefly, then eagerly shook the creek water from his fur all over Maggie and the porch.

"Ugghh, had to share it with somebody didn't you big guy?" She grimaced and tried to wipe the creek water off her legs. "Come on, we've got a lot to do today. We won't get finished if we don't get started early, so let's get started."

She paused by the edge of the woods before she headed up the trail and observed the place where she saw the silhouette of the man lurking in the woods by her cabin several nights before.

"Whoever was here the other night must be an excellent woodsman," she whispered to herself as she scanned the ground for signs. "No trace of the midnight visitor anywhere, no tracks, no broken twigs, nothing obvious at all."

Maggie learned to track from Digger. He was an excellent woodsman and started to teach her at a very young age. She began to walk in a circle around the site as Digger taught her during one of her first tracking lessons. Each time she walked around the circle, she stepped out a little bit to widen her search. She carefully searched the ground with each lap. It was not until she reached the edge of the clearing that she saw something unusual. Here she saw the faint imprint of a boot of some type. An odd shaped boot print which appeared to have the sole worn down on the outside of the heels. As Maggie began to scout the trail of the midnight visitor through the woods, she learned very little about him.

*Whoever this stranger was, he was very good in the woods*, she told herself. *Even Digger would have a hard time tracking this one.*

Even as she thought about the visitor, she was not sure why she knew, perhaps intuitively, she just knew it was a male. As she walked along the trail, she could only see partial boot prints here and there along the outside of the path. The large size of the prints indicated to her that the stranger in the woods was most likely a man. The soles seemed almost worn out because the bottom of the boots appeared to have very few ridges left in the soles. She rarely found broken branches or crushed grass.

"I wonder where he was going?" Maggie wondered. "Where would he go from here?"

She continued to look for signs along the path that might give her more information about the stranger. The trail she followed was barely visible. It seemed to parallel a trail that led from her cabin to a more often used trail maintained in the National Forest. There were numerous trails along the Cherohala Skyway maintained by the National Forest Service personnel. Staff of the National Forest Service and many volunteers created these trails for tourists who wanted to get out of their cars and stretch their legs a bit before they continued the 68-mile drive through the mountains to North Carolina. Only experienced hikers and woodsmen traveled off the trails as skillfully as this person was able to travel.

Along the Tennessee/North Carolina border, there was a beautiful campground where people from miles around came during the camping season. Maggie was always amused at the number of "weekend warriors" as she called them, made their way to the park with loaded-down vehicles. Every time she saw the enormous four-wheel-drive vehicles pull pop up camp vehicles filled with radio, TV, microwaves and the works, she was amazed. It just did not make sense to her that someone would travel to such a beautiful mountain location just so they could stay inside and watch TV.

Maggie was always fascinated when she watched people and how they acted. She concluded that very few people respected each other much less the mountains and nature. Even fewer people revered the mountains. Digger always taught her to respect the mountains and "leave no trace" when she camped. Naturalists called it "low impact" camping.

Whatever you wanted to call it, the intention was to enjoy the mountains and leave as little trace of human intrusion as possible. When Maggie hiked or camped, she was careful to bury any human or food waste. True-blue Naturalists dug out the top layer of sod before they dug a hole in the ground, and then replaced the sod after they buried the waste. In this way, the forests had little obvious impact from the passage of humans.

"I've got to stop for a minute, Max and catch my breath," she commented, as Max trotted in the woods nearby her. "We've been hiking for several hours now." She was now on one of the main trails maintained by the National Forest Service. "This trail is a lot steeper than I remember it being last year," she gasped as Max ran past her. Although the morning was cool when she left the cabin, the spring sun started to warm things up. She took off her jacket and tied it to the base of her pack.

"Got ta be careful to make sure ye don't get too warm when ye're hikin', girl," Digger always told her. "Ye don't want to break out in a sweat if ye kin help it." Maggie knew the temperatures on this ridge could drop suddenly with the sunset and wearing damp clothing during the night could be dangerous for a hiker.

A nice shade tree just off the trail made an inviting place to take a break for lunch. More than an hour passed since she was able to see any obvious trail signs left by the midnight visitor and she began to feel tired and hungry.

Maggie sat in the shade and pulled off her pack. She pulled out a peanut butter sandwich and an orange and began to eat lunch. Max dove into the bushes near her and completed his version of a perimeter check before he came over and plopped down beside Maggie. Although Max was panting heavily from the long trek, he was always alert and on guard when she was around. She never felt afraid when she had Max with her.

Maggie poured some water for him into the lid of her water bottle that he eagerly lapped up. She always tried to carry enough water for the both of them in case there were no streams nearby when they hiked.

"Come on, boy. Drink up. We've got a long ways to go yet and I don't want you giving out on me."

Suddenly, his ears picked up. They heard voices from hikers as they came up the trail from the campground. Four young people appeared around the bend of the trail. They were all enjoying their hike as they laughed, talked eagerly and seemed to be having quite a good time. Max stood and hesitantly wagged his tail as they walked closer to where he and Maggie sat. He loved to play and these hikers looked like they might be potential playmates for him.

*Trekkies,* Maggie thought as soon as she saw them.

"Trekkie" was the term she used to describe genuine hikers who walk for the pleasure of walking and for the sheer delight of being outdoors. Many of the hikers who came to this remote region were here for the experience of being in nature and far away from crowds.

*Minimalists, naturalists, those requiring nothing but their boots and a trail to follow... these were the kind of people who were kindred souls,* Maggie thought as she smiled and greeted them when they rounded the bend in the trail.

"Oh, how cute!" One of the girls squealed with delight when she saw Max. "Come here, baby," she cooed as she stepped away from her hiking companions and started to giggle when Max began to lick her hands and face. "Look guys! He's just a big old teddy bear!"

One of Max's best qualities was his ability to judge character. He made fast friends of the four hikers. Amy sat on the ground and started to laugh when Max crawled in her lap and continued to lick her face. Justin sat down beside her and played with Max while Colleen sat on the rock by Josh and pulled out her canteen. They all seemed to enjoy the fun.

Josh, oldest of the four, appeared to be guiding the group. He wore faded jeans, a flannel shirt and hiking boots that looked as though they had plenty of use on the trails. He seemed so relaxed, completely at ease and comfortable in his surroundings as he leaned against a rock. Constantly aware of everything around him; he seemed to drink in everything he observed.

"So, where are you guys headed today?" Maggie smiled as she watched Max enjoy the attention he was receiving from the girls.

"We were on a break from school and decided to complete a trek along the Skyway while we're off. We're not sure where we'll end up," Josh commented as he watched his companions play with Max. Amused with their play; he sat down to relax on a nearby rock. He pulled out a pocketknife and began to slice an apple to eat while he talked to Maggie.

"That's an admirable feat," Maggie commented. "The Skyway is steep and difficult even under the best of weather conditions. In the winter and sometimes in the spring it can almost be formidable. I admire your ability to take such a huge challenge."

Maggie loved to hike, but tackling a 68-mile hike through elevations that exceeded 5,000 feet in less than a week was a little more challenging than she wanted during this time of year. As they sat with Maggie and Max, the hikers swapped news of the trails they had crossed.

"Gosh, it's great to be able to exchange news with other people who have experience with some of the risks and dangers involved when you hike. You four seem to know what you are doing," she said, admiring their skills. "I can tell you have lots of experience."

"Thanks, Maggie, hope we get the chance to hike as much as you do," Amy commented. Maggie smiled at the compliment.

Max began to get restless and ready to move on again. As much as Maggie enjoyed the visit with the four hikers, she knew she had a long way to go before she reached home and a special purpose for her trip. She needed to know whom she was tracking and who might be lurking in the woods near her cabin. She felt a chill and strange foreboding as she rose to start her hike again.

"Oh, by the way, be careful when you come to the next high overlook," Josh warned. "There's something odd going on up there."

"Yes, please be careful," Justin agreed. "There are some real strange characters on the trail there. One of them has a real problem with his attitude. He doesn't seem like he is someone to mess around with if you are hiking alone."

"What do you mean?" Maggie asked hesitantly.

"Those guys gave me the creeps!" Amy shuddered. "They smelled horrible! Their whole campsite smelled like a sewer!"

"I thought the forest service didn't allow overnight camping in that site," Maggie commented. She knew most of the forest service workers in the area and they usually kept her informed of the new camping areas. As far as she knew, that was not an overnight spot.

"They don't, but remember, they've cut back on their employees this year and they don't have enough personnel to hike all the trails every day to see if someone's in the wrong place," Josh reminded her.

"Those guys were on some kind of bad trip or something," Justin said as he shook his head. "I'm not sure what it was. All I know is we were real glad to get out of the area where they were camping. The place just gave us a creepy feeling."

"One of them, the short, blonde headed one, kept making eyes at us, too," Colleen shuddered. "He was so gross."

"The taller one could be the dangerous one, though. He was very restless and kept moving around kind of like he was trying to block us from going into their campsite or something," Justin added with a serious look in Maggie's direction. "They acted like they had something to hide, but I'm not sure what."

"His eyes were dilated, too, like he was on drugs or something. They were as big as saucers! He was pretty high," Josh warned. "Just be careful." Maggie could sense genuine concern in his voice. His eyes were dark, deep and intense. As they started to leave, he paused and seemed to hesitate.

"Watch your back, Maggie, you can't be too careful when you're alone, although I know you are already are aware of that."

She smiled, then nodded her head in agreement as she and Max headed down the trail again. It was late afternoon and she needed to be on her way, night would come all too soon.

Max darted in and out among the bushes and shrubs along the trail and stayed a few steps ahead of her. Maggie's mind began to wander. Spring always reminded her of her grandmother's cabin in the mountains. She loved living with her grandmother. That time of her life seemed so long ago.

The spring flowers at this higher elevation were starting to come up and redbuds were ready to bloom. She grasped a branch from a redbud tree as she walked past a large one that grew along the trail. They seemed to be scattered throughout the forest. She always thought it was a little funny they named the trees Redbuds when they were such a beautiful shade of purple when they were in full bloom. The only time they actually had any red on them was when they were in the budding stage.

"Which probably accounts for their name," Maggie smirked and shook her head idea.

Her thoughts wandered then to the purpose of her trek today, the midnight visitor. She and Max were already tired from the past few days on trails and today's journey seemed to sap their energy more quickly than usual. Maggie thought carefully about the past few days' events as she plodded along the trail.

"I wonder where that fella went, Max," she pondered while she hiked. "He must have turned off the trail somewhere and I just missed it. My tracking skills must be slipping. Just think about it for a minute, Max. Not many people know where our cabin is located. It's very remote." She talked to the dog as she walked.

"Unless he just happened to walk up the forest service road and see the path to the cabin, there's no way he could have found it from the Skyway trail. No one else knows about that trail except for Digger and maybe the Rangers," she talked to herself. "But someone else MUST have known about it, Max." She tried to rationalize her thoughts with the dog. "We certainly had a visitor the other night, or maybe I was dreaming," she mused. "No, I saw the boot prints, you saw them too didn't you, Max."

Max wagged his tail as if in agreement and trotted along beside her. Maggie shivered as she remembered seeing the man's silhouette against the trees that night. A sudden realization flooded over her.

"Oh, I forgot to tell Digger that the stranger looked like he was wearing a miner's hat! That's why he reminded me of that silly old folk tale about Dynamite Dan! Ohh, geezze, this is great!" she said aloud to herself. "Now it sounds like I'm crazy! I have decided it could not possibly be a dream because it was a 100-year-old man blown up by dynamite who continues to walk the ridge tops at night! Is this delusional or what!" Maggie laughed.

She was not paying attention when Max came to a dead halt in the middle of the path. She absently mindedly bumped into him and stumbled over him before she landed on the path, knocked her chin on the ground and scraped the skin off her hands and knees. Every bone in her entire body jarred as she fell. She groaned as she tried to sit up and gingerly felt the bones in her legs and arms. Nothing seemed to be broken, although her palms and shins were full of dirt and grime. She delicately tried to brush some of it out.

She started to reach for the water bottle from her backpack when she noticed Max remained in the middle of the trail. He rigidly blocked anyone from passing him and also kept Maggie from going any further for that matter. She could hear the deep rumble in the back of his throat as he lowered his head and stared straight ahead.

Instantly aware there must be some kind of danger and fearing it might be the stranger she was tracking; Maggie looked for a place to hide. She said nothing to distract Max as she slowly and cautiously slipped off the trail and into the woods. She quietly lay down among the leaves, her Khaki pants and olive jacket blending into the forest.

Maggie softly whistled for Max. "Come on boy," she whispered. Max quietly moved back from the trail and lay under the bush beside her. Maggie could barely hear him breathe. She held her breath when she heard the voices in the distance and wrapped her arm around Max when he began to growl again.

"Shhhh, quiet."

Two people stumbled nosily up the trail. She could hear their voices, but could not quite make out what they said. It was the sound of someone cursing, an argument of some sort. One man seemed to be very angry with the other man. Quietly she waited, hidden in the darkness of the forest as two men who looked like they were in their late twenties clumsily staggered up the trail. They struggled to carry a large wooden crate the size of an ice chest between them. The crate appeared to be quite heavy as both men groaned under its weight on the steep trail.

*This must be the two men the kids warned me about*, Maggie thought with alarm.

She barely breathed as she watched the unusual pair struggle with the heavy crate. Just before they reached the turnoff from the trail to the overlook parking lot, the shorter of the two men dropped his end of the crate. There was a great racket as it fell to the ground.

"Sounds like it's full of some kind of jars, Max," Maggie whispered softly as she wrapped her arm around him a little more tightly and scratched behind his ears.

The taller man set his side of the crate down while he continued to curse and thrash his arms about wildly. He stepped toward the shorter man and shoved him down on the ground, which knocked the man's head on a rock and caused it to bleed.

"You're an IDIOT, Frank, an IDIOT! What the heck are you doing! You trying to get us killed or something!" the tall man screamed, followed by a long tirade of expletives. "Get off your rear end and help me with this. It's almost dark. And BE careful!" he shouted.

"I'm sorry, Wes, I'm sorry, I'm sorry," Frank said as he cowered on the ground rubbing his head and trying to focus his eyes. It took a few moments before he was able to regain his balance and stand back up on his feet. When Frank was able to stand again, he and Wes continued their struggle with the chest until they came to the section of the trail that led to the overlook parking lot.

Maggie and Max waited and listened from under the bushes until they could hear no more sounds. Then, Max started to get up and follow the pair across the trail to the overlook.

"No, Max, wait!" she whispered as she held him back. "We don't know where they are right now and I don't think they're gone."

In a few moments, the pair stumbled back down the trail again. Wes, the taller of the two men was carrying an empty crate. They both disappeared into the woods at the base of the hill again. Maggie waited and watched as the sun began to set over the mountains.

"It's going to be dark soon," she whispered, alarmed. She knew it was going to get dark very quickly, but was afraid to move. "These two characters seem like they're up to no good, but if we move now, they'll see us for sure," she whispered to herself as much as Max.

Dark shadows began to fall between the trees and in the deep crevasses of the ridges as Maggie heard the two men labor back up the trail again with the loaded crate. Both men breathed heavily and strained from the weight of the crate. They paused as they reached a level spot across from where she and Max hid. Maggie listened intently as the pair continued to argue about something while they rested on the trail.

"I told you not to talk to those hikers! What do you think we are here in the middle of nowhere for anyway?" Wes yelled.

"She smiled at me first, I think she liked me," Frank protested. He kept his head down, his long stringy blonde hair hanging in his face. He was extremely unkempt and dirty. His worn jeans looked as though he had not washed them in a very long time.

Wes wore his jet-black hair in a slicked back fashion similar to an Elvis style. He wore a white tee shirt and jeans that looked washed and pressed.

"Ain't no girl like that gonna look at you twice! Come on you little twerp," Wes said angrily. "If you don't put some muscle in it we won't make it to the car before dark."

Frank seemed to sway a little as he tried to stand. As he started to pick up his end of the crate, he looked across the path to the area where Maggie and Max hid. He seemed to hesitate then squint his eyes as he peered into the bushes where they lay. Maggie averted her eyes and held her breath. Frank shook his head as if he was not sure of what he was seeing, picked up his end of the crate and the two men continued up the trail to the parking lot.

Maggie waited for the distant sound of the car engine as the daylight faded. It seemed as though it took forever before Maggie heard the roar of the motor when the two men revved up the engine and noisily drove away.

"Sounds like they're gone," Maggie whispered. She looked at Max as darkness enveloped them. "Boy, we're sure in a mess now, big guy." Maggie whispered as she ruffled his neck. "Guess we will be camping out because it looks like we're here for the duration of the night."

She crawled out from under the bushes and tried to brush the dirt and leaves from her clothing while she searched for ticks and other uninvited critters that might have joined her.

"I itch all over, Max. Hope there wasn't any poison ivy in there." Although, she wanted to be home in her own bed, the risks of hiking here at night were too great. The trail was treacherous in daylight, at night it would be even worse. It looked as though a fog was moving into the area and she did not want to make the mistake of taking a wrong turn and step off the trail into a ravine.

"What do you think we should do, Max?" she asked. "Using the flashlight is out of the question right now." She knew that on these high ridges a person could see the light of a flashlight from miles away. "Guess we'd better just stay where we are till the sun comes up so we can see what we're doing. I don't want anything to happen to you."

They moved a short distance down the trail until Maggie found a clean level spot. Using her backpack for a pillow, she zipped her jacket, pulled her hands inside the sleeves and curled up to try to sleep. Max thumped his tail and lay his head down on the leaves beside her. Maggie drifted off into another restless, fitful sleep. She could not seem to get out of the halfway stage between wakefulness and deep sleep. She dreamed the dream she dreamed since she was a child. The one she dreamed whenever something was on her mind...

...the child was alone, surrounded by darkness. In the distance Maggie could see a small light. She could hear the sound of footsteps behind her as heavy footsteps, the sound of leather shoes walking on pavement headed for the child's hiding place. She shivered and wrapped herself into a ball and tried to make herself very small. A deep masculine voice called out. The sound of the voice sent chills through her body. The child was in trouble again. The child looked up to Maggie for help as the shadow of a man in a black suit stood over him and held a whip. The man stood in front of the light so she could see its warm glow no more, only the outline of the man as the light shone around him. Fear raced through her veins and her heart began to pump at an alarming rate. She couldn't catch her breath and started to pant as she broke out in a sweat and began to run away. The sound of a 'child's muffled cries and footsteps of the man followed her

and came closer and closer no matter how fast she tried to
run – no, wait....

Maggie awoke with a start and gasped as she tried to orient herself to her
surroundings. It took a few moments for her to orient herself to the reality of
her situation. She tried to remember why she was on the trail.

"Something isn't right." She tried to blink her eyes.

Darkness surrounded her. Slowly she began to think clearly. Gradually,
she began to remember she was on the Skyway trail on the mountain, not at
home in her bed. She felt confused and a little disoriented. The fog of sleep
began to lift from her brain as she slowly remembered where she was.
Consciousness slowly dawned on her. She was on the mountain, not at home
in her own bed. She was here with Max and they were outside in the dark.

"Gosh, that dream was so real!" she spoke aloud. She shook her head as
she wrapped her jacket a little tighter around her. She turned to look for Max
and could see him nowhere.

*Where is he?* she wondered. *He was right here just a little while ago.*
*That scoundrel must be off gallivanting in the woods.*

She opened her mouth to call him and decided against it. Something
stopped her even as the thought crossed her mind, a premonition or intuition
perhaps. She often had strong feelings she could not quite define that guided
her in difficult situations.

"He'll come if I need him." She tried to reassure herself hoping he was
close by in case she needed him.

Suddenly, a cold chill ran through her body. She heard the sound of
footsteps - real footsteps on the path, walking toward her. They were not the
same footsteps she just dreamed about, they were real. She felt around on the
ground for a stick or a rock, anything to use for protection if she needed it.
There was nothing nearby.

"Remind me to kick myself if I get out of this," she whispered to herself.
"And then, remind me to give Max a piece of my mind for leaving me alone
on the trail like he did."

Fear paralyzed her as she heard the sound of the footsteps briefly pause
in front of her hiding place. She shuddered as she heard the footsteps slowly
disappear when the unknown person continued to walk down the trail.
Breathless, Maggie waited until she could hear the sound of the footsteps no
longer, then she waited through the long endless hours until dawn, barely
sleeping any during the night.

Sleep was difficult and only came in brief, fitful spells. She dreamed of a shadowy figure that lurked in the woods and followed her wherever she went. Sometimes the figure looked like a man and other times it looked hunched and bent over as it scurried among the trees. The cryptic words of the crooked old woman floated through her thoughts - *a blockage in there*, and *clear up your head*. Like an annoying song, they played over and over again in her head.

Maggie tossed and turned through the rest of the night. She woke up as the first rays of sun rose over the mountains. She ached all over, partly from sleeping on the ground in the cold air all night and partly from the tumble she took on the trail during the night. As she shook the leaves out of her clothes and straightened her jacket, Max bounded up the trail to greet her.

"And what happened to you last night, Mister? You left me all alone!" she demanded. Max seemed oblivious to her irritable remarks and sat down in front of her. He wagged his tail and watched her expectantly.

"I suppose you want me to believe you were here all along and I was only dreaming, huh?" She smiled and shook her head. "Guess you're pretty hungry aren't you fella. Let's see what we have for breakfast," Maggie said as she scoured through her backpack for something for both of them to eat.

She gave Max the peanut butter crackers and started to munch the last apple in her pack as she headed down the trail. When she reached the bottom of the trail, she immediately smelled the stench before she noticed the area where limbs and crushed grass lead off the trail to the unauthorized campsite. Trash and debris filled the camping area. It looked as though someone was living on the site for weeks and for some reason made a hasty retreat.

"This place is disgusting!" Maggie burst out angrily, "There is nothing more despicable than someone who has such complete disregard for other people, animals or just nature in general. I can't believe they would leave the campsite like this."

She kicked one of the old cans across the clearing. The anger rose inside her as she stood and looked at the old cardboard boxes that now were crumpled and soggy from the rain. Mason jars and empty drink cans were crumpled and tossed around the site. Dozens of empty canisters of camping fuel rusted as they lay in a pile tossed to the side of the clearing.

"They must have camped here all winter to use so much fuel," she said, as she shook her head. "Even when this place is cleaned up, it's going to take forever to get rid of that smell!" she said aloud to herself. The sight of the ruins, the stench of urine, rotting food and human decay permeated the air and sent Maggie into a rage as she viewed the damage in the area.

"The little twits! I cannot believe anyone would be so STUPID! It has ruined this place for everyone! It is blatant disregard for everyone, animals and humans alike! I would like to get a hold of the jerks right now, tie them to one of these trees for a few days and see how they would like to live around this awful smell. Then, I'd make them stay here till they had it cleaned up!" Furious, Maggie kicked another of the fuel cans across the small clearing onto a pile of debris frightening Max as it landed and clattered into the rubble.

Maggie could feel the blood pumping in her veins. Her head pounded, her temperature boiled and she felt tense inside. She quickly scanned the area for damage around the campsite.

*I have to calm down,* she told herself as she started to take in deep breaths and count to ten. She took deep breaths as she slowly tamed the anger that boiled inside her.

Involuntarily, she wrinkled her nose as nausea and bile rose in her throat. She grimaced and decided to report the site to her friend Sam, who worked with the National Forest Service as soon as she could get into town. First, she wanted to get home to a hot bath and something good to eat! Camping on the trail was one thing she loved to do, but it was much more enjoyable when one had their sleeping bag and plenty of food on the trip.

# River Run

It took an extra amount of time for Maggie to nurse and soak her sore, aching muscles in a hot bathtub and ease some of the pain she felt from her night on the ground in the woods. The steamy waters and herbal cleansing ointments helped soothe her arms and knees. She examined the areas now swollen and bruised from her fall on the trail. She took extra time to cleanse her wounds and treat them after her bath to prevent them from developing an infection. A huge blue welt developed along her jaw and chin. She winced when she dabbed at her jaw and tried to soothe her tired eyes.

"Today might be one of those days I really need to wear some make up," she told the face in the mirror as she examined the puffy bruise on her chin. "It doesn't exactly compliment my face does it?"

Rarely, did she wear makeup, she just wanted to be natural and felt comfortable being who she was, gray hair, wrinkles and all. Something about wearing makeup felt false to her. When she wore it, she felt as though she was trying to be something she was not. She just wanted to be herself. Being comfortable with herself showed in the clothes she wore and things she did. She rarely wore anything but old faded jeans or khakis, although she did have a few cotton dresses she wore on special occasions. Maggie was average height and size, 5'6" tall and around 145 pounds.

"Not bad, but nothing to write home about," she often told herself. "Average - at least I don't stand out in a crowd," she reasoned.

The most notable things about Maggie were her eyes and her genuine smile. Her eyes were a soft gray color that seemed to reflect her mood and the colors around her. Some days they appeared to be a deep pensive green color; other days they were a bright blue, even lavender at times. She wore an infectious smile that invited even the coldest person to smile in return.

Max lay in the shade as she headed out the door of the cabin. "You be good, Buddy. I won't be gone long." He thumped his tail as she walked past him. "Stay out of trouble!"she cautioned.

She rolled the window down while she drove to help dry her hair. Maggie's long dark curls were beginning to show signs of gray along the top and sides. She usually wore her hair long and loose allowing the natural curls to do as they pleased. It was easier for her to keep it this way than to continually try to control her hair.

Frustrated with attempts to tame her curls a long time ago, she now just preferred to allow her hair the pleasure of being natural. It was a form of the philosophy to "choose your battles". She chose to allow the natural curl in her hair to have free reign and avoided fighting it. It was too frustrating and usually a losing battle for her.

When she reached the bottom of the mountain, she turned left on River Road and headed toward the Ranger's station. She wanted to talk to Sam about the unusual characters and the ruined campsite she saw on the trail. There was only one vehicle in the parking lot as she pulled up to the ranger's station. She opened the office door to find Ranger Stratton behind the desk almost buried behind a stack of files and papers near the computer.

"Hey, Maggie! Long time no see, pull up a chair and join me here. I'm a little swamped."

Maggie laughed. "At least things are normal then, Stratton," she teased. Stratton always seemed swamped with paperwork. He loved being outdoors and typically put off his paperwork until his desk was so covered he could not see it anymore.

"You looking for Sam?"

"Yep, I thought I'd give him a report on one of the trails I hiked yesterday. Is he working today?"

"He's up the river." He paused while he waited for her to catch his attempt at humor.

Maggie smiled. Stratton was always trying to slip something funny into a conversation. She had to listen, or sometimes she missed his remarks. "He's always up the river, Stratton." She grinned.

Pleased with her response he added, "He's making sure the crowd stays in control during the kayak competition at Baby Falls. They're having one of those kayak rodeos today."

"Ok, thanks Stratton, I'm going to try to find him. Good luck with your paperwork." She grinned and waved goodbye.

She watched the twists and turns of the river as she followed along on River Road. They built this road over two hundred years ago for logging companies who wanted to tap into the area's virgin forests. Later, an iron works company moved into the area and mined iron to make huge pots for the confederate army during the war. General Sherman destroyed the iron company during his march to Atlanta.

Today, the riverbanks were full and overflowing with water from recent rains. Maggie watched eagerly to see kayakers as they maneuvered down the river. Every time the water levels were up, the river was flooded with daring young people who loved to ride the rapids and waterfalls as they competed in treacherous feats.

Nearing the waterfalls, she paused. It was almost impossible for her to cross the stone bridge that spanned the river in front of Bald River Falls without stopping to watch the power and majesty of the falls. Today, they were even more breathtaking than usual.

"This is spectacular!" she said aloud. "I think it's more beautiful every time I see it."

The sound from the falls was deafening as Maggie sat in the jeep and watched the power of the water rush over the boulders in the stream. The falls were so full and overflowing from spring rains the spray from the rush of water over the falls almost reached the jeep. The stone bridge was wet from the mist that rose from the falls. She took a deep breath and inhaled the fragrance of fresh water and damp ground. The woods were always a little darker and deeper here by the falls. Lush undergrowth of the forest and stream banks filled the area with the mysterious feeling of a long ago place and time.

She could almost drink in the beauty as she looked along the sides of the falls where the rosy pink color of Mountain Laurel and the deep lavender shade of Rhododendron blossoms filled the edge of the stream. The sun touched only the tops of the trees in the woods bringing a bright spring green to their leaves.

"This is one of my favorite places in the whole world," she said. She closed her eyes and listened to the sound of water as it rushed over the stones. "This is probably one of the few places that remained the same over the centuries."

She loved to come here and watch shadows deepen in the evening while she listened to the sound of the water. This place was one of her own perfect places she kept hidden in her heart. She often remembered this place in her meditations. She smiled as she thought of coming here with a group of friends in the seventies. They sat on the bridge, played folk songs on their guitars and sang of peace, love, and their hopes for the future.

*Those were the days,* she thought to herself. *We were able to sit on the bridge for hours at a time with no other traffic attempting to cross the bridge. If anyone sat on the bridge these days, someone would probably run them over with a car.*

Traffic and visitors increased dramatically in this area since the seventies. She smiled, and sighed; satisfied she was able to return to her paradise for a few moments and dream. She traveled on the road again for another quarter mile. Maggie then drove to a small parking area and overlook around Baby Falls. The lot was crowded and filled with people. Cars filled all of the parking spaces, so, she had to park along the side of the road in a ditch.

Maggie got out of the jeep and walked to the edge of the Baby Falls overlook. Groups of people in every type of river gear possible filled the steep banks along the river. Some of the visitors were in swimsuits, others wore wet suits, and many carried kayaks. The impromptu competitions, which often took place after a big rain, now took place at the top of the falls. Kayakers took turns floating off the top of Baby Falls into the deep torrent of water in the pool below.

Cheers rose from the crowds as each competitor went over the top. Some competitors ended up going down sideways, some nose first, some even backwards. The more difficult the maneuver, the louder the crowd roared their praise. No one seemed to heed the sign posted on the opposite bank of the river that stated, "Hazardous Waters, 8 people have died here."

The area was a favorite spot for swimmers and kayakers alike. Each group boasted their own brand of daredevil feats to perform from the top of the falls. Swimmers liked to jump or slide from the top of the falls into the deep pools below. The problem that seemed to place people at risk was swimmers who tried to swim while intoxicated. Some people even tried to jump into the water in a place where the pools were not deep enough below the falls.

Maggie searched through the crowd looking for a familiar face. She noticed Hubert T. Brown as he worked the crowd and handed out business cards to any of the spectators who listened as he talked. He seemed to have found an audience in several men who stood around him. They nodded and appeared to agree with something he dramatically relayed to them.

*Hope they really listen to what he is saying. He is like a wolf in sheep's clothing leading the blind astray,* she said to herself as she shook her head and continued her search of the crowds.

She finally saw the khaki uniform of one of the forest service personnel as he walked among the swimmers. She watched until she was certain it was

Sam, then, weaving her way through the crowd, worked her way forward until she reached him.

"Hey, Ranger," she greeted as she stood beside him on a stone near the river. "Looks like you have your hands full of tourists today."

"That's an understatement!" he said with a smile. "They sure are having fun. Wish I could keep them out of here though. Somebody gets hurt every time the water's up at this level."

They watched one of the competitors complete an Ender by using the force of the water to enable him to stand his boat on end. He completed his moves by placing the bow of his kayak headed upstream in the water. The water forced the front of the kayak completely under a wave. This forced the other end of the boat up into the air. The crowd roared their approval.

Sam turned to look at her and was surprised to see her bruised chin. "What in the world have you been up to, Maggie? You look like you've been wrestling with a bear!"

She blushed. "Nothing much, just took a tumble when I was hiking. These big 'ole feet get in the way sometimes."

Sam was a ranger with the Tellico District of the forest service for about four years. Disillusioned by the fast-paced city life, he and his wife moved to this area with their girls as soon as he accepted a position with the forest service.

They watched one of the kayakers take his craft parallel down the face of the falls, then maneuver it into an Ender position in the pool at the bottom of the falls. He began to demonstrate a Pirouette by completing a 180-degree vertical spin and landing upright for his stunt. The crowd again cheered their approval.

Sam laughed. "I'm not sure if it's the arrogance of youth or the ignorance of youth that keeps these guys from being afraid to do a stunt like that," he said admiring their skills.

"Whatever it is, I don't think I ever had it," Maggie commented. She watched the next competitor line up for his trick.

The kayaker aimed his boat directly for the center of the undercurrent in the waterfall. As the front end of the boat began to sink, the kayaker paddled furiously and caused the water to dramatically lift and spin the boat around and out of the water.

"Wow!" Maggie was amazed.

Sam nodded agreement. "So what's up with you today, Maggie?"

"Oh, that's what I came to tell you. There's something strange going on the trail over on Brush Mountain."

"What do you mean strange?" Sam asked. He only halfway listened as he continued to watch the competition, preoccupied with the difficulty of the stunts.

"Well, I was hiking Springs Gap Trail yesterday and met four hikers who just came up from the Citico area. They gave me a strange warning about some guys they'd seen on the trail." She went on to tell him about the commotion she saw during the night and the disastrous campsite they left behind.

Sam quickly turned around and faced her. "What?" he said in sudden awareness. "Say that again."

He stared at her intently and continued to question her. "Now, where was this?" He demanded to know, now suddenly alert and attentive.

"I told you. It was on Brush Mountain, right where the trail intersects with the South Fork Trail. There is a small parking area there right above the trail. They were camped in an area that was kind of hidden in a little glade off the trail."

Sam watched her intently now. "Think carefully, Maggie. What kinds of things were left behind?"

"Well, trash, you know, glass jars, plastic bottles, old medicine bottles, rubber hoses, all kinds of things." Maggie adjusted the socks in her boots as she talked. "When I saw it, I thought they must be camping there for a long time because there were so many fuel cans. There were dozens of those old red fuel cans you can buy to refill your camp lanterns and stoves. They were pretty dented and rusted. It looked like they were there for a long time."

"What else, Maggie, think!"

"Well, it's hard to remember because there was so much, but some of the stuff was really weird. There were things that you wouldn't think about people having at a campsite."

"Like what?" Sam was urgent.

"You know, stuff like drain cleaners and things like that. Who needs a drain cleaner in a campsite that doesn't have restroom facilities?" Maggie laughed. "Oh, and one of them may have been sick for a while or something. There were lots of old medicine bottles for colds, things like that."

Sam grabbed her by the arms. "Maggie, are you sure?"

She nodded. "Of course I'm sure."

"Do you think you could recognize the same men again if you saw them?" Sam asked urgently.

"I guess so, it was starting to get dark though," she said hesitantly, as she tried to remember things exactly as she saw them.

"Did either of the men see you?"

"I don't think so, but I can't be sure." Maggie had a queasy feeling when she remembered the way Frank had peered into the bushes where she and Max hid.

"Listen, Maggie, I've got to go check it out. I'll catch up with you later," he said as he quickly disappeared into the crowd.

She watched the competition for a few more minutes before she decided to leave. She wanted to head into town before the crowd started dispersing after the event, otherwise it would take her twice as long to drive the few short miles. River Road was extremely narrow and winding. Often, campers and fishermen parked along the side of the road while they fished or swam in the river which made travel in a vehicle a little more difficult and much more time consuming.

As Maggie passed the Ranger Station, she noticed there were several forest service vehicles there now. An ambulance and a hazardous waste materials team van headed up the mountain with their lights flashing and sirens blaring.

*It's a good thing I'm not headed that way now*, she thought. *If there is an accident somewhere, there will probably be a traffic jam and a long delay in getting home.* Maggie did not see Sam's jeep anywhere, so she drove into town. *Probably some sightseers or tourists that don't know how to drive on curvy roads*, she thought with disgust as she headed her jeep in the opposite direction.

"I may as well go ahead and run some errands while I'm in town," she said as she drove into town.

The small road into town was crowded with cars of tourists who often came to the area on weekends to enjoy nature or to purchase souvenirs from the local gift shops. As with many of the national tourist sites, some of the shop owners quickly learned to find items that were fast sales. Many were on display for people just passing through the area who wanted to take a souvenir home to others as a reminder of the area. Hats, visors, mugs and key chains that broadcast the name of the town were hot items in this area much as they were in many other summer vacation areas.

It was much more difficult to find genuine articles made by local artists and craftsmen made in the traditional methods passed down through generations and generations, but they were there if you looked for them. The area had many local craftsmen who were excellent weavers, potters and basket makers. Some of the local artists who made baskets from slivers of hand split white oak splints were among of the finest baskets in the world. Maggie pulled into the feed store parking lot and went into the shop to purchase the supplies she needed.

# Wani'nahi'

Her broad round face is creased with
the lines of many years of joy and tears.
Bright blue eyes glisten and sparkle as she eagerly
waits for the child to make her way through the field.
A butterfly halts the child's steps
as she tries to follow its flight.
Golden wisps of hair blow in the summer breeze
as she makes her way thru a sea of grass.
A flower here, a pebble there,
everything she sees must be investigated.
Soon the child's hands are full of treasures
found on her journey.
Suddenly, she looks up and sees
the gentle old woman as she
patiently waits and rocks on the porch.
Her face brightens, her heart leaps with joy.
She runs quickly to her grandmother's arms.
The old woman's eyes fill with tears.
Lines and creases on her face deepen with joy
as the child climbs into her arms.
A handful of daisies wilted from the warmth of the sun,
a shiny stone and a woolly worm
all spill into the old woman's lap.
The child peers into her eyes.
Tiny little hands stained with dust and grass
clasp the woman's wrinkled old face.
Eye to eye and soul to soul
they speak the language that has no words.
They smile and embrace.
The child nestles into her grandmother's soft bosom
as she gathers the treasures of the day into her tiny hands.
Gently, eyelids begin to flutter softly against her cheeks
as she dreams of cotton clouds and crystal streams.

Smoothing the lace on her worn cotton gown
with fingers swollen and crooked with age,
the old woman slowly begins to rock,
and sing a soft, sweet lullaby, while in the dusk,
the songs of the night greet the end of the day.

# Springtime Yearnings

Maggie placed a large bag of dog food by the counter at the feed store alongside a bag of wild birdseed. She meandered through the store and gathered first some vegetable seeds and then a few tomato plants for her garden, a package of nails and finally a box of new jelly jars for the jam she would make. As usual, her decision to walk through the store without a buggy was a mistake. Her arms were full and overflowing with supplies by time she made it to the checkout counter again.

"Need any help there?" a deep mellow voice asked.

Maggie jumped with surprise. She tried unsuccessfully to grab several items that fell from her arms and tumbled to the floor. The only sound that came from her mouth was, "uuhhh," when her heart seemed to leap up and stick in her throat. She turned to see Doc's gentle face smiling at her.

"Here, let me help." He leaned to pick up the items she dropped on the floor.

Blushing, Maggie tried to regain her composure. "Thank you." Her heart was beating so loudly in her ears she quickly looked around to see if anyone else could hear it.

"Here, let me carry these things for you." Doc gathered some of the things out of her arms and started to walk with her through the store to the checkout counter. "How've you been, Maggie? I haven't seen you for a while."

"I, uhh, I've been good," she stammered, as she tried to regain her composure again. "I've been doing some hiking."

"Looks like you've been doing more than hiking," Doc chuckled, noticing the large bruise on Maggie's chin.

She grinned and blushed. "Yeah, guess you could say the trail rose up to greet me." She could not bring herself to say more. After she made her purchases, Doc helped Maggie carry the supplies and load them into her jeep.

"I was hoping I'd run into you, Maggie." He gazed intently into her eyes.

"How about having dinner with me tomorrow? I'm making my special Marinara sauce."

Maggie remembered their last conversation. Doc made it very clear he was interested in seeing her. She did not know what to say, so, she avoided him. She ran, afraid of the intense emotions she felt. She and Doc formed such strong feelings for each other during the snowy night when they worked together to deliver Rena's baby it now almost overwhelmed her. It was such a long time since Maggie allowed herself to care for someone she was not sure how to allow herself to feel again.

During that storm, they talked and shared their innermost feelings with each other throughout the night. They shared more than Maggie planned to share with anyone. Over the years, she built such a thick wall of protection around her heart. She convinced herself she would be alone for the rest of her life when she moved back to the mountain. It caught her by surprise to meet someone who so openly shared with her, someone so much like herself.

Being a very private person made it difficult for her to feel completely comfortable being so open with anyone. Yet, during that night, she felt as though he was a part of her soul, a part that had been missing for a very long time. The closeness with another person frightened her so, she hid away in her secluded mountain cabin afterwards and avoided seeing him whenever possible. She feared her heart might become vulnerable again if she cared for someone.

A commotion in the parking lot interrupted their conversation. Two men began to fight with each other while three others watched and taunted them to continue. The taller of the two wildly jumped around, waved his arms and fists as he cursed the shorter man.

Maggie and Doc watched the taller man throw a punch so hard he knocked the shorter man off his feet and onto the ground. The crowd cheered him. The taller man looked wild. The frenzy of the fight seemed to fuel him and pump him up as he jumped around the man on the ground while he screamed and cursed.

Maggie shivered as she looked closely at the two men who were fighting. "I'm not sure, but I think I've seen those two before."

They watched the shorter man roll on the ground and try to get up. He swayed as he stood, unsteady on his feet. His nose was a bright shade of red and bled profusely. Maggie was shocked to see Hubert T. Brown look up at her from among the spectators in the crowd that gathered to watch the two men fight. He hurriedly made a few gestures and spoke to the two men as the taller man shoved the blonde headed man again and gestured to a car. The crowd began to break up when they realized the fight was over and the men were leaving. Mr. Brown glowered at Maggie; then straightened his jacket before he returned to the crowd.

Both men climbed into an older model dark blue station wagon with a dark tint that shaded each of the windows. The motor roared as a plume of gray exhaust smoke bellowed from the back of the car. As the taller man backed the car up and sped away, the blonde headed man rolled down the window on the passenger side of the car and laid his head in the breeze. He held a bandana over his nose in an attempt to stop his nose from bleeding. Just when they drove past, recognition and panic flashed across his face as the car passed the place where Maggie and Doc stood by the jeep. The car sped up and passed them.

Shaking, Maggie leaned against the jeep.

"It's them, the same two characters I saw on the trail."

"Are you Ok, Maggie? You look as though you've seen a ghost." Doc wrapped his arm around her protectively.

"I'm fine, just a little shaken up. I didn't think they saw me on the trail, but he seemed to recognize me." Maggie wrapped her arms around her waist feeling a growing knot of fear in her stomach. She laughed to herself. *Well, at least that got rid of the queasy feeling I had from being around Doc,* she thought to herself.

"I kind of had a run-in with that heavyset guy at the BP the other day, too," Maggie said with a growing sense of anxiety.

"What kind of a run-in?" Doc laughed. "I didn't think you had an angry feeling in the world," he grinned. "I'm sure you must have some very good reasons when you get riled up about something."

Maggie shook her head. "Oh, there's plenty of things that I get riled up about - pompous, arrogant, jerks that take advantage of innocent people is one of the main ones." Then almost to herself, she said, "I've had too many experiences with people like that in my lifetime. Experience can be such a bittersweet teacher."

"Sooo, about dinner," Doc gazed down at her, his soft gray eyes full of concern.

"Oh, yes," Maggie stammered. "Umm, what time would you like for me to come?"

"Let's make it seven o'clock, tomorrow night." He smiled warmly.

"I'll be there." Maggie smiled as she climbed in the jeep and waived goodbye to Doc. *I need some Rolaids, Maggie* thought to herself. *My stomach is already doing flip-flops; I cannot imagine what it is going to do tomorrow night when I go to Doc's house for dinner.*

One last stop at the grocery store to pick up some milk and snack cakes for her two little bandits, the McCutchen boys and she was on her way home. Maggie tried to stop by and check on Rena and the boys as often as she could. She knew it must be difficult to raise three children alone. Even though Maggie could come up with many reasons for stopping by to see the little family, the truth was, she always enjoyed seeing them, too.

As Maggie began the long drive up the mountain, several emergency vehicles and a forest service jeep drove past her on their way back down the mountain. She pulled over onto the shoulder of the road to give them clearance.

*I wonder what has been going on up there for so long,* she asked herself as she looked for Sam's jeep. *I need to look him up tomorrow and see if he found the ruined campsite I told him about at the river.* Maggie turned onto the rough service road towards her cabin. As she passed the turnoff that led to Doc's cabin, she felt queasiness return to her stomach when she remembered their dinner date.

"Gosh, why did I say yes!" she moaned, yet, even as she asked herself the question, she knew she wanted to go. "Like a moth to a flame - that's exactly what I am."

Maggie groaned. "I don't know what's gotten into me, I was doing just fine all by myself and then he had to go and speak to me and get my stomach all messed up." Unconsciously, she rubbed her stomach and tried to ease the knot that formed there since her meeting with Doc.

As she pulled in front of the McCutchen's home, Maggie looked for Jonah and Zack. The area was amazingly quiet. She halfway expected them to jump out from a bush or tree somewhere.

"Hmmm, no apparent ambushes today," she mused as she remembered some of their antics. She grabbed the packages she purchased for the boys and walked toward the house. The guineas scattered and cackled as they heralded her arrival when she neared the front porch.

"Hello there," she called. "Anybody home?" Hearing no response, Maggie knocked on the door. "Rena? Zack, Jonah...hello in there..."

The tire swing looked lonesome as it dangled in the breeze from a limb of the maple tree. The huge calico cat jumped off the front porch rail and ran into the house as Maggie opened the door. She walked into the small kitchen and placed the bags she brought on the table. No one seemed to be home.

"I wonder where they could be," she said aloud. Everything appeared to be neat and in order. She put the gallon of milk and some eggs in the refrigerator, then placed some flour, cornmeal, cereal and other groceries on the table. She left a note for Rena on the table.

> "Hi all, ran into a big sale at the grocery store and thought you guys might be able to use some of these things. There's too much for just me. Maybe you would let me trade them for some of the fresh herbs you are gathering right now. Tell the boys the strawberries are ripe if they want to come by in the morning and help me pick them. Talk to you later, love, Maggie"

One last look around, everything seemed ok. She grabbed the cat and walked out the door, closing it gently behind her.

"Come on Gertie, you can't stay in here by yourself. You and I will both get into trouble for that!" The big cat jumped out of her arms and ran under the front porch.

*This is a little strange*, Maggie thought to herself as she drove home. *Rena doesn't leave the house very often; hope the baby is ok.* She decided to check on them tomorrow on her way to Doc's house for dinner if she did not hear from them before then.

Maggie drove through three streams on the way to her cabin. Two of them were fairly small and easy to cross. The third one was a little more difficult. After a big storm, or several days of rain the third stream usually raised so high it was impossible to pass through it. She then either had to wait a few days for the water to recede or take the longer service road that wound around to the top of the mountain and joined the Skyway to get in or out of her cabin. Max heard the jeep long before Maggie pulled up to the cabin. He began to leap and jump through the field as he ran to greet her.

"Hey there Max," she smiled as he bounded his way to greet her. Maggie held up her palm to him as he neared.

Max sat down, his whole body wiggled with excitement to have her home again. When he was a puppy, Maggie taught him to sit down when she put her palm up so she could greet him without him accidentally knocking her down. Sometimes in his excitement to see her, Max couldn't stop fast enough and accidentally plowed into her.

"And what have you been doing today, buddy?' she asked him as she ruffled his neck. Max lifted his paw to shake hands with her. "Been out playing with Basil today?"

Max barked and ran to the corner of the cabin. She followed him to find a dead rat and a mole lying in the grass. "Did you catch those two critters?" she asked. Max thumped his tail and licked her hand. "You did great! Good boy!" She patted him on the head.

Max loved to bring Maggie things he caught for her approval. It took a while for him to learn which things she was happy for him to catch and which things she was unhappy for him to bring home. She did not want rats in the cabin or moles in the garden, so she always praised him when he was able to capture one of those. It took a while for Max to learn to leave the birds alone and cats, but he finally learned which critters were OK for him to hunt.

"You did good, boy," Maggie praised him as she patted him on the head. "Now, take them away."

She waived her hand in the direction of the critters so Max would know she wanted him to take them away. Max jumped up and grabbed the mole. He carried it under a tree to enjoy his snack in the shade. His patience was finally paying off.

"Ick!" Maggie thought.

*I know it is gross, but it's a little more normal for Max to do what comes to him naturally as a predator than to use a trap or poison to get rid of the moles and rats.*

After she stored the groceries, Maggie made a salad for dinner to go along with some beans, brown rice and wild mushrooms. While she waited for a pot of chamomile tea to brew, she built a fire and began to work on the quilt she was making. As a child, she spent countless hours around her grandmother while she quilted. Now, quilting always seemed to be a source of comfort for her, kind of a place where she nurtured herself and took time to think.

Quilting, always reminded her of home. So much had happened in the past few days; Maggie felt the need for something familiar to steady herself again until she could sort out her feelings.

*I need to relax, let my soul go home for a while and reminisce about something comfortable,* she told herself.

Home for Maggie was the time with her grandmother in their mountain home. Those were the happiest days of her life. She was only three years old when she went to her grandmother's house to live. She could not think of another time in her life when she felt more loved or more secure than she had during those days. Maggie learned about important things in life while she lived with her grandmother. She made life long friends with the mountain folk as she learned their simple ways. She learned to revere nature and every creature while her grandmother taught her about love and spiritual things.

"Maggie," her grandmother often said in her kind, gentle voice, "Everything in life is connected. We are all a part of everything we know and even a part of things we don't know. Not everyone can see it, but we are all connected. God made us all different parts of the same creation but made us in a way that we need each other in order to survive. What affects one of us will affect each and every one of us in some way." She kept this philosophy near to her heart always.

Maggie lived with her grandmother until her death the day after Maggie graduated from high school. Then her whole world changed. As much as she wanted to stay on the mountain and never leave, she knew her grandmother wanted an education for her, so she left the mountain to attend college. Far from the mountains and the things she loved and cared about, far from the things she knew the best, she often struggled - emotionally and physically.

She was frequently labeled as a troublemaker in school because she questioned the school administration, because she meditated or simply because she slipped out of the dorms to look at the stars and play with the animals. Maggie continually seemed to be doing something someone did not approve of her doing. Her first experiences with life outside her sheltered mountain community were often difficult.

Maggie remained true to her beliefs as she completed school. Wani'nahi', always taught her how important it was to nurture each other's "spirit" in love, to use meditations to "center" oneself and to heal and grow. Maggie used her grandmother's words to help her through the most difficult times while she was away. In fact, her grandmother's guidance was one of the reasons she entered a helping profession with her career.

Although she loved the work she did with children, she prayed for the day she would be free to return to her mountains. She longed to return to the comfort and beauty of the simple life she remembered with her grandmother. It was a different way of life and part of the reason Maggie wanted to return to these mountains.

It took Maggie almost half a lifetime to return permanently. She worked her way through school, and then worked two and three jobs at a time to save enough money so she could put a little aside each month. She visited her friends in the mountains as often as possible through the years and stayed in contact with them until she had the funds she needed to return to the cabin. Maggie's life filled with many twists and turns since her days in school. All of that was behind her, now. She was finally able to come home again.

"Life is good here," Maggie told herself. "I don't think I was meant to be here to get away from it all, though. Things keep falling in my lap." When she thought about it, she knew it was that way with her grandmother, too. "The only problem right now is I'm just feeling a little unsettled," Maggie told herself. "My stomach has been in knots for days." Thoughts of the midnight visitor bothered her. Something about him nagged at her consciousness but she couldn't quite grasp the thought and bring it into awareness.

"I know I am always concerned about Rena and the boys. I'm afraid they won't have enough to eat. Then, there is always the anxiety over Doc. He certainly keeps my stomach in flip-flops. How can I ever trust him? I never cease to have concerns about Digger, too. He is always traipsing off into one of those dangerous mines - and what about the two strangers I saw on the trail? I'm getting too much on my mind," she said aloud. "I'm getting boggled, or muddled, as grandmother would say." She shivered as she remembered the words of the strange, crooked old woman who sold the herbs.

*Boggled - she said they were my words, not hers. Maybe she is right. Grandmother used those words. I guess she reminds me of Wani'Nahi' in a way - something about her - I am not sure what, just yet. Sometimes she seems to be able to see into my head, just like Wani'Nahi' did when I was a child.*

"What I need right now is a good cleansing," she told herself. "A cleansing was Grandmother's prescription for everything that ails a body. A good cleansing can move you out of the old self and into the new, gets rid of the stuff inside you don't want around anymore, sort of a rebirth. I wish she was here, she would know what to do."

Maggie's grandmother knew all of the herbal remedies to cure just about anything that made a person ill. Long considered a healer, even a shaman by some, everyone respected her Grandmother. People who lived in the mountains came from miles around to receive treated from her. She always seemed to know just what to do. Maggie's great grandmother was a Cherokee Indian considered to be a strong a medicine woman among her tribe. Members of her tribe and local mountain folk alike respected and revered her grandmother. She passed the skills and knowledge of spiritual and physical healing along to Maggie's grandmother in the traditional way, from mother to daughter. In turn, Grandmother was teaching Maggie's mother the old ways until her mother's death.

Teaching Maggie's mother was difficult and frustrating for Wani'nahi'. Her mother just did not seem to have the gift. She never seemed interested in learning the old ways. She never wanted to know how to heal anyone, much less have sick people around her. They all saw the gift in Maggie, though, even at a very early age.

"Some people are chosen, child and some people aren't. You are one of the few. You have many special talents, which is why you are one of the few chosen. You have the gift."

Maggie did not understand clearly what it meant to have the gift until later in life. The things her grandmother taught her seemed to come so naturally. It was a part of Maggie's person, her "being". Learning to nurture and develop the gift took time and training. She tried to learn as much as she could while she lived with her grandmother. It was something that was a part of her soul and a part of something so natural within her it couldn't be separated from who she was, which sometimes made life a little more difficult for her when others didn't understand.

It took a long time for Maggie to realize many people were afraid of her and feared people who like Maggie were a little different from what they considered "normal". It was a part of the reason she had such a difficult time in school. Many students and teachers considered her healing chants and meditations an act of the devil and shunned her for them. Although their actions were often hurtful, she knew their actions stemmed from ignorance, fear and because they did not understand her. She knew nothing they could ever do would damage her spirit.

"Yes, a cleansing and a healing, that's what I need right now." Maggie decided to have one of the special ceremonies her grandmother taught her to use in special situations and began to make the necessary preparations.

Before she began her ceremony, she took a long, hot, bath. She scrubbed and cleansed every part of her body as she hummed one of the cleansing chants her grandmother taught her to sing while she bathed. She dried, then covered her body with an ointment she had made from natural oils and herbs. Maggie braided her hair in one long braid then walked into bedroom to get the things she needed for her healing ceremony.

She took out a wooden box from under her bed and lifted the lid. Inside she found the soft deerskin tunic made by her grandmother when she was twelve. It was so large when her grandmother first made it for her, now it was a perfect fit. The tunic was a soft golden brown color decorated with a few simple stones she found in the mountains as a child.

She slipped the tunic over her head and closed her eyes as the softness of the deerskin draped around her body. The fragrance of the leather flooded her with memories of her grandmother and the many spiritual lessons she had given to her. She wrapped her arms around her waist as memories of her grandmother and the love she felt when she they were together rushed through her. Maggie fought back the tears as she reached inside the box to pick up the small leather pouch filled with treasures from childhood, her totem pouch.

"It's so lumpy now," Maggie smiled. She slipped the small bundle over her head and around her neck. After she gathered one of her grandmother's quilts, a small pottery bowl and a few matches, Maggie made her way outside to a small area at the edge of the woods. She spread out the quilt and lit the two small bundles she brought with her, one of sweetgrass and one of sage.

She closed her eyes, then began her prayer chants, one for each direction of the earth. After she finished her chants, she sat down on the quilt to pray and meditate on the things that transpired during the past few weeks. Softly as she meditated, she began to chant unconsciously. She sang the soft rhythmic melodies of ancient songs her grandmother taught her years ago, songs of the ages that had no beginning and no end. Slowly, she allowed the worries and concerns of the day to melt away and ease her fears.

Maggie sang the songs of the earth, prayer songs, songs of praise and thanks. The sing - song melodies of the chants seemed to lull her into another plane of existence. She felt her body and soul lift up towards the heavens. All the burdens and worries of the world seemed to fall away. Her spirit drifted higher and higher until she felt she was floating, then soaring across the sky. A wonderful peace came over her as all of her worries and cares drifted away.

The prayers and meditations cleansed her mind and soul of worries. For the first time in as long as she could remember, Maggie felt free of stress and concerns.

*I may not have solved any major problems, or come to any earthshaking decisions, but at least I have cleared the fog in my mind.* Feeling refreshed and renewed, she was thrilled when she opened her eyes to see a shooting star zip across the sky.

"Thank you Grandmother Earth," she whispered aloud.

Max came over and lay down beside her on the quilt. He waited patiently for her to finish her meditations before he nudged her.

"And thank you, Max, for waiting so long." He often knew when Maggie wanted to be alone and waited for her until she was finished.

As she sat under the stars in the crisp night air, she thought of people in her life that helped her become the person she was today. She reminisced about people in her childhood and on into her work career who left an impression on her one way or another.

"Even the most difficult situations can help us grow. That is what Wani'nahi' always told me Max. I wonder how I'm supposed to grow right now." Max nuzzled a little closer. Maggie watched the stars until it became too chilly for her to stay outside any longer.

"I've got to go inside buddy; I'll see you in the morning." Max wagged his tail and trotted off into the woods, his mission to befriend Maggie in her time of need accomplished. Now, he was off for a night of adventure again.

Maggie gathered her things together and headed into the house. The night was dark and cool. She could see a million stars twinkle in the sky as she walked along the dirt path.

"Nite Max, see you in the morning," she called as she headed inside the cabin, crawled under the layers of handmade quilts on the old iron bed and quickly went to sleep.

# Strawberry Fields

Maggie woke to the unusual sound of something as it hit the top of the cabin then rolled down the roof until it dropped onto the ground. Usually, when something struck a tin roof, the metal of the roof made the object sound a lot larger than it probably was. Whatever this was, it sounded extremely loud. She was not sure exactly what she heard this morning.

"Thump...ch, ch, chch, ch,ch..." Another object rolled down the roof. Maggie tried to imagine what it could be. In a few moments, she heard two, then three. Puzzled, she pulled on her sweat suit and tennis shoes and walked to the door. She heard a telltale giggle as she opened the door.

"HUMMM, I wonder what in the world that could be," she said as she walked on the porch. "Maybe the sky is falling! I should call the President or someone like that and tell them so they'll know what's happening and have time to get ready for it." Giggles came from the bushes.

Max stood facing one of the bushes beside the cabin, wagging his tail. His long, dripping tongue hung out of his mouth as he waited for something to slurp. He looked as though he wanted to play with whatever was in the bush. A small leather boot suspiciously stuck out from underneath the leaves as a little hand tried to wave Max away.

"Well, whatever it is, I guess I need to eat some breakfast first. If the sky is going to fall today, I need my strength." Maggie eyed the unusual movements in the bush and walked into the cabin.

She gathered up the orange juice, cereal and blueberry muffins before she headed for the porch again. "Let's see, I guess I need some bowls and plates," she said aloud. "I sure do wish I didn't have to eat by myself this morning. If the sky is truly falling, I really wouldn't want to eat my last meal alone."

She went back into the cabin to get the rest of the things she needed. As she opened the door again, both of the McCutchen boys jumped out from behind the door as they laughed and yelled.

"Ha, haaaaa! We got you Maggie! You really thought the sky was falling didn't you!" they shouted with glee.

"Ohh my!" Maggie exclaimed in exaggerated surprise. "You scared me to death!" Both boys jumped up and down as they laughed.

"Do you mean to tell me the sky's really NOT falling? Oh, Wow, thank goodness! I am so happy!" she laughed. "But, I've brought all of this breakfast food out here. What am I ever going to do with it?"

"We'll help you eat it, Maggie! We'll eat it!" they both shouted in unison as they sat down at the table.

"Good, I could sure use the help." Maggie fixed bowls of cereal for the boys. She filled their plates with fruit and muffins, then poured them some milk. "So, what are you guys up to today? Did you come to help me pick some strawberries?"

"Yep, Mamma's gonna make us some jam," Jonah said. Milk dripped down his chest as he drank the milk from his bowl.

"How is your Mom doing? I stopped by to see her yesterday, but no one was home."

"Mamma's fine. She just had to take the baby in for a check up. The van came to the house to pick us up," Zack replied as he stuffed half of a blueberry muffin in his mouth.

*There are some good things about social services,* Maggie thought. As a child's advocate for many years, she devoted a lot of her career to working with children. Designing programs to benefit the ones who were disadvantaged or needy was one of her specialties. She became a voice for those who could not speak for themselves, an advocate for the underdogs in life. Her experiences with children in boarding homes or placement sites fueled many of the things she did in her life and career.

Because Rena was unable to drive and could not afford to do so, a social services van picked her and the children up for doctor's visits and took them where they needed to go. It was a wonderful service. Maggie doubted Rena could have afforded to take her children to the doctor without it.

"I'm finished, Maggie." Jonah had a huge milk mustache on his lip. Maggie laughed as she wiped it off for him.

"Great! as soon as we get the table cleared, we'll get started," Maggie said as she started to carry things into the kitchen.

"Zack, if you'll look in the potting shed over there, you'll find the berry buckets. If you don't mind getting them for us, we'll get started right away."

Zack left to get the berry buckets while Jonah played with Max. As Maggie carried the dishes into the cabin, she thought about how nice it felt to have someone else around the house, especially children.

When they were ready to begin, Jonah ran ahead. Max leaped and jumped by his side while Maggie and Zack walked to the strawberry patch a little more slowly. They laughed as they watched Max's version of holding hands with Jonah. Max tried to hold Jonah's fingers in his mouth while they walked. When Jonah started to run to the strawberry patch, Max immediately followed and tried to grab hold of his fingers again. Jonah's hands were so small his whole hand disappeared into Max's mouth!

"Aaahhhh!!!" Jonah shouted when he looked down and saw his hand disappear into the dog's mouth. His eyes looked as though they could pop right out of his head.

Zack and Maggie giggled. "It's ok, honey. He just wants to hold hands with you and the only way he can do it is with his mouth. He has to walk on his paws." Maggie patted Max on the head. "You don't have to be afraid, he likes children." Jonah eyed Max skeptically as he rubbed his hand.

"Here, just introduce yourself to him again and he'll shake paws with you." Maggie instructed Max to sit down and shake with Jonah. Max was about eye level with Jonah when he sat down in front of him. He wiggled with excitement as he watched to see what Jonah was going to do next.

"Max, this is Jonah. Shake paws with him." Jonah tentatively held out his hand. Max held up his paw to shake which brought a big sigh of relief from Jonah. "See, I told you he loves children." Maggie smiled, pleased with the greetings.

Max wiggled with excitement. Hardly able to contain himself, he leaped up and licked Jonah from the bottom of his chin to the top of his head! Jonah's eyes almost popped out of his head!

"Eyyyeeee, help!" he shouted. By this time, Jonah was convinced Max would now swallow him completely. As much as he wanted to run away as fast as he could, he could not move a muscle!

Maggie and Zack could not stop giggling at the sight. Zack laughed so hard he ended up rolling around on the ground, which tempted Max to roll around on the ground with him while he licked Zack all over! Max playfully placed his paw on Zack's chest and pinned him to the ground then began to lick his face. Jonah joined in the merriment as soon as he could move. They leaped and played together until they were all too tired to move.

"I think he likes the way you taste, Zack," Maggie laughed. "You must taste like breakfast."

When they were finally tired of playing, Maggie and the boys gathered up their buckets again and began to pick strawberries while Max ran down to the stream to cool off. The spring sun warmed them as they worked the field and filled their buckets with the luscious red berries. Of course, it took most of the morning to fill the buckets, as they had to sample one each time they placed a handful of berries in the buckets.

The warmth of the sun and the pleasant chatter of the boys as they worked lulled Maggie into a wonderful feeling of peace and total contentment. She laughed as they began to sing some of their most favorite country songs while they worked. She began to hum softly to herself as she picked berries and thought of her dinner date with Doc. An eagerness to see Doc and spend time with him again soon replaced her nervousness and anxiety over the dinner.

*What a wonderful feeling,* she thought. She closed her eyes as she remembered his gentle touch, his soft kind eyes. She allowed herself to drift into dreamy thoughts about dinner and being with him again, about feeling his arms around her once more.

She turned around as a still quietness surrounded her when a soft twangy melody drifted across the field and caught her ear. Jonah was sitting in the middle of a row of berries with his arms wrapped round his knees. He gently rocked back and forth, while Zack stood behind him, an arm placed across his shoulder.

A gentle, slight breeze gently fluttered their hair as they softly sang the heart wrenching notes to a country song, "...in the mines, in the mines, where the sun never shines..." Maggie held her breath as she listened, trying to catch every word they sang.

Zack rubbed Jonah's shoulders as they finished the last verse of the song, their heads hanging low. Maggie was spellbound with the touching scene.

"That was so beautiful." She was at a loss for words.

"That was Poppa's favorite song." Zack commented.

"Him wuved stwahbewwies," Jonah said in a tiny baby voice.

Maggie fought back tears as she watched the close tenderness between the two boys and felt their grief. "What a wonderful song to sing for him," she said as she walked to them and wrapped her arms around them both. She smiled as she hugged them tightly.

She brushed back the hair from their foreheads as she said, "Hey, what do you say we stop picking strawberries and wade in the creek for a while. I am kind of hot. Then, after we swim, I'll make some sandwiches."

"Oh, boy, that would be fun!" Jonah said as he took off his shoes and ran to the creek. Zack walked beside Maggie as they watched Jonah leap and run through the field.

"Are you ok, Zack?" She asked.

"I'm ok, I just miss Poppa," he said as he hung his head down.

"I know you do honey," Maggie said as she put her arms around his shoulder. "You are being very brave about it. It's good to talk to someone about the things that make us feel sad. If you ever want to talk about your dad, you know you can come and talk to me."

Zack nodded his head. "Thanks Maggie." He laughed as he watched Jonah in the creek play a game of splash with Max.

Maggie and Zack joined in the fun and played in the creek until everyone was famished. "Let's go eat guys, I'm starved!" Maggie called to the boys after they had been in the water for over an hour. "I'll get you some towels so you can dry off on the porch."

They had a lively conversation while they ate a lunch of lettuce and tomato sandwiches and fresh strawberries. As they prepared to head back home, Maggie reminded the boys to come back and pick more berries when they had time.

"We will, Maggie, we will!" they both said as Jonah bounced down the steps of the porch and ran to the buckets of berries.

Maggie laughed. "Oh, what I'd give for the energy you two guys have!" She watched as they tried to carry the buckets of berries they picked. "Looks like you guys have too much to carry," Maggie said as she looked at all the buckets of berries. "Would you like to borrow my little red wagon to carry your berries home?"

"That'd be great, Maggie." Zack smiled.

"Guess that means you'll have to bring it back soon, so I can use it in the garden again."

"Oh, boy! We get to come back to Maggie's house!" Jonah yelled as he jumped up and down.

Maggie laughed. "Of course you can!"

The boys loaded the wagon up with buckets of berries and got ready to head back down the mountain to their home when Zack suddenly stopped. "Oh, Maggie! I almost forgot, Mamma told me to tell you to be real careful!"

"She did? Whatever for Zack?"

"Don't know for sure. All she said was some guy was asking questions about you yesterday in town and you needed to be careful."

Maggie shivered and held her waist. "Ok, thanks for telling me Zack. You tell her I'll be just fine, I have Max with me."

"OK," Zack said as Jonah ran over to give Maggie a big hug.

"Thank you, Jonah. That was a big 'ole Bear Hug! That's my favorite kind!" She grinned at him as he bounced across the yard to the wagon again.

Zack blushed and held out his hand to shake hands with Maggie. "Oh, my! You mean I don't get a Bear Hug from you, too?" she asked as she shook his hand. Suddenly, a bashful grin crossed Zack's face as he then eagerly hugged her as tightly as he could.

"Thanks, Zack. You give great Bear Hugs, too."

Zack ran over to the wagon and began to push it from behind as he made the sound of a motor with his mouth. Jonah hurried to pull the handle and down the mountain they went. Maggie smiled as she watched the two little boys head down the gravel road. A cloud of dust stirred around them as they scooted the wagon over the dirt road and made sounds of car engines in their throats.

*I hope this place is always here for them and their grandchildren, too, just the way it is today. There is something so special and unique about the freedom of growing up so close to nature in this area, it makes you appreciate the simple things in life.*

She was a little tired from her day's adventures so far and knew it was not over yet! She thought about the evening in store for her as she headed into her cabin to get ready for her dinner date with Doc.

# Visions of Paradise

Maggie turned off the forest service road onto the small dirt and gravel road that led to Doc's house. As she drove the winding road up the side of the mountain, she noticed the special care and attention Doc gave to details along the road. She knew just from looking at his handiwork on the road that Doc loved nature and the natural setting of his home.

Someone took special care along the entire road to beautify it naturally. Native stones placed in areas where the road washed out during storms prevented further damage to the road. Areas along the curves in the road were cleared of underbrush so native ferns and bushes could get more sunlight. In some areas, cleared trees and brush gave an opening for beautiful views of the mountain range in the distance. Maggie was amazed. Everywhere she looked there seemed to be something special or unique to see.

The road wound back and forth in switchbacks and hairpin curves until she neared the top of the ridge. As she topped the ridge, the woods opened up to reveal a natural Bald that spanned the top of the ridge. Maggie saw a few of the natural Balds through the mountain ranges, but did not know one was here so close to her home. She learned from Digger some time ago that a Bald was a natural occurrence through the mountains where the top of the mountain or ridge had no trees at all, only a field of grass or small brushes.

Wild blueberry bushes covered one of the Balds on the Cherohala Skyway. She loved to travel there in the fall and pick blueberries. There was much speculation about what exactly causes a Bald to form, no one knew for sure. Native Americans and people who grew up in the Appalachian Mountains alike had many folk stories about how they formed, but nothing was certain. Even geologists from local colleges who studied them were puzzled.

As the road rounded the top of the ridge, Maggie gasped. The view was unbelievable! Centered in the middle of the clearing, Doc's house came into view. Perfectly situated on the crest of the mountain, the house sat in such a way a person could have a 360-degree view of the mountains all around.

"Sunrises, sunsets, he can see it all from up here," Maggie said as she admired the location.

The cabin he built was beautiful. It was made entirely of materials native to the area. Logs, cut from the woods near his house, fieldstones and slate were throughout the structure. A huge, front porch overlooked the eastern sky and a large deck seemed to hang out over the ridge on the back of the house as it faced the western sky.

Throughout the yard around the cabin were areas where stones were nestled into circles or half circles around old tree stumps or natural crevices then filled in with dirt. Each area was alive with color from the flowers and small shrubs that filled them. Some had flowers that draped over the sides of the stones and cascaded down onto the path beside them. Herbs completely filled several areas.

Posts and supports formed a grape arbor on one side of the Bald. The vines of the grapes looked graceful as they twisted and turned their way around the posts and through the arches. This season's leaves were just beginning to sprout and turn green. The other side of the yard had a series of raised beds that contained rows of vegetables and berries. Maggie was spellbound as she tried to take in everything she saw.

*It would take a long time just to see everything he has done,* she mused. *There is so much here, you can see his hand everywhere.*

Maggie picked up a basket of fresh strawberries from the front seat as she climbed out of the jeep. She started to walk toward the house and noticed for the first time a dog that stood watch at the top of the stairs on the porch. It was a beautiful dog who wore the white legs and facial markings of an Alaskan husky; although Maggie thought, it looked more like a wolf than a husky and may have some wolf breeding.

As Maggie approached the porch, the dog silently came down the path to check her out. She had one blue eye and one eye that looked almost black.

"Wow! A mystical eye! Hey, girl, you are beautiful!"

Maggie set down the strawberries and held out the back of her hand for the dog to smell her scent. The dog took a few hesitant steps toward Maggie and sniffed the back of her hand, then looked up and barely wagged her tail. Maggie smiled.

"You don't know me yet girl, but I won't hurt you. You'll see." She brushed the back of her hand against the dog's jaw and smoothed the fur around her ears. The dog moved closer and brushed against Maggie as she nudged her head against Maggie's thigh. She laughed and sat down beside the dog while she talked and ran her fingers through the dog's thick fur.

The door of the cabin opened and Doc stepped out on the porch. He wore faded blue jeans, a soft denim shirt and a long white chef's apron. He looked as though he was cooking all day long.

"Hey, Maggie!" he smiled. "I thought I heard you drive up. I see you've met Dakota."

"Hi!" Maggie smiled as she rubbed Dakota's neck. "So that's your name. Hello, Dakota." She rubbed behind the dog's ears. "She's a beautiful dog," Maggie complimented. "I love her eyes."

"She came to my campsite in the middle of a snowstorm once when I was hiking in the Dakotas a few years ago. She was just a pup then, and looked like she had nothing to eat for days. She followed me everywhere. I looked for her mother and den, but couldn't find it. So, I brought her home with me and we've been together ever since."

"She's a wonderful dog," Maggie smiled.

Dakota began to wag her tail harder and act as if she wanted to tell Maggie something. "Arr rouw rouw rouw," she said as she rubbed Maggie with her head.

"Wow that sounds important!" Maggie tried to imitate Dakota.

"She's trying to tell you about dinner. She smells the pasta. It's her favorite meal," Doc laughed. "I think I've spoiled her, she thinks she is supposed to eat everything I eat."

"I see, a taste for Italian, huh?" Maggie gave Dakota one last pat as she picked up the basket of berries and headed up the steps. "I love your place here, it's beautiful!"

"Thank you, it took me a while to get it this way, but it's worth the effort. I feel completely at peace when I am here. It's like my own little piece of heaven."

"I know exactly what you mean." Maggie stood on the porch and gazed out toward the east. The base of the mountains below the Unicoi Trail were a beautiful deep periwinkle blue fading to a light silvery blue along the mountain crests. Soft silvery clouds hovered over the crest of the ridges.

A soft breeze blew her hair as she watched a hawk soar through the sky and land on a treetop nearby. His movements looked so graceful as he floated effortlessly in the sky. Maggie felt drawn to his movements and amazed by his grace. It looked so liberating to soar and float among the clouds through the sky. She almost wished the wind would lift her so she could join him as he soared through the air.

"Such freedom," she sighed.

"Here, let me help you with that." Doc lifted the berry basket out of her arms and stood beside her on the porch gazing into her eyes. "You look beautiful, Maggie."

She blushed under the intensity of his gaze. "Thank you, Doc." She quickly looked away as her heart pounded.

"You can call me Chris if you'd like," he said as he turned to look at the mountains again. "This is where I eat breakfast in the mornings. There is something about watching the sunrise that feels like a renewal, or maybe a new beginning. I never get tired of watching the sunrise or the sunset. Seems like they are each a little different each time I watch."

"Yes." Maggie cherished the sunrise. "That's so true." Maggie watched the colors deepen, as the mountains seemed to change shape and depth with the setting sun. "This is so peaceful, I hope it never changes. There are so few places left like this one."

"What makes you say that, Maggie? Why would you think it might change?" Doc asked curious about her statements.

"It's just that I've kind of heard some undercurrents about some newcomers in town who want to change the area and make it more industrial to bring new jobs in for the young people," she said as she gazed off into the sky. "I don't want to keep people from having jobs, but I know industry and natural areas just don't mix."

"I agree, but don't be too concerned. I don't think that will ever happen. This whole area is protected under the national wilderness protection laws and you know as well as I do that most of the people in this area would fight to their last breath to keep it that way."

"Yes, we can't be too careful though. That's one thing that concerns me about Herbert T. Brown, I'm afraid people aren't being careful enough about examining the issues. The sad thing is he is running for office. He has something up his sleeve. I am not sure what it is yet, but I will find out. I seriously doubt he has selflessness or public interest at heart when he's campaigning for his political office."

Suddenly a female voice called out from inside the cabin, "Merryberry, where are you?" Maggie jumped with surprise. Then she heard it again, "Yoo-hoo, Merryberry."

"Ohh gosh! Did I come on the wrong day?" Maggie asked, shocked to hear a female voice come from inside the cabin. She immediately grasped her stomach to keep the knot growing there from getting any worse.

*What do I do now?* She thought, embarrassed that she may have made a mistake and arrived when another visitor was present. Alarmed, Maggie was ready to bolt down the steps and drive away as quickly as possible.

Doc started to laugh. "Come on in and I'll introduce you to Polly. She's a little forward at times." Doc led the way into the cabin.

"Aawwwkkk, pretty girl, pretty girl." the loud voice came from the corner of the cabin.

Doc walked over to a huge birdcage and held up the slice of an apple to a giant Macaw inside a cage. The parrot was a brilliant green color with yellow at the tips of his wings and breast. The bird was pacing back and forth across a bar in the middle of the cage.

"Aawwwkk," she squawked. Then very clearly said again, "Yoo-hoo, Merryberry."

Doc laughed. "This was my father's bird. Mother used to hang her cage in the garden while the gardener worked. His name was Merryberry. Mother would go out to check on the gardener often and say, 'Yoo-hoo, Merryberry, where are you?' I guess through the years the bird caught on to what she was saying."

Maggie laughed. "It certainly sounded convincing. It sounded like another woman was already here. I was beginning to think I was here on the wrong day."

Doc laughed. "Come on and I'll show you around while dinner cooks." Doc clasped Maggie's hand and walked toward the fireplace. "I want to show you something."

Maggie noticed there were beautiful Navaho rugs that adorned the log walls and floor of the cabin. Each one a little different, yet each followed the same color scheme and blended nicely. She paused to touch one especially beautiful rug that hung on the wall near the fireplace.

"This is beautiful, Doc."

"Chris...," he grinned.

Maggie blushed. "Uumm, Chris, yes, I'll try to remember."

"That's ok, you can call me whatever you like. I've been called Doc for so many years. I sometimes forget my own name, too."

Cherry wood shelves covered one end of the cabin from floor to ceiling. Each shelf contained beautiful arrangements of carvings or pottery that looked as if it was hand made by a fine artist. There was a shelf of unusual stones, some of them geodes and a shelf of unusual wooden roots, feathers and tiny beads.

Maggie gasped when she saw the shelf of hand carved animals. A beautiful hawk looked so realistic she almost expected him to fly off at any moment. An owl with beautiful eyes that seemed to follow her around the room, a wolf and a bear cub all adorned another shelf.

"These are fantastic! Where did you find them?"

"I carve a little in my spare time," he replied modestly.

"You made these yourself! Wow, I am really impressed!"

Chris reached over the mantle, brought down an elk antler, and handed it to Maggie. She could see a skilled craftsman intricately engraved the front of the antler. Maggie could see the carving of a high ridge that overlooked a distant mountain range. A lone grizzly bear stood looking out over the vast expanse of the mountain range. Maggie gasped.

"This is amazing, Chris! It's the most beautiful carving I've ever seen!"

She gently touched the outline of the grizzly bear and closed her eyes. A tingling sensation surged through her veins. For as long as she could remember, she always wondered what it would feel like to stand alone on a precipice such as this and gaze out over a vast mountain range. She dreamed about the same image all of her life. She felt as if he carved an image from her own imagination - alone, yet not lonely, just alone in the vast wilderness of the world, looking off into the distance for something unseen.

"I'm glad you like it, Maggie. I made it for you."

"What? I can't take this. This is too amazing. It's too much. I could never repay you for such a beautiful piece."

"I don't want you to pay me for it, Maggie. I made it especially for you. It belongs with you. A long time ago, I lived in the Rocky Mountains and worked as a lumberjack. I found this horn one spring after the elks had knocked the antlers off their heads." Chris guided Maggie to sit on the couch.

"Something compelled me to keep it through all these years. I always knew there would be some special purpose for it, some destiny that was just right. It's perfect for you, Maggie."

Chris put his hand on hers. "I started carving it after we worked together to deliver Rena's baby. We shared so much that night. It is kind of strange, but I felt as though we knew each other for a long time, for many lifetimes in fact. The grizzly bear reminds me of you, Maggie. You are always traveling the wild and lonely places; so protective of the things you love. For some reason, I felt I had to carve it for you. Please, take it, it's yours. It belongs with only you."

Maggie was overwhelmed. "I, umm, I don't know what to say," she stammered. She felt as though someone turned the heat up in the cabin and she desperately needed some air. Her face began to flush as she fumbled with her coat.

Just then a buzzer rang in the kitchen. "Dinner's ready," Chris smiled. "Let's eat, we can talk more later, I'm starved!"

"Saved by the bell!" Maggie grinned, relieved to change the subject.

They ate a wonderful dinner of Caesar salad, pasta with a marinara sauce Chris spent two days cooking, and homemade Italian bread. Maggie watched as he moved around the kitchen. He seemed so comfortable and at ease in the role of nurturer and chef.

"This is delicious! You get the 'yumm, yumm' award for the day, even the week!" Maggie smiled. "Pasta is my favorite meal."

"I thought it was," Chris said. Pleased with the success of dinner, he began to wrap a cloth around the bread. "Now, how about some coffee and desert? I've made a pound cake we could have with the strawberries you brought for us."

"That sounds wonderful," Maggie said as she started to help clear the table of dishes and food.

"Just leave that, I'll get it later," he said as he brought out coffee mugs and desert plates. "Go ahead and sit by the fire if you'd like and I'll join you just as soon as the coffee's done.'

Maggie walked into the den and began to look around the room. Everything she saw seemed so fascinating. A half carved tree stump sat in the corner by the fireplace. Its abstract shape fascinated her and caused her to wonder what the final shape would become. A handmade drum made of a hollowed out tree trunk and covered with deer hide sat beside it. Several unusual sticks made into walking canes were in a pottery urn by the door.

Chris entered the room with coffee and desert. "Ready?" he smiled as he set the desert tray on the table in front of the couch.

"Yes, it looks wonderful!" She sat beside him. "I was admiring your collections. It looks like you have carved for a long time."

"I've carved since I was a child. It has always been a passion of mine. My other passion is collecting rocks." Chris brought out several trays of rare and unusual rocks he found when rock hunting on some of his camping adventures. There were trays of turquoise, sapphires, rubies, and golden emeralds he had found on some of his treks.

"These are beautiful. What do you do with them after you find them?" Maggie held up one of the geodes. Doc had cut the geode in half exposing the beautiful crystals inside.

"Some of them I just store away until I know for sure what they are destined to become. Others I cut into gemstones or place on the shelf. I love them in their natural beauty most of all."

Maggie relaxed as they sat by the fire and talked of their favorite things. Eventually, they began to talk of things that lay deep in the recesses of their hearts and souls. They spoke of the things in their lives that compelled them to make the choices they made in life. Chris told her of his life growing up on his father's farm, of the hard work and harsh expectations there. He spoke of medical school and his passions about being a doctor.

"I love being a doctor. There's something special about being able to help people when they're sick or hurt that compels me to keep going and stay in the business." He stood up to stir the fire and add another log.

"I don't think I ever wanted to do anything else. Being a healer is a big part of me. Who knows, maybe I was a healer or a shaman in another life." Maggie smiled at the thought. The image of him as a shaman in any time era seemed to fit him just right.

"For a while I worked with special forces in the government. That changed my life. The amount of pain and hurt we as humans do to each other is almost overwhelming. Troops would blow each other up and I would try to patch them back together again. It was something that just did not make sense to me. During that time, my whole world changed. I had to take a break for a while and do something different."

"Painful situations in my personal life and the stress of working in the intensity of Special Forces became almost too difficult to bear and I had to escape for a while." When he told Maggie of his decision to leave the medical field she could feel his pain and anguish.

"How did you escape?" curious, Maggie asked.

"I left the big city, moved to the Rocky Mountains and worked as a logger. The need to be alone, to find solace in a wild lonely place and get myself together was stronger than my need to be a doctor. "

Maggie nodded her head. She felt connected to him. She felt she knew the part of his soul drawn to the wild and lonely places when he felt the need to be completely alone.

"Anyway, I spent a few years there before I realized I really did miss being a doctor. It is like the old saying goes, 'healer, heal thyself'. I had to learn to heal my own wounds before I could heal anyone else. So, when I was ready, I returned to heal again; this time a little stronger and a little more patient with others."

He sat down by her on the couch again. "I've retired now. I only work on an emergency basis at the local clinic when they need me. For the most part, I stay up here in my little corner of heaven and work on the gardens and gemstones."

"We've traveled similar roads, different, but similar in their affects on our lives," Maggie commented. "The experiences may have been in different times and different places, but we both seem to be drawn to the lonely places."

"Maggie, I -" Chris moved closer to her as he spoke.

Immediately, her guard went up. "Don't say anything, Chris, not yet. This is a little new for me. I have always been a very private person and sharing the part of me I've spent a lifetime protecting is a little difficult. I think we share something special, but it will take some getting used to before I'm very good at relationships."

"Ok, I'll be patient." Chris smiled and gently touched her cheek with his finger.

Maggie felt her heart start to pound when he gazed into her eyes. *Wow, this is such a wonderful feeling. It is going to be hard to keep my heart protected if I stay around him much longer.*

"Thanks for understanding, Doc, umm I mean, Chris and on that note, I'd better head home," she smiled.

Chris walked her to the jeep and closed the door after she climbed inside. As he handed her the elk's antler he said, "I've enjoyed the evening, Maggie. Please keep this, it's important to me." He stuck his head inside the jeep and gently kissed her on the cheek.

Maggie blushed. "Oh, Chris, I don't know what to say, it's so beautiful. I don't have anything to return for such a valuable gift. "

"There's no need to repay it, Maggie. It's like I told you earlier, it was always meant to be with you." He smiled and leaned on his arms in the open window of the jeep.

"Thank you, Chris. It is beautiful. I will cherish it. I really have enjoyed dinner, too. You are a great chef! Next time, we will have to have dinner at my place. I'll introduce you to my dog, Max and our resident groundhog, Basil, too, if we can get him to pop his head out of the den long enough to say Hi."

"Ok, I look forward to it," he smiled. "Goodnight then, please drive carefully on the way home." He waived as she backed up and began to head out of the driveway on the road that led home.

Just before she left the clearing by Chris' house and entered the service road, she passed a small wooden tool shed at the edge of the woods. Something flashed as her headlights passed by it. Curious, Maggie slowed down. It was dark, so she could not see very well. She backed up the jeep until the headlights of the jeep shown on the tool shed again.

Blood rushed to her head and her heart began to pound so hard it felt as though it was going to burst. She broke out into a sweat and thought she would lose her supper when she saw the glow of a shiny miner's hat as it hung on the wall of the shed. Fear paralyzed her as she stared at the shiny silver hat hanging on the wall. Behind her, Maggie could hear Chris take a few steps toward the jeep.

"Is everything ok?" he called with concern in his voice.

Maggie gulped and tried to force her voice into action.

"YES!" she said a little too loud. "I, uhh, I dropped something. I'm ok. Thanks for asking, uhh, I'll see you later," she stammered as she tried to regain control of her senses and start on her journey down the road again. Maggie raced down the road as quickly as she could. Panic almost overcame her. She could not get the image of the silver miner's hat hanging on Chris's tool shed out of her mind.

*Was he the person I saw lurking in the shadows in the woods near the cabin? Was HE the midnight stranger?* She asked herself. *I cannot believe I spent the whole evening with him! I was just beginning to trust him. DANG! Why did I have to see that miner's hat! Why did he have to leave it there, right out in the open for me to see,* she asked herself as she felt the nausea and bile churning in her stomach.

As soon as she was on the main service road, she quickly pulled the jeep over to the side of the road and lost her supper as a cold sweat burst out on her brow.

"Dang," she repeated again, a little more softly and sadly.

Finally, Maggie was able to drive again and completed the trip home. She pulled into the driveway by her cabin and climbed out of the jeep. Max was nowhere around.

*He must be off on one of his midnight prowls.* Maggie thought as she quickly went into the cabin and bolted the door behind her.

# Delusions of Peace

The heat from the sun began to beat down strongly on her back while Maggie worked in her herb garden. She needed to trim some plants and then needed to thin and transplant ones that were overcrowded. She cut some to dry for use in the winter. Curiously, she checked on the patch of ground she filled with the seeds and plants from Ms. Cates's garden. She was surprised to see that many of the plants were thriving. They seemed to be growing and maturing into something although she wasn't sure what, yet.

*Who knows what they'll be*, she told herself as she left them to grow in peace. *Maybe they will all be unique and magical cures for all my needs..*

After she weeded and trimmed the herb garden for several hours, Maggie was ready to take a break. She wiped the sweat off her brow, pulled her shirt off and walked to the stream. Tossing her shirt and shoes aside, she waded through the chilly water until she came to a large moss covered stone in the middle of the creek.

The stone was dappled with sunlight and shadow, the perfect place to sit in the middle of the stream and think. The large pink blossoms of Mountain Laurel bushes hung out over the water in places making it look dark and mysterious. The heavy purple Rhododendron blooms were faded and almost spent. The stream gurgled past her spot on the stone in the stream. Water lapped the sides of the stone in its hurry to travel to parts unknown.

Maggie sat on the stone and began to splash the cold water over her body. Icy drops of water trickled down her back as she scooped one hand full of water after another from the stream and poured them over her body. She wiggled her toes in the sand and watched as the crystal clear water circled her ankles then bubbled and gurgled away. The stream looked so inviting she could not resist the temptation to swim. She removed her shorts and tossed them aside as she waded deeper into the stream. Maggie plunged under the water when she neared the area where the water was deep enough to swim. The icy water felt exhilarating as she swam a few strokes in the small pool.

Maggie spent some time when she first moved to the cabin arranging some of the rocks to form a small swimming hole. Perfectly hidden in the stream, away from the road and the trail, it was the perfect swimming spot. It was a secret hiding place where she could go skinny-dipping as often as she liked. Feeling refreshed and renewed, Maggie made her way to the large stone in the middle of the creek. She climbed on the stone, which was warmed by the sun all day long.

After being in the icy water, the warmth of the sun and the stone was so inviting. She lay on her stomach and allowed the warmth of the stone to seep through her body. The sun shone on her back and filled her with a peace and contentment she had not felt in days. Maggie allowed her fingers to dangle in the water.

She began to think of the past week's events as she watched the water flow past her. She tried to clear her head of the confusion she felt. Maggie threw herself into work around the cabin in the days following her dinner with Doc. Sometimes it was easier for her to apply herself with hard work when she did not want to think about something disturbing.

"I had such a good time," she said almost wistfully.

Seeing the miner's hat on the side of the tool shed shook her more than she realized. She did not want to think about the possibility that Doc could be the person who was watching her house from the woods. In the days after the dinner, she threw herself into work in the yard and tried to work out the fear and frustration she felt.

As Maggie lay in the sun, she began to doze and remember the dreamy feeling she had when she sat by his fire that night. Being close to him, near him, the way he gazed into her eyes - she drifted off - and began to dream...

> She and Chris were walking hand in hand along
> the crest of a ridge. They came to an overlook
> that opened into a view of a vast mountain range
> that spanned as far as the eye could see. As she
> looked across the mountains, a lone hawk soared
> through the sky then turned and headed toward
> them. She slipped as she tried to step back from
> the edge of the cliff and tried to reach for his
> hand. When she turned, the last thing she saw
> was Chris smiling, wearing a silver goldminer's
> hat on his head, as she began to fall....

Cold drops of water and a huge wet slurp awakened her abruptly from the disturbing dream when Max eagerly splashed through the water to greet her.

"Umm, I was just about dry, Max!"

She splashed him back as she waded to the stream bank to retrieve her clothes and shoes. She dried her arms and legs with her tee shirt before slipping it over her head. She finished dressing while she tried to decide what to do next.

Max's ears perked up and he began to run toward the service road that connected to Maggie's driveway. Maggie watched cautiously as she walked slowly to the cabin. A forest service jeep pulled into the yard under the oak tree. Max barked and pranced around the jeep to make his presence known. He jumped up, pressed both his paws on the driver's door of the jeep, started to bark and wag his tail, obviously pleased with the arrival of the visitor. His whole body wiggled with excitement.

"Hey there, Max. How are you, fella?" Sam reached out of the window to pet Max on the head.

"Hey, Sam, this is a nice surprise!" Maggie greeted him. "Are you checking out the roads today?"

Sam laughed when Max started to jump around the jeep in an effort to get Sam to come out and play.

"I can't play today fella, I'm working right now." Sam opened the door of the jeep and walked with Maggie to the porch of the cabin. "I just wanted to check on you and make sure you're ok," he said as he sat in one of the rocking chairs on the porch.

"I feel great right now. I've just had a wonderful swim in the creek. The water feels great today. Would you like some lemonade?" Maggie offered as she stepped into the cabin to fix something cold to drink. "It's a long way to the next rest stop."

"That sounds great! It's kind of hot out here today."

Maggie returned from the cabin with two glasses of ice and a pitcher of fresh lemonade. She sat in a rocker beside him and poured them both tall glasses of the tangy sweet drink.

"So, what are you up to today, Sam?"

"I've been doing a quick check of all the service roads and campsite areas. Stratton and several of the other rangers are hiking on the trails and checking out the backwoods campsite areas. We've been in a big mess since I saw you the other day." Sam paused as he took a long drink of his lemonade and wiped his brow with the back of his hand.

"Really? What happened?" Maggie asked curious about the flurry of activity with the rangers. This season was busy for the rangers, but rarely were so many in one area at once.

"Remember the campsite you found the other day that was in such a disaster?"

Maggie nodded, watching Sam curiously.

"Well, we're pretty sure that site was used to make illegal drugs. We found waste products usually found in illegal meth labs. We didn't find the actual substance, but we found enough evidence to indicate it was made in the recent past."

"Are you serious!" Shocked, Maggie stood up, walked to the rail of the porch across from Sam and sat on the rail.

"Sam, do you think those guys I saw on the trail had anything to do with it?"

"Well, that's why I stopped by, Maggie. I need you to tell me again exactly what you saw. We've started an intense investigation and have to fill out a ton of reports."

"It's been a few days since it happened, but it's still pretty clear in my mind. Max and I were hiking. Well, actually we started out tracking some boot prints from the yard here. We were trying to see if we could find who was hanging out around the cabin."

"Someone was in your yard?" Sam asked as he tried to learn the details of things Maggie saw in her yard and on the trail.

Maggie shivered. "Yes, it was the middle of the night and Max was barking at something. When I went out to see what was upsetting him, I saw a man standing at the edge of the woods over there. I looked away for just a moment and he was gone when I looked back."

"What happened then?" Sam asked.

"Humm, let me see. I didn't have time to do any tracking or scouting the trail right then because Max and I went on a little hiking trip with Digger. I didn't get to check out the trail until I got back two days later." Maggie poured more lemonade into their glasses.

"So, it was two days before you could check out the trail after you saw the stranger?"

"I checked it out on the third day. Max and I followed the boot prints as far as we could. Then we took a little path we've made from here through the woods that connects to the Skyway trail." Maggie paused as she remembered the events of the excursion.

"I met some really neat kids on the trail. They were on a spring break or something. They all seemed to be genuine 'Trekkies' out looking for natural adventures." Anyway, we all talked while we ate lunch." Maggie sat down on the porch floor and started to pet Max.

"They warned me about a couple of guys they passed on the trail. Evidently, one of the men made advances towards one of the girls. They all felt uncomfortable and left as soon as they could. Oh, and they were the ones who told me about the ruined campsite."

"What happened after that?" Sam asked.

"I was in kind of a hurry to get home because it was late in the afternoon. So, Max and I took off again. Then, just as it started to get dark, I accidentally fell down pretty hard. Something ahead of us on the trail had Max on guard because he blocked the trail and would not let me around him. Anyway, when I realized what was happening, I backed into the edge of the woods to get off the trail just in case there was some real danger. That's when I saw the two men."

"Ok, I need you to tell me everything you remember from that point, Maggie." Sam leaned forward in his rocking chair and listened to every word Maggie said.

"Well, I saw the two guys carry a big crate of something up the trail. They made two trips. Both of these guys fit the same description the kids gave me of the men they ran into on the trail. One of the guys looked like he was kind of a dope head or something." Maggie tried to remember every detail.

"He was dirty and unkempt, walked kind of 'woozy' like he was on some kind of drug or something. The other guy may have been on something, too. He was a little wild. He kept cursing and jumping around. He even punched the shorter guy a time or two."

"You say they made two trips?" Sam asked. "Did they see you?"

"They made two trips. Both times, they carried a huge crate up to the parking lot that looked like it was full of something. Once, they dropped the crate and it made a huge rattling sound. The taller guy seemed to be very upset when that happened."

"No wonder, if they were carrying what we suspect they were carrying it could be extremely dangerous, even explosive," Sam exclaimed. "Do you think either one of them saw you?"

Maggie shuddered, "I didn't think so at first, but it's possible." Maggie told Sam about the incident in town when she and Doc saw the fight between the two men and one of them acted as though he recognized her.

"You need to be extremely careful, Maggie. We haven't found the people involved in the drug lab yet." Sam paused, "If it's the same two men and they saw you, they may feel as though you personally reported them. One of the characteristics of meth use is paranoia, hallucinations and irrational behavior. You could be in danger. Do they know where you live?"

"Oh, no, they didn't follow me home. I stayed in the woods until I heard their car drive away. In fact, Max and I ended up having to sleep on the trail because it was so dark by time they left. So, they couldn't have followed me home." Maggie thoughtfully nodded her head as she tried to reassure herself the strangers had no idea where she lived.

"Ok, just be careful. Guess I had better get back to work, I have to drive to the end of the service road and check out all the off the road campsites on the way. If you see anything unusual, just inform Stratton or me about it and we will do what we can to help. He's on the case, too."

Maggie stifled a giggle. "You mean Stratton finished all of his paperwork and you guys let him see daylight again?"

Sam laughed. "I wouldn't say that! We just need him on the trails more right now than in the office."

"Ok, I'll be careful and I'll let you know the instant I see or hear anything unusual."

Maggie smiled as Sam waved and pulled the jeep back onto the service road again. She sat on the porch for a few more minutes as she thought about Sam's visit and the events of the previous week.

"I'm getting boggled down again. It's about time for me to do something a little different for a change. I've been hiding out here too long Max, and I am a little tired of my own cooking. I need a female's perspective on things." She tied the laces in her shoes. "Think I'm going to stop by and see Rena for a few minutes. Maybe, I will even take a basket of fresh strawberries in to 'Old Lady Cates' and see how she's doing, then I'll drive into town for some dinner tonight, Max." She gathered her things together and walked toward the jeep.

"You stay here and take care of things for me while I'm gone." Max wagged his tail and tried to put her hand in his mouth as she walked down the path. Maggie laughed. She climbed into the jeep, started the engine, then closed the door and drove away.

# Friends and Strangers

"She's getting so big now!" Maggie said. She played with the baby while she and Rena enjoyed a glass of iced tea. Abigail cooed and giggled while in Maggie's arms. "I've been meaning to come by here and see her for a while now and haven't had the chance. It feels good to spend time talking to each other now and then. Have you been doing ok Rena?"

"We've been doing pretty good, Maggie. It's been tough on all of us since Jess died, especially on the boys, but we're making it." Rena brought out a platter of homemade sugar cookies.

"Do the boys ever ask any questions about their dad?"

"They used to, but now, it's almost as though Zack thinks he's the man of the house. He tries to do everything around the house just like his daddy did." Rena looked out the window facing the front yard at the two little boys swinging on the tire swing under the maple tree.

"It may be good for you to talk about it with them, Rena. One of the really great things my grandmother did for me was talk to me about my parents and remind me of the good things about them so I wouldn't forget. Sometimes when you are as small as they are, it is easy to forget, or to get things confused. They need to remember their dad as much as you do."

Rena nodded in agreement. "They loved their Poppa, he was everything to them."

"I'm sure he was. You don't have to make him more than he was, but it may help sometimes for them to talk about their memories. That way, you can keep them real and they won't become distorted. Plus, it will help them talk to Abigail about her dad. She didn't have the opportunity to even meet him."

"My Grandmother raised me and she was so great about telling me stories about my Mom and Dad. They were funny little things she remembered about them, so I wouldn't forget. Digger did the same thing. He was my Grandmother's best friend and always seemed to show up if there was a situation where a man's perspective was needed." Maggie said as Rena handed her a bottle so she could feed Abigail.

"Do the boys have any adult males they can relate to that would give them some influence from a man's perspective?"

"My father comes by and gets them once a week or so to take them to church and that sort of thing," Rena said as she blushed and looked away. "Then, one of the forest rangers stops by sometimes to make sure I'm ok. He took the boys fishing one day to teach them how to catch rainbow trout. Their dad just started to teach them how to fish when he had the accident."

"Really! That is wonderful Rena. Which ranger is it?"

"Ranger Stratton." Rena blushed and walked to the kitchen.

"He's a good man, Rena. He will be a good role model for the boys. I'm sure they enjoy going with him to fish." Maggie watched Rena's reactions carefully as Rena returned to the table.

"He's very nice, Maggie. I'm glad he's taking an interest in the boys." Rena picked the sleepy baby out of Maggie's arms and placed her in the crib.

When Rena became obviously quiet, Maggie decided not to say anything else on the subject and leave it for Rena to continue if she wished. She did not want to invade Rena's privacy, or make her feel pressured to talk if she wasn't ready.

"Well, I guess I'd better go, Rena. I have a few errands to do before I head back to the cabin. Is there anything you need from town while I'm out?" Maggie asked as she headed for the door.

"No, but thank you. Fred is watching out for us."

"Who?" Maggie asked, surprised.

"Stratton, Fred Stratton," Rena said as her blush deepened.

"Ohhh, ok." Maggie's eyes sparkled. She gave Rena a knowing look. "Well, I'm glad things are going so well." Maggie smiled and hugged Rena as she walked out the door.

"Oh, Maggie," Rena stopped her, "I almost forgot, there's some guy in town whose been asking around about you. Please be careful. He looked like a pretty mean character," Rena warned.

"What did he look like?" Maggie asked, curious.

Rena snickered. "The boys said he looked like Elvis. He was hanging out at the BP the other day when we rode the van to the doctor's office. They had to refuel at the gas station there and this fella was asking everyone who got off the van if they knew anything about you. We all said we didn't know what they were talking about, but it's just a matter of time before someone tells him something about you. Just be careful," Rena warned. "Please be careful."

"Ok, I will, Rena, thanks." Maggie felt a little unsettled as she walked out the door and said goodbye to the boys.

"Hey, Maggie, guess what! We went fishing the other day," Zack said excitedly as he jumped off the tire swing.

Jonah stood up on the swing. "We went whiff a forrwest wainger!" His eyes were as large as saucers and full of excitement.

"You did! Wow, that is wonderful! I heard Ranger Stratton took you fishing. Bet that was lots of fun! Did you catch any big ones?" Maggie asked as Zack came over to her and picked up the cat.

"Zack did," Jonah replied excitedly. "He caught him a BIG one, an' Mamma fwied it up! It was SOO good!" Jonah started to rub his stomach and smack his lips as he stood on the tire.

"That sounds yummy!" She patted Zack on the shoulder. "WOW, Zack, that's terrific!"

"We're going to go again, too, Maggie." Zack smiled a satisfied smile. "I think Ranger Stratton likes to do things with us. He even helped me bring in the wood when he was here."

"I'm sure he does like to do things with you, Zack. He's a real good man, too and he knows a lot about the forest. You both could learn a lot from him." Maggie cuddled the cat for a moment, then let her jump down to the ground. "Bye Gertrude, see you next time."

"Are ya leaffin', Maggie?" Jonah asked as he stuck his feet inside the tire, turned upside down and began to swing. The tips of his fingers trailed in the dust as he began to swing back and forth.

"Yes, and I won't be able to come back until late this evening so I can't stop by on my way home today."

"Will ya come back 'nother time so you kin stay 'n play whiff us?" Jonah slipped lower in the tire allowing the top of his head to brush through the dirt under the swing. A small cloud of dust puffed around him with each swing.

"Of course I will," Maggie promised. "Have fun on your next fishing trip." She smiled and waved goodbye as she headed to the jeep to drive down the mountain towards town. Jonah grinned and waived goodbye as she left.

As Maggie neared town, she noticed a small crowd swimming in the local swimming hole at the Beach. This was one of the favorite places for locals and tourists alike. Here, the waters from the Tellico River broadened and formed the perfect area to wade or swim in the water. A small sandy area formed the area called the "Beach".

Many parents brought their small children here to learn how to swim for the first time. Teenagers came to sunbathe or to order chilidogs and milkshakes from the Beach Diner, which was one of the first drive-in or walk-up diners in the area. There always seemed to be something going on at the Beach. Tall trees lined the banks of the stream; their limbs often overhung and drooped into the water. Sunlight dappled through the trees and onto the water.

Some time in the past someone climbed one of the tall trees on the opposite bank of the river and secured a rope to the top of the tree. Now, those who dared to take a risk could swim to the opposite bank, climb the tree, grasp the long rope and swing out into the current of the river.

Maggie pulled the jeep under one of the tall trees that shaded the parking area for the beach and ordered cherry lemonade from the Beach Diner. While she sipped on the cool, tangy drink, she walked down to the swimming area to watch a group of young boys as they swam across the stream to climb the tree and swing out on the long rope. A Tarzan contest seemed to be going on as one after another swung out as far as they could while they yelled like Tarzan.

She laughed when one of the boys fell a little too soon and landed in a belly flop on the water. She winced when she heard the smack of his stomach strike the water from where she stood.

"Ouch!" she said aloud, to no one in particular. "That had to hurt." Completely engrossed in the competition, she did not hear the man as he walked up behind her.

"You'd better believe, Ouch." A deep, masculine voice whispered in her ear as he moved in behind her, pressed his body next to hers and gripped her arm so tightly it hurt.

Surprised, Maggie jumped and started to turn around. The man prevented her from turning when he grabbed her arm even more tightly and moved so close Maggie could feel the heat from his breath against her neck.

"And you'd better believe it's going to hurt if you go messing around in other people's business again," he snarled.

Anger flared inside her as the initial shock and surprise of being held and threatened by this man wore off. Instinctively, she slammed her heel down on the top of the man's foot and plunged her free elbow into his ribs.

"Don't EVER threaten me again!" Maggie shouted as she spun around to face her attacker. The man fell off balance and landed on his rear end on the ground as Maggie turned. Instantly, she recognized him as the man she saw

124

on the skyway trail that looked like Elvis. Quickly, he jumped off the ground and lunged toward Maggie. His eyes bulged wildly and veins pumped on his face.

"Listen here, little missie," he snarled as he reached to grab her arm again. "You'd better mind your own business!"

Maggie threw her lemonade in his face and thrust her knee forward as he lunged towards her. Wes fell to one knee and groaned as he clutched his crotch. Shaking, Maggie took a step backward as she watched him moan on the ground. As she took another step backwards, she bumped into someone else behind her. She stiffened unconsciously, ready to defend herself again.

"Hey, Maggie, is everything ok?" Doc's soft voice came from behind her as he gently touched her shoulder. Maggie spun around quickly. "Is this man giving you any problems?" He protectively stepped beside her, blocking Wes from moving any closer to Maggie.

Maggie gasped, surprised to see him. "Doc!" She began to tremble uncontrollably, relieved to see him and still shaken from the attack. He gently wrapped his arms around her to protect her. Hesitantly, she stepped into his arms, not sure if she could trust him.

Wes began to stand up and straighten his clothes as he wiped the lemonade from his face. He glared at Maggie and Doc as he pulled out a comb and began to comb his hair.

"You remember what I said, little missie," he snarled as he tried to regain some dignity.

"I think you'd better move along now, mister," Doc said firmly.

Wes glared at him, "You'd better mind your own business, Buddy. This is between me and the little lady."

Maggie could feel her anger rising again. She started to reply to his slur when Doc stepped in front of her and faced Wes, steady and unflinching. "I'm making it my business. It's over," he said in his calm soothing voice. "It's time for you to move along."

Wes glared intently for a moment, then spat on the ground. He then turned and began to walk stiffly through the small crowd gathered around the commotion. Everyone wanted to see what was going on between the three.

"It's ok, folks, it's all over, everyone's fine." Doc smiled to the crowd as everyone started to disperse. He turned to Maggie to make sure she was ok and unharmed. "What happened, Maggie? I just happened to see your jeep, so I thought I would stop and talk to you for a few minutes if you weren't busy. Then, I saw that man as he followed you around. It looked like he was trying to attack you. Are you sure you're ok, you aren't hurt?"

"He was threatening me and grabbed my arm."

"I came as soon as I could, but you already had him on the ground before I could get through the crowd." Doc chuckled as he brushed a loose curl off her forehead. "You're pretty tough for a girl. I don't think I'd want to cross you the wrong way." He grinned at her and gently held her in his arms again. "Did you know that man?"

"Not really, but I've seen him a few times before. He's the one we saw in the fight on town square a few days ago."

"I remember now." Doc started to walk with Maggie to her jeep. "That was just the other night, but why would he threaten you?"

"It's kind of a long story." Maggie hesitated, remembering she first saw Wes on the trail when she tracked the man who lurked around the woods near her house.

"The only other time I may have seen him was on one of the trails near where they found the meth lab last week. I told the forest service about the campsite. I don't know if that has anything to do with it or not."

"Are you ok, Maggie? We can go file a report with the police department or, I can stay with you for a while until you feel safe, if you would like me to do that. What would you like to do?"

Maggie was torn. She felt so safe and protected in his arms but seeing the miner's hat on his tool shed still loomed in her memory. She felt queasy and unsettled just thinking about it.

*How can I care so much about this man and have such doubts about him?* she asked herself. *I want to trust him so much.*

"Thanks, I'll be ok. I'm just a little shaken up." Maggie rubbed her arm as she got into the jeep. "I'm safe when I'm at home; Max is there to protect me. I don't think anyone could get close to me with him around if he felt I was threatened in some way."

Doc smiled and leaned in through the window of the jeep. "You know I'll do anything you need me to do; all you have to do is ask." His soft eyes full of concern. "You know how much I care."

She smiled and impulsively kissed him gently on his cheek. "Thanks, Chris." They gazed into each other's eyes for a moment before Maggie broke away. "I guess I'd better go. Thank you for coming to my defense, it meant so much."

"Anything, Maggie, you know that. I just wish I was able to get there a few moments sooner, maybe I could have helped."

Maggie smiled and started the jeep. "I'll talk to you later."

"Promise?" Chris grinned, his soft gray eyes glowing.

"Yes." Maggie grinned. She felt herself melting as he looked at her. "I promise." She waved and felt her heart pounding as she pulled onto the road and away from the beach.

*I feel so comfortable when I am with him,* Maggie thought, *so, why am I so confused? I just have a hard time trusting anyone, especially men. It is going to take a while for me to trust again.*

Maggie's difficulty usually related to the fact that she trusted *too* easily. She assumed that everyone had her best interest at heart as her grandmother, Digger and all of her mountain friends had.

*And that isn't always true,* she nodded her head, agreeing with her own thoughts. *Sometimes people are out for their own best interests and innocent people get hurt.*

Maggie had an innocent view of people during the first few weeks at school after her grandmother died. She believed the social workers and guidance counselors when they advised her that to go away to school and live in the dormitory would be the best place for her. They all seemed to feel it would not be good for Maggie to live alone in the woods when she was so young.

"It would be so much better for you to live in the dorm than to live in a tiny two room log home far away in the mountains," they said as they smiled at her. They did not understand Maggie's love for the mountains and her need to live there; or her need to be around the people and things she loved. Maggie wanted to stay with Digger who was like a father to her, or one of her grandmother's other mountain friends; but she realized if she didn't take the opportunity to get an education right after high school graduation she might never leave the mountain at all.

Far from her mountains, the people she loved so much and the way of life she held dear; Maggie felt lost and alone. Only the regular letters from Digger and her visits back home during school breaks kept her from feeling completely lost. It felt as though everyone was so different and she could find few people she felt really knew her.

"Grandmother always said everything happens for a reason." Maggie sighed as she remembered those days so long ago. "Being in that school probably made me a stronger person and much more determined to take care of myself and follow my own convictions."

Maggie lived in the dormitory at school until she completed her undergraduate degree, then was able to find a small studio apartment where she lived while she completed her Master's Degree. From then on, Maggie made it her mission in life to try to help the people in life who could not help themselves. She became passionate in her efforts to help children especially.

Maggie saw many heartbreaking situations during her career. Some situations were so painful they left lasting impressions on her. One child in particular was a little boy named Timmy who desperately wanted to come home with Maggie one day. He lived in a terrible home environment that needed improvement. Maggie spent much time and energy with his parents teaching them new parenting skills as she tried to help them find resources to improve their living situation.

The parents never seemed to follow through with suggestions from Maggie or try to improve their situation beyond doing the things they absolutely had to do to comply with the court's requirements. Maggie often suspected they somehow abused little Timmy, but could never prove it. That snowy night when he asked to come home with her, it almost broke her heart to have to tell him no. She politely told him there was nothing more she could do and he must stay in his own home. Later in the week, when he died from a severe beating from his stepfather; Maggie felt as though she would die herself. She felt she could never forgive herself for leaving him in his home that night.

"No child should ever have to experience pain or disappointment when adults or life lets them down without having a way to get out of the difficult situation with their own resources," she vowed. She decided she would help every child she could and spent her entire career diligently fighting for their protection and safety until she finally decided she needed a break herself and needed to return to the mountains.

Maggie pondered her past as she drove into town. The healing ceremony cleansed her and healed her to a certain extent, but there was still a need, something deep in her soul that she had not quite fixed. She was not sure what it was yet. She yearned for the ancient wisdom and guidance of her grandmother, still unaware of her own abilities to cure herself.

*I wish Wani'Nahi' was here. She would know how to help me. She always knew exactly what to say to get my thoughts headed in the right direction. Sometimes it seems as though I will never be able to shake the memories of the children I was unable to help. I feel their memories are ingrained in me and I will never be able to get them out of my head no matter how many cleansing ceremonies I go through.*

# Old Lady Cates

Maggie drove into town and located the small driveway filled with ruts and holes that led to the crumbling old home where the crooked little woman lived. As she carefully drove down the mountain, she thought about her last visit with the old woman. She assumed it was the person Sharon called "Old Lady Cates". When she arrived, the house was just as dark and dreary as it was on her first visit. She pulled up and parked the jeep in the driveway beside the house.

Remembering her earlier experience when she came to purchase herbs, Maggie carefully examined the bushes and shrubs around the front of the house before she opened the jeep door. She knew the woman could scurry around just about anywhere and was apt to pop out of hiding from behind the shrubbery at any moment.

Seeing no one in the front of the house, Maggie took her basket of strawberries and walked through the gate to the rear of the house. Everything inside the house again seemed dark and forlorn, as if no one was home. No lights burned anywhere Maggie could see. She knocked on the door of the porch on the back of the house. She felt a little skittish about being in the back of someone's house when no one seemed to be around. An eerie feeling gnawed inside her.

"Hello, Ms. Cates, are you there?" she called, as she tried to peer through the window of the house. "I brought you some berries, hello."

Hearing no response, Maggie glanced around the weed-cluttered yard to see if the little woman was hiding in one of the hidden herb gardens behind the house. Seeing no one, Maggie gently pulled on the door of the porch. It seemed to stick at the bottom somewhere. She pulled a little harder, tugged on the handle and tapped the bottom of the door with her foot.

It was jammed fairly tight, swollen from moisture in the air or warped with age perhaps. She grabbed hold of the handle and yanked the door as hard as she could. Maggie fell off balance as the door jerked free, swung open wide and caused her to fall onto the porch floor. She dropped the basket and spilled her berries all over the floor leaving bright red bursts of color everywhere.

"Gggrrhh, what a klutz I am," Maggie said as she got down on her hands and knees to pick up the strawberries.

"A klutz you say," a familiar, crackly voice came from behind her.

The hair stood up on the back of Maggie's neck and Goosebumps popped up all over her arms. Her heart felt like it dropped to the bottom of her feet. She gasped and turned around so quickly it cased her to fall on her rear end on the porch.

"Ohh, Ms. Cates!" she stammered as her tongue felt like it stuck in the back of her throat. "I, I, um, I was looking for you!"

"Looking for me you say." The crooked old woman eyed her up and down with her piercing bird like eye. Her disheveled hair straggled out of a net. She seemed to be wearing the same three old fashioned dresses. She wore a purple sweater not buttoned just right with a red scarf tied in a bow around her neck.

"Uhh, well, yes," Maggie stammered as she tried to stand up without stepping on the berries that spilled around her feet. "I thought you might like some berries from my garden, but I, umm, well, I spilled them you see." Maggie fumbled with the basket in her hand and the rest of the berries fell to the floor.

"I see." The crooked old woman chuckled as her eye began to twinkle. "You pick them up and I'll make some tea."

"Oh no! I can't stay!" Alarmed, Maggie tried to protest, afraid of what the old woman might put in her tea.

"You'll have tea, my dear," she said with a sly, funny grin. "Just follow me."

"Ok, I guess." Flustered, Maggie quickly picked up the rest of the strawberries while the knot in her stomach grew hard and tight. "How do I get myself into these messes!" she whispered to herself then followed the old woman into a mysterious old-fashioned kitchen.

The woman pulled a string and turned on a light bulb that dangled from the ceiling over the table. A dull eerie glow filled the room and cast a dim glimpse of green plaster walls that were cracked and broken. As Ms. Cates filled a large old teapot and placed it on the stove, Maggie slowly and carefully looked around the cluttered room.

Black iron kettles hung from a rack above the huge wooden chopping block. Old withered plants grew in pots on the floor and strands of ivy vines climbed up the walls and around the room. Dried peppers and beans strung by threads hung to dry from nails on the thick ceiling beams that stretched across the room. An old kitchen cupboard set back in the corner seemed crammed and filled to overflowing with dozens of half full canning jars. Maggie stared in amazement as she looked at the jars.

*This is probably where she keeps the eye of newt, dried frogs and bat wing dust,* she thought, *or whatever gnomes and witches might use for potions and spells. I'll probably be a toad my morning. Fat chance of finding a prince then!*

The old woman placed a beautiful china teapot on the table and walked to the corner cupboard to retrieve some jars. She mumbled to herself as she turned them around and tried to decide which one to use. "Umm hmm, this one will do," she said to herself. "Not enough there; we'll have to make do."

One jar she shook, but the contents did not move, another she held up to the light and squinted her eye as she tried to see what was inside the jar. She gathered together three or four jars, brought them to the table and set them beside the teapot. Maggie watched with her eyes open wide as the old woman took her crooked gnarled fingers and reached inside each jar for a pinch full of ingredients. When the kettle on the stove began to whistle, the old woman poured hot water over the mysterious ingredients in the china teapot and allowed them to brew.

"There, that will do us just fine," she said with a sly grin.

"So, have you been making tea very long?" Maggie asked with a nervous laugh, unsure if she wanted to drink anything new. "I'm a vegetarian you know." She averted her eyes and nervously tried to clear her throat, "ahhemm".

The old woman became very still as she slowly turned her head around. She gave Maggie a piercing, quizzical glance. Maggie felt a chill run through her spine as the old woman's intense gaze felt as if it would bore a hole right into her.

"I mean, umm, well...," Maggie stammered as she squirmed uncomfortably in her chair.

*Oh great! That was stupid. Now she really WILL turn me into a toad. When am I ever going to be able to keep my mouth shut.*

"I, I just meant, well - I just thought you should know," Maggie said with a silly, weak smile as she shrugged her shoulders and straightened her shirt.

"Um, hmm, I see," the old woman said. She squinted her eye as she placed cups and saucers on the table for the tea.

Shocked, Maggie stared at the china saucers. *Those look just like the ones grandmother had when I was a child. They have the same delicate pattern of tiny flowers.*

Maggie watched intently as Ms. Cates filled the cups with a rosy red liquid that smelled almost heavenly! The delicate fragrance of raspberries and cloves with a hint of orange rind drifted to her nose.

"This smells wonderful!" Maggie exclaimed as she leaned over the cup to smell more clearly. She closed her eyes as she slowly breathed in the spicy, sweet steamy aroma of the raspberry tea.

"Indeed it does," the woman said with a satisfied smile.

Maggie waited and watched carefully while Ms. Cates took the first sip. She drew in a long, noisy taste and smacked her lips, licking the corners to catch a drip.

*She doesn't seem to be frothing at the mouth or in any kind of pain,* Maggie thought. She watched from the corner of her eyes as the gnarled old woman took a second sip from her cup of tea. *It smells so good, I would love to try some, she really seems like she is ok. These cups remind me so much of Wani'Nahi' and the wonderful times when we talked and drank tea. Maybe if I try just a tiny bit, I will be ok.*

Maggie hesitantly lifted the cup to her lips and looked intently at the rosy brew. Then slowly, carefully took just one tiny little sip.

"KKAACCKKK!!! KKAACCKKK!!!" A loud choking sound came from the old woman as she grabbed her throat and began to turn red!

Maggie dropped her cup and leaped from her chair as she gasped for air.

"OHH, GOSH! OH, NO!" she shouted at the top of her lungs. "Don't turn me into a toad! I have a dog at home!" she gasped as she wildly turned around the room and tried to decide what to do.

"Heh, heh, heh," the old woman slowly laughed as she slapped the table. "HEH, HEH, HEH!"

She laughed a little louder and more strongly now. Then, she slapped her thigh so hard she rocked the table. Her eye sparkled as she looked up at Maggie with her face full of glee. Shaking her old crooked, gnarled finger, she continued to laugh.

"A toad you say - hee, hee, hee."

Slowly, realization dawned on Maggie. "You're ok! You're not sick!" she gasped, as her mouth fell open, shocked with surprise. "Why, why - you tricked me!"

"The look on your face!" she said in her crackly old voice. " Haa, Hahh,

Hahh," the woman laughed so hard her whole body shook until she was consumed with glee and her laugh became a rolling, uncontrollable roar.

Maggie tried not to giggle, embarrassed by her own thoughts and actions, but the old lady's laugh was so completely contagious, she eventually laughed just a little. Then, just thinking of the funny hilarious scene made them both laugh out of control. When one calmed down the other laughed more; they fueled each other and laughed until they cried.

Finally, they sat side by side and finished their tea as time floated by. For the time, Ms. Cates seemed lucid and fairly sane. She told Maggie stories of her days as a teacher when she worked with mountain children in a one-room school. They discovered they had quite a bit in common in the way they worked and their desire to help children find the life they deserved.

Ms. Cates told Maggie of the children who walked down the mountain each day to her one room school. The tattered clothes they wore and the skimpy lunches they brought did not seem to hinder their desire to learn and come to her classroom. As Maggie lifted her cup to take the last sip of the wonderful brew, Ms. Cates put her hand on top of the cup and covered Maggie's hand with hers.

"Your journey is a long road my dear, that won't be smooth. It is the way for those who have a special gift. Only one who has endured great sadness and suffering can become a true healing woman, but first you must overcome your fears."

Maggie trembled when she heard the old woman's words. Their cryptic message seemed to drive right into her heart and the heart of the struggles she dealt with for the past few weeks and years. Flustered, and wanting to avoid what the crooked woman said, Maggie brushed back her hair and tried to dismiss what Ms. Cates said.

"I'm not sure what you mean."

"Ummm, I see," Ms. Cates slowly said as she settled in her chair and gazed into Maggie's eyes. "Then a story I'll tell to help you see."

A spark of excitement flowed through Maggie's soul as she remembered the stories her grandmother told. She watched the old woman as she swirled her tea and cleared her throat before she began:

> "Many, many years ago, long before those with the pale skin
> and sky blue eyes arrived, there were five civilized tribes of
> the Peoples who honored the earth: the Choctaw, Chickasaw,
> Cherokee, Creek and Seminole. One small clan of the

civilized People lived high up in the eastern mountains. It was the most beautiful place filled with lush green gardens and plenty to eat, almost like heaven. The hunters found deer, turkey and fish whenever they went out on a hunt. They always had something good to eat. The People were happy and wanted for nothing."

"The People were guided by a wise old woman who had special gifts and healing ways and a wise old shaman. The People had a secret that they told no one outside their clan. They lived near a special cave with walls that shimmered and glowed when they lit their ceremonial fires within its walls near the pools of water. Inside the cave also lived a great sacred white snake with emerald green eyes. The People believed if they honored the snake with meditations and fed it, their land would continue to prosper and grow. They made a special medicine bundle and placed many of their treasures and powers in the bundle to give to the sacred white, green eyed snake."

"One day an evil man, one of the 'Others', came and killed the old woman and forced the People to be his slaves. He found the medicine bundle in the special glowing cave then moved into the cave and forced the sacred snake to go away. The People were very sad and heartbroken as their crops withered up and died. The turkey and deer went away. Fish would not bite. Hunger and sickness were everywhere. The People were very sad. Everyone was afraid of the Evil One who lived in the cave, but no one knew what to do. Everyone was filled with sadness and despair."

"Finally the old shaman realized he had to do something because his days on this earth were short. He had to recover the treasure. He decided to enter the cave to retrieve the People's powerful medicine bundle. If this happened, the sacred snake would return with its special powers and the People could be healed. Then, the gardens and hunting game would return. So he sneaked down the mountain and entered the cave. He knew he was on a dangerous mission and death was probable, but he wanted to risk it all to save his people."

"One of the young maidens heard the old shaman had entered

the cave to steal the medicine bundle from the Evil One so he could save the People. She threw down the basket she was weaving and quickly ran after him because she knew the Evil One would kill him just as he killed the old woman. She ran inside the cave just in time to see the Evil One knock the old man down to the ground."

"He held a stone over the old shaman's head ready to crush his skull. The young maiden let out a blood curdling scream and fearlessly rushed into the Evil One causing him to drop the stone. Furious, the Evil One fought the young maiden. He knocked her down into the water and tried to drown her."

"Just at that moment, because the old man and the young maiden had shown such great courage and selfless love to save the People, the great white snake returned and stuck the Evil One on the arm. He fell into the water and sank out of sight. The old man and the young maiden helped each other as they returned to the People. When they emerged from the cave, the sun was happy again."

Maggie wrinkled her brow and tried to absorb the story the old woman told. She tried to decide what to say as Ms. Cates began to gather up the dishes.

*Ok, this is a story like my grandmother always told when I was a child. There must be a hidden meaning in here somewhere that I am supposed to know - but where?*

"What happened to the People after that?" she asked, hoping for a clue. "Is there more to the story?"

"More, there's always more, I say," Ms. Cates mused and wistfully began to hum a little fragment of a tune. "You'll know when there's more," she said in a confusing tone.

She seemed distracted as she moved around the kitchen and washed the dishes. Then, Ms. Cates began to move around the room as if Maggie was not there. Her mind seemed to be somewhere else, almost a million miles away.

"Carry a rake if you see a snake" she started to laugh and talk in a gibberish manner again as she moved around the kitchen. "Better watch out, watch out for the snake!"

Maggie watched Ms. Cates pull out the Mason jars from the cupboard and place them on the counter, then return them to the cupboard once more. In and out, again and again as she talked to someone else who was not really there.

Maggie raised her eyebrows and let out a long sigh. She stood up and started to walk to the door. "Well, Ms. Cates, looks like it's time for me to go. I've enjoyed having tea with you today." As she reached the door, Ms. Cates scurried past her and out into the yard, then disappeared into the herbs and weeds in the back of the house.

*It really was good to talk to her for a while, she does have her good moments and she is a great storyteller if nothing else!* Maggie thought to herself as she waived goodbye, then returned to the jeep and drove away. *She is a little delusional, perhaps and I would probably diagnose her with a few additional things along with the Alzheimer's disorder if I were still practicing. She may even qualify for a few mental diagnoses categories that are uniquely her own!* Maggie laughed to herself as she drove away.

# Treacherous Descent

The sound of the metal pick strike against stone made a distinctive ringing noise as it echoed through the small valley and up the steep walls of the ridge. A faint smell of flint followed the tiny spark that flared each time the pick struck quartz. The man worked diligently late into the afternoon digging out a rich section of gold in the vein of quartz that flowed through the side of the cave.

A cloud of dirt and dust covered his head, hat and shoulders as a section of the cave crumbled and fell on him. He adjusted his metal hat and brushed the dust off his shoulders then carefully stepped around the rocks that tumbled to the floor of the cave with each strike of the pick. He stooped to pick up one of the golden stones, which were almost the size of a softball.

His eyes glistened as he fingered the streaks of gold that riddled through the white quartz. As he licked his lips he looked intently at the wall of the cave, tempted to pick more gold out of the stones but aware of the need to complete his task soon.

Quickly he glanced at his watch. Alarmed at the time, he stopped his work and began to fill his backpack. He chose only the stones with the largest streaks of gold. The light on his hardhat flickered and began to grow dim as he loaded the last of the stones into his pack and heaved it across his shoulders. The weight of the pack was awkward and caused him to stumble and lean forward as he walked toward the small opening at the entrance of the cave.

He removed the pack from his back as he slowly crawled though the tunnel to the entrance of the cave and emerged on the outside. He blinked to allow his eyes to adjust to the late afternoon sun. There he slowly stretched, then glanced around the small clearing. He looked carefully for movement of any kind that was out of place.

Suddenly, a burst of dust erupted from the opening of the cave. He heard the sound of rocks fall somewhere deep within. Quickly, he reached inside the cave and pulled out his knapsack now heavy with quartz stones. He struggled to lift it across his back and over his shoulders. The weight of the pack bore him down and caused his boots to leave a distinct imprint as he walked away from the cave.

One more glance across the small valley floor and he began the long journey up the ridge again. With the late evening sun setting, twilight seeped over the valley floor. The late afternoon heat bore down on him as he climbed out of the valley and made travel difficult.

He stopped frequently to rest and drink from his canteen. The man slowly worked his way to the top of the ridge by time the valley was in complete darkness. He slowly walked to the trail head close to the Skyway trail and waited there in the shadows of the forest until completely cloaked in the darkness of night.

# Anonymous Gifts

Maggie arrived home much later than usual, exhausted from the day's activities. She was ready to take a long, hot bath and go to bed. Her mind was busy sorting out the day's activities.

*This has been one heckofa day*, she thought as she closed the door on the jeep and walked to the cabin. *First, the warning from Sam, then the visit with Rena and the warning from her, the incident with Wes and Doc at the Beach and then the thing with Ms. Cates.*

"I don't think I could have done much more even if I tried and to think it all started with me wanting to get out of the house for a little while! I was so busy, I even forgot to eat!"

Maggie looked around for Max and wondered what he was doing as she walked toward the cabin. He was usually somewhere close by waiting to lick her as soon as she got home. She started to walk up the steps to the porch when she noticed a lumpy burlap sack wadded up and laying on the floor by the door. A long Bowie knife stuck through the opening of the sack pinned it to the floor.

"How strange - I wonder what that could be?" she asked herself.

She looked at the sack more closely when she reached the top of the steps and saw a small piece of paper pinned under the knife near the front of the sack. She reached down and lifted the paper up so she could see it better. The knife fell over to the side of the sack as she removed the piece of paper.

The words, "MIND YOUR OWN BUSINESS, OR ELSE!" were scrawled across the paper in a handwriting she never saw before.

A little frightened, Maggie read the note two or three times and tried to decide who might have written such a note and left it at her door. After everything that had happened, this was a little more than she wanted to deal with at the end of the day. Suddenly, she froze when she heard a distinctive sound she never wanted to hear. She slowly lifted her eyes and looked without moving a muscle at the rattlesnake that slithered out of the burlap sack and coiled itself by the front door.

*Three coils, four, maybe more - that has to be a timber rattler five or six feet long or more.* Frozen in her place, she stared at the snake without moving a muscle. *Ok, keep your head about you, cannot make a single mistake.*

Her mind raced as she tried to remember the things Digger taught her about snakes. Moving only her eyes, she quickly looked all around the porch. She could see nothing nearby she could use to defend herself from the fangs of a poisonous snake.

*Can a person die from fear?* she thought as she stood frozen in time. *Could an animal have more power over you if it can smell your fear? How can a person rid himself or herself of the smell of fear, anyway?*

Maggie watched, as the next few moments seemed to go by in slow motion. Each tiny movement became a glimpse of time, frozen one moment at a time, slowly clicking away like a slide show. She looked back at the snake and watched, as it seemed to tighten its coil. Its head arching up and backward as it opened its mouth and bared its fangs. Its tail straightened up as the bone chilling sound of the rattlesnake's alarm began.

*I'll dive over the porch rail*, she thought as the snake drew back its head and prepared to strike. *At least then, I will have a chance.*

Instantly, a streak of black fur flashed before her eyes as a powerful force knocked her down on her side and almost knocked the breath out of her. As she rolled from the porch to the ground below, Max landed near the snake diverting its attention from where Maggie landed. Max viciously fought with the snake. Skillfully, he charged it, then backed off when the snake came his way. Each time the snake tried to strike; he ferociously barked and bared his teeth as he moved back and forth. He darted around from one side to the other and continued to keep the snake off guard.

Tiring, the snake tried to lie down and slither off the porch in an attempt to get away from the loud, noisy beast. As it moved, Max leaped forward and clamped his jaws down in the middle of the snake's back. It writhed and squirmed in his grasp. He tossed it around then threw it in the air, snapping it again in his massive jaws each time it fell back down to the ground.

Maggie grabbed the shovel from the side of the house and ran back up the steps to try to help Max. She hit the snake's head with the back of the shovel and tossed its body out in the yard. Shaking with fear, she leaned against the side of the house and tried to catch her breath as she allowed the fear and panic she felt to subside. Slowly she turned around to see Max lying in a limp pile on the porch.

"MAX! Oh, gosh, no!" she cried as she rushed to his side.

His tongue hung out of his mouth and lay on the floor, while his beautiful brown eyes rolled back in their sockets until only the whites shone in the moonlight. His heavy, labored breathing came in slow infrequent breaths. Weakly, he struggled to lay a paw on her arm.

"Oh, Max, don't die," she moaned. "Please don't die." She fell to his side and gathered him in her arms, gulping and sobbing with each of his labored breaths. "I need you, Max," she sobbed as she rocked him back and forth in her arms. "We've got to get help," she said as she came to grips with the need for urgency. "I'll take you to Chris; he'll know what to do."

She desperately tried to lift him off the porch. Struggling, she realized he was too heavy for her to lift. Frantically, she opened the cabin door, ran to the bedroom and brought out a quilt. She worked the quilt under his body and wrapped it around him as tightly as she could, then slowly, carefully slid him down the steps.

"Hold on big guy, I'll be right back." She smoothed the fur on his nose, which was now swelling from the bite of the snake.

Quickly, she ran and started the jeep, then backed it up to the steps. She opened the back door and struggled to slide the bundle of quilt with Max inside.

"I'm sorry, Max. I don't mean to hurt you." She tugged and pulled until she had him in the jeep. Closing the tailgate, she ran around to the driver's side gasping for air. As she fought against the panic that rose in her chest, she clumsily dropped the keys beside the jeep and desperately fumbled in the dirt before she found them so she could leave.

"It's ok, Max, we're going now. You hang on; we'll get you some help," she said as she turned on the headlights and sped down the road. The jeep careened and rocked around each curve as she practically flew down the road.

Dust flew around the jeep as she took the sharp turn in the road that led up the ridge to Chris' house. Driving as fast as she possibly could, she sped to the top of the clearing where Chris lived. She blew her horn and called for him as loudly as she could.

"Doc, Doc, come quick!" her voice began to get hoarse as she continued to yell until she topped the ridge. "Hurry! Doc, where are you!" she wildly yelled as she sped to a stop in front of his house. She blared the horn three more times then jumped out and ran to the back of the jeep. As she opened the door of the jeep, her adrenalin pumped wild strength through every vein.

Without thinking, she lifted Max from the back of the jeep and struggled with the heavy bundle as she ran toward the front porch.

"Maggie, Maggie! What's wrong?" His voice came from the shed.

"Hurry Chris, Max was struck by a rattlesnake," she gasped, her voice now raspy and hoarse. She turned toward his voice, her face wet with tears, as he reached her side and slid his arms under the bundle with Max inside.

"I," she started to say, when she turned and saw his face.

The last thing she saw as she collapsed to the ground was Chris holding Max, a shinny, silver miner's hat on top of his head.

# Intensive Care

"Maggie, Maggie," the soft gentle voice seemed as though it called to her from some far away land. "Maggie, come on, wake up."

*It is the voice of an angel, calling to take me home.* Her eyes fluttered as consciousness slowly began to return. She blinked several times and tried to clear the fog in her head. Slowly, she tried to sit up. She clasped her hands over her face as a rush of dizziness and nausea almost overpowered her.

"Whoa, just wait there for a minute. You'll be ok." Doc sat down beside her and handed her a glass of water. "Here, try to drink a little of this, it might help a little."

"Where am I?" she asked, still a little confused.

"You're in my house. I brought you in here when you collapsed outside. You've been through quite an ordeal."

"Max! Oh no, Max!" she suddenly remembered his battle with the snake. "Is he -" she could not say the words. She felt her stomach wrench into a knot.

Chris smiled and gently held her hand. "He's fine, Maggie. You got him here just in time. I don't think the snake was able to get much venom in his cheek." He got up and walked to a rug by the fireplace where Max lay sleeping by the fire.

Maggie gulped and tried to hold back a sob. She saw his chest rise and fall as he slept on the floor. The dizziness returned as she tried to stand up, causing Chris to rush over and help her walk across the floor. As she lay down by Max and wrapped her arms around him, he began to lick her hand with a tiny, weak flicker of his tongue. She sobbed uncontrollably. She held him in her arms and gently stroked his nose as she slipped her fingers in his mouth.

"You big goofball," she sobbed as she stroked his fur. "I can't believe you tried to take on a rattlesnake."

"He's going to be fine, Maggie, just a little sick for a while, but he'll be just fine. I don't think much of the venom had time to get inside him. He must have been quicker than the snake," Chris said as he crouched by her side. They watched as Max returned to sleep. Slipping his arm around her, Chris helped Maggie stand up and return to the couch. He sat beside her and gently wiped away her tears, his eyes filled with care and concern.

"Now, tell me how you feel, do you hurt anywhere? You took a pretty hard tumble." He gently stroked her hair.

Maggie felt completely drained, whipped and filled with the type of exhaustion that comes only after such emergencies. It was a feeling that occurs when all of a person's physical and emotional resources are tapped into and used for an extended amount of time. She did not have words to express how she felt. Her emotions were a jumble as she thought of the frightening experience and nearly loosing Max. Tears began to stream down her face again.

"Just a minute, I think I have just what you need." He smiled gently. He got up and left the room. Maggie sat on the couch in a daze, her brain still not quite working or remembering all the events of the day.

*Everything still seems to be in a haze*, she thought.

Chris returned and set a tray on the small table in front of the couch. He handed her a mug of hot chocolate and wrapped a blanket around her legs.

"Here, take a few sips of this. Not too much, I've made you some soup," he said as he stirred a steamy bowl of homemade vegetable soup.

"Umm, this is delicious," Maggie said as she gingerly took a few bites. "I didn't realize I was so hungry." She eagerly gobbled down the warm hearty broth, scraping the bowl down to the very last drop.

"Would you like some more?" Chris asked with an amused twinkle in his eyes. "I have a whole pot full."

Embarrassed, Maggie quickly set the bowl down on the table and wiped her mouth with a napkin. "Oh, No, that was just right. Thank you very much." She smiled and pulled the blanket closer around her legs then reached for the mug of hot chocolate.

"Now, tell me how you're feeling," Chris said as he looked seriously into her eyes. "Do you remember what happened?"

Maggie took in a deep breath and tried to recall the events that led her to his house. She took a sip of hot chocolate as she tried to remember.

"Well, when I got home tonight, I noticed there was a sack of some kind on the porch by the door, burlap I think. It had a knife stuck in it holding down a note. I didn't think much about it at first because Digger leaves things on the porch sometimes. When I picked up the note, the knife fell over and the next thing I remember was a huge rattlesnake coiled up by my front door."

She shivered as she recalled the huge timber rattler coiled and ready to strike. The sound of its rattle still rang in her ears.

"How did you get away from the snake?" Chris asked as he sat beside her. He wrapped his arms around her shoulders.

"I was frozen; couldn't move. I just stood there and listened to the sound of the rattle. It was almost as if the snake hypnotized me or something." She trembled as she remembered the chilling sound of the rattles. "The next thing I knew, that big lump of fur over there just plowed right into me and knocked me off the porch."

She glanced over at Max to reassure herself he was still in the room and breathing. A tear escaped and ran down her cheek. She quickly wiped it away and paused to take another sip of her drink.

"He saved your life, Maggie," Doc said gently.

"I know," she said weakly. Her face wrinkled and she began to cry again. She grabbed the handkerchief Doc handed her, wiped her tears and blew her nose.

"He's a brave dog, and a very skilled hunter."

Maggie gulped and nodded her head. "It was a very vicious fight. It seemed to go on forever. Max already killed it by time I thought about using the shovel to help him. When I realized he'd been struck, the first thing I could think of was getting him here."

"I'm glad you did, Maggie. You got him here just in time. He will be fine in a few days, he just needs to rest."

He wrapped his arms a little tighter around her as she laid her head against his chest. The crackle of the wood as the fire burned low, the warmth of the hot chocolate and the closeness of another human being helped her relax. Slowly, the tension of the day eased and left her finally at peace. She closed her eyes, and then drifted into a deep peaceful sleep.

*To sleep, and to dream - to dream of warm sunny fields and a soft summer breeze, of daisies and watermelon and someone to walk beside me hand in hand -* Maggie began to drift into a dream.

Chris gently slipped a pillow under her head and covered her with a blanket as he moved off the couch. Once more, he checked on the large black dog asleep on the floor before he tenderly leaned down and kissed Maggie on the cheek as he whispered in her ear.

"Goodnight, my love, my beautiful love."

Maggie woke abruptly to the loud baritone sound of Max's bark as he pranced back and forth in front of Polly's cage. A loud squawk erupted from the bird each time Max came near the bird. Little feathers flew around the cage each time Polly paced back and forth on her bar or jumped to the top of the cage in alarm.

"Max, Max! Shhuuush!" Maggie called, "It's just a bird." She jumped up and ran beside him as she tried to calm him down.

Chris ran in from the porch just as Max bumped into a table. The contents flew into the air and over the floor. Startled, Polly began to squawk again and flap her wings inside the cage.

"Hey! Good morning everybody! Looks like the whole household is up and at 'em early this morning," he said with a broad smile.

"Oh, Chris, I'm so sorry. Max isn't used to being in the house," Maggie said as she quickly tried to pick up the things Max knocked down. "I doubt he's ever heard a bird that talks before." She held him by the collar as he wiggled and thrashed his tail in an attempt to get closer to the noisy bird. She looked at Max.

"Sit down!" she instructed him sternly. He sat, but continued to bark and wag his tail at the bird. He could hardly contain his enthusiasm for such an unusual opponent.

"Well, here then," Chris laughed as he reached for Max's collar and walked him out the front door. "Let's go outside and get some fresh spring air so Polly can rest for a while."

Maggie followed the pair out the door and watched Max immediately leave the porch and trot down the steps to check out Dakota. The two sniffed each other and wagged their tails then they walk around the yard together.

"Looks like it's the social hour," Maggie laughed.

"This is a real treat for Dakota, she doesn't usually have house guests." Chris smiled. He pulled a chair out from the table on the porch. "Here, come have a seat with me. I was just having a cup of coffee while I watched the sunrise. Would you like some?"

"Oh, no thank you, I don't usually drink coffee." She smiled and tucked her feet under her as she sat in one of the chairs placed around the table that faced the sunrise.

"I could make you some tea or hot chocolate," he offered.

"Hot tea would be nice, thank you." She wrapped the end of her sweatshirt over her knees and around her legs as she curled up in the chair and tried to soak up the beauty of the morning.

Maggie laughed when she saw Max and Dakota chase each other in the yard. An energetic game of tag was going on between the pair. Max seemed to tire easily and finally stopped to rest under one of the large shade trees. He tried to get up and play again each time Dakota came over and butted him with her head.

Chris returned with hot tea, fruit and bagels on a tray and set them on the table in front of Maggie. "I hope you don't mind bagels for breakfast, as you can see I don't often have very many guests." He laughed, "Sometimes I forget to stock the refrigerator until my stomach reminds me I've neglected it again."

Maggie smiled. "This is wonderful! Really, it is. It's just like something I would have at home." She eagerly began munching on a bagel while she held the mug of hot tea in her hand.

"Looks like those two are becoming good friends," Chris commented as he watched Max and Dakota lay under the tree. "They must have worn each other out, they're already resting."

"I think so." Maggie smiled. "Max seemed to wear out more easily than usual, though," she commented, concerned about him.

"He'll be tired for a few days, Maggie, and you may have to watch what he eats. He may have a sensitive stomach for a while, but he will be fine. I don't think enough of the venom got into him to cause any permanent damage. Before you know it, he'll be up and ready to tangle with Basil again."

Maggie shuddered when she remembered the horrible scene with the snake the night before. "I don't know what we would have done without you, Chris. Thank you so much for taking care of Max," she said sincerely, then with a small, embarrassed laugh, "and for taking care of me, too!"

"It was my pleasure!" he said with a broad smile.

"I must seem like a real wimp!" she said as she shook her head.

"Maggie, you went through a stressful day even before you got home. Then to go through the experience you had with the snake and the fear of loosing Max, too. It's no wonder you passed out," he said as he refilled her cup.

"Sometimes, when we have been through an extreme trauma or shock like that, our body just shuts down. Click! It shuts down, just like that, to keep us from being overwhelmed. It is a self-protection mechanism sort of built in with our system. It's sort of like the power going off in your house when something is wrong with one of the circuits to prevent a fire from happening."

"It's a good idea it's built in automatically then. I couldn't think of anything when I first saw the snake. Then all I wanted to do was get help for Max." She watched tiny specks of tea grounds swirl in her cup as she remembered the overwhelming feeling of helplessness when she didn't know if Max was going to make it or not.

"Thank you again, Chris." She reached for his hand, her eyes moist again.

"You know I'd do anything for you Maggie," he said as he gently held her hand and gazed into her eyes.

"Yes, I believe that." She felt swept up in his warmth, in the intensity of his emotions. Her heart began to pound as he leaned forward and tenderly kissed her on the lips. She touched him gently on the cheek. "You're quickly becoming a special part of my life."

"I hope so, Maggie."

She smiled and cleared her throat as she broke away from his intense gaze. "So," she began, trying to change the subject away from one she was not ready to get into yet, "What do you have planned for your day today? Anything special?"

"Well," he began slowly as he straightened in his chair, "I'm mostly going to work around the place here. I have some new gemstones I need to sort through and then I need to work in the gardens for a while." He took a long drink of coffee as he turned his eyes on the distant mountains. A sad coolness passed over his eyes as he watched the hawk fly over the trees.

Feeling uneasy, Maggie began to fumble with her sweatshirt. "Umm, well, I guess we should go soon then. I have a lot to do at home and I need to get rid of the snake in my yard."

"Make sure you report it to the rangers, Maggie. Someone threatened you with a deadly snake. Whoever is doing this isn't playing around." He looked at her his eyes filled with concern.

"I will Chris," she said as she reached for his hand. "Thank you, for everything you've done. I don't think either one of us would have made it through such a traumatic event without you." She leaned over and gently kissed him on the cheek. "We'd better go. If I stay too much longer, I don't think Max would go home with me, he seems to get along with Dakota very well."

Chris laughed. He watched the two dogs lay in the shade under the tree. Dakota barked and wagged her tail. She seemed grateful to have a visitor at home she could play with, too.

"Yes, they are doing great together." He walked with Maggie to the jeep as she called Max to climb inside with her. "Don't be a stranger." He smiled, tenderly hugged her and waved goodbye as she drove back down the mountain.

# Dangerous Reports

The first few moments at home were a little traumatic while Maggie searched to find her shovel and bury the dead snake that lay in the yard. She carefully lifted the snake carcass into a bucket and carried it to a corner of the yard near the woods she dubbed "Boot Hill". Here, she buried the remains of all the critters that lost battles with Max through the years.

A couple of ground hogs, a squirrel, snapping turtle and a few rabbits all found their final resting place under an old pair of boots Maggie hung from a stick in the ground. A large wooden sign nailed to the post under the boots stated simply, "Boot Hill". Several comical epitaphs written on the crudely made wooden crosses adorned the small graves.

Max, obviously upset when he saw the snake, barked and charged the dead carcass until Maggie placed it securely in the ground and covered it with a large pile of dirt and rocks. He seemed to know Boot Hill was an area designated for the remains of things he killed and brought to Maggie. He often checked on the area to make sure all the critters stayed in their place once Maggie buried them.

"You want to make sure he doesn't get out again don't you, big guy," Maggie commented as he paced around the snake's grave. Max wagged his tail and trotted off to check out one of the new groundhog dens when he was sure the snake was securely in the ground.

"What do you think we should put on this one, Max?" she asked as she took out a small board and a marking pen. "How about, 'Slower than the dog,' does that sound good to you?" she asked as she made a sign and stuck it in the ground by the snake's grave.

Maggie spent the rest of the morning working in the garden and yard around her cabin. She trimmed the herb garden and cut many of the tender new shoots to hang in the breeze to dry. She would use these dried herbs during the winter to season many of the stews and breads she made. Some of the herbs she preserved to use in her homemade remedies.

Digger always insisted on having several bottles of one of the tonics that she made using her grandmother's recipes to help him make it through the winter. She had a strong suspicion he added about fifty percent of one of his own "home brews" to her tonic before he actually used it for anything - medicinal or pleasure.

"Got to add a little something to give it some *punch*," he always said before he downed a swig or two.

Maggie laughed. She often wondered about a small jug filled with some kind of tonic that sat between her grandmother's rocking chair and the fireplace when she grew up. Wan'nahi' simply said, "It's good for what ails you," and left it at that. As a child, Maggie always thought it must be powerful stuff because when Grandmother and any of her friends drank some of it, they seemed to feel pretty good, especially Digger. He always seemed to dance a whole lot more after he took some of Grandmother's tonic.

After she spent most of the day working in the yard and around the cabin, Maggie decided she needed to shower and drive in to town to report the incident with the snake. She left Max resting on the porch as she drove down the mountain to the forest ranger's station. When she pulled into the parking lot, only one official service vehicle remained parked near the building.

Sam was busy at his desk with one computer while another was busy spilling out paper from the printer. "Hey, Maggie," he paused and looked up from his work as she walked into his office. "Want some coffee?"

"Hi, Sam. Thanks, but I think I'd rather have a diet cola if you have one," she said as she walked around the desk and headed to the back of the office.

"Help yourself. You know where they are."

Maggie took a frosty drink from the refrigerator, then picked up a package of peanut butter crackers from the basket on the table before she dropped some change in the honor jar on the table and returned to the front room.

"Tell me something good, Maggie. I am up to my eyeballs in paperwork. Since fishing season started we've been so swamped with getting the licenses registered, we hardly have time for anything else." Sam shuffled one stack of papers together and filed them in a drawer before he started to work on a new stack.

"Well, the good news is, I'm OK. The bad news is - I think someone wanted something really bad to happen to me," Maggie replied in a mater of fact manner as she sat down on an old green vinyl chair across from Sam's desk.

"What!" Sam immediately stopped what he was doing. "What are you talking about?" He turned, faced her and intently listened to every word she said as he poured himself another cup of coffee.

Maggie hesitantly told him of her battle with the rattlesnake left on her doorstep, the wound Max received and her frantic trip in the middle of the night to Doc's cabin for help.

"Are you ok? Is Max?" Alarmed and concerned, Sam jumped up from his seat. "I warned you about this, Maggie! There have just been too many unusual things happen recently. I have been very concerned about your safety for a while, and now THIS! You have to be more careful. What if Max hadn't been there!"

"I'm ok, Sam, really I am. Max is there with me all the time. Besides, I know how to take care of myself, really, I do. I never would have made it this long if I didn't."

"I heard about the incident at the Beach yesterday from several people who were there. It's already all over town. Everybody has been talking about it. You're quite the hero among the locals now, but I don't think you have a friend with the newcomer."

"Well, I hope they're all saying I came out on top," Maggie quipped and laughed in an attempt at humor to lighten Sam up.

"That's not funny." Sam glowered. "You could have been hurt."

"You know how people are, Sam. They are going to talk no matter what! It wasn't a big deal, anyway. That guy threatened me and grabbed my arm. I just let him know I didn't like it too much. Then Doc came up and made sure the man left me alone. It could have been worse if Doc hadn't been there."

"Was it the same guy you saw on the trail?"

"Yes, I think so. One of the men I saw anyway. His name is Wes, I think. He's an Elvis wanna-be, tries to dress like the "King". I saw him and his partner, Frank when they were involved in a fistfight with each other in town the other day. They seemed like they were hanging out with that guy who's running for city council, Mr. Hubert T. Brown, himself," Maggie said with a smirk.

"You need to be careful of him, Maggie; he seems to have some powerful backers from somewhere pretty high up the political ladder somewhere in the state. I think he is one character that could cause us some problems in this area. He could be mixed up with those two characters somehow, although we may never be able to prove it." Sam watched her reaction. "I was concerned after we found the meth lab on the mountain and this guy, Wes, started asking people around town how he could find out where you live. Several people said Wes left messages around town that you'd better 'watch out', and now he has personally threatened you at the Beach. It's important you tell me when something new happens," Sam said his voice full of concern. "He's probably the same person who left the deadly present on your doorstep; either he or his partner could have done it."

"We don't know that for sure," Maggie replied hesitantly. "Wes doesn't strike me as the 'woodsy' type. I doubt he ever gets very dirty much less goes out to hunt for snakes."

"What more evidence do you need?" Sam asked incredulously, then, after thinking, "But you're right, we don't have enough evidence to prove anything."

"Well," Maggie hesitated, "Whoever it was did leave a note."

Sam shot her a serious look. "Do you have the note with you?"

"Yes," she nodded her head, pulled out the note and handed it to Sam as she stood and walked around the room thinking.

"I can fill out a report, Maggie and keep this on file. You need to be very careful for the next few days. I think these two men have split up. They have not been seen together since you saw them fighting in the town square last week. In fact, no one has seen the one called Frank since then at all. They may be operating separately, or they may just be laying low for a while."

Maggie nodded her head.

"Hey," Sam looked at her intently, "I'm serious! Be careful! They may blame you for discovering their meth lab, if they were the ones operating it. They may think you are the one who turned them in to the authorities."

"Ok, Sam, ok, ok," Maggie answered, a little aggravated with his persistence. "But, I'm NOT going to be a prisoner in my own home!" She paused and looked irritably into his eyes before she said her goodbyes, walked out and quickly closed the door.

Sam pulled out the official forms as he watched Maggie close the door on the jeep and drive away. "Too dang independent for her own good," he mumbled to himself as he began to fill out the report.

"I don't know what it is about a man that makes them think women can't take care of themselves. I have been taking care of myself most of my life and have done a pretty good job of it too, even if I do say so myself! Dang! How can we ever get them to see us as capable if they think they can keep telling us what to do!" Maggie argued with herself, a little sensitive about Sam's attempts to caution her. "You know, there is such a fine line between trying to help someone and trying to control someone," Maggie continued to argue with herself as she drove into town.

# Impatient Errors

Digger pulled his truck under the shade tree in the yard near Maggie's cabin and paced back and forth around the yard while he waited for her to come home. He sat on the porch for a while, played with Max and checked out the herb garden before he finally became impatient and decided to go ahead and leave without her.

He walked to his battered old truck and scrambled around in some of the jumbles and piles of junk and debris. He searched for a scrap of paper and a pen to leave a note for Maggie. Finally, after he found the things he needed; he scribbled a short note and stuck it to a nail by the front door. After he rubbed Max on the head, Digger lifted his knapsack across his shoulders, adjusted the weight of the pack and headed down the trail past Maggie's cabin.

"Max, ah gots ta go down to the mine. They's sumpthin' wrong, real wrong 'n ah gots ta check it out. Ah'll be lookin' fer ye when Maggie gits here. Don' ye go leavin' without 'er now ye hear! That's real important!"

Max barked, growled and tried to get in Digger's way to keep him from leaving. He then followed Digger down the first hill before Digger irritably turned around and scolded him sternly.

"Ye best be waitin' fer Maggie! Now, go back home, ye hear!"

Max whimpered and sat down on the path. He miserably watched Digger disappear over the edge of the trail. Max waited until he could hear Digger on the path no more; then slowly walked back to the cabin to lay in the shade beside Digger's truck and wait for Maggie to come home.

# May Day

Town square was crowded and overflowing with cars and trucks when Maggie tried to make her way through town to the Tellico Pride. Signs tied to the storefronts welcomed visitors to the May Day Festival and heralded the onset of spring. When Maggie found it impossible to get on the other side of town, she decided to park the jeep and enjoy the activities. Multicolored ribbons and balloons blocked off the main streets around the central square of town. Twangy notes of bluegrass music came from a band that played in the bandstand in the middle of the square.

A woman in white Levi jeans, white boots and a white leather jacket decorated with fringe and silver spangles sang into a large microphone. Her long, curly blonde hair spilled out from under an enormous white cowboy hat which was adorned with feathers and silver spangles. Several couples danced in a roped off area in front of the colorful bandstand. Some of the couples were involved in a Texas Two Step competition. One couple in particular, she recognized as one of the young couples she saw hiking on the Skyway trail several days before.

"That's Justin and Amy," she said aloud as she moved closer to the dance area for a better view.

She watched as they swayed and swirled to the music and kept step with every beat. Their bodies looked as though they molded together as they moved through the crowd of dancers.

"Hey, Maggie," a voice called from behind her. She turned to see Josh and Colleen sitting on the delivery ramp of the Co-op feed store. They enjoyed a root beer and a caramel apple while they watched the dancers spin around the dance floor.

"Hey, Josh! I thought you might be here. I was just admiring the way Justin and Amy dance. They look great together don't they!" she said as she slid up on the wall beside them. "How come you guys aren't out there with them? It looks like there's plenty of room for more competition on the dance

155

floor."

"I'm not much on dancing," Josh said with a shy smile.

Colleen grinned, "He needs one of those bumper stickers to wear on his backpack that says, 'I'd rather be hiking.' He'd rather do that than anything." She nudged Josh on the shoulder and kissed him on the cheek. Josh blushed.

Maggie smiled at the exchange. "Did you have a good time on your hike the other day?"

"Oh, it was wonderful, Maggie. The flowers were great and the weather - everything was just about perfect. We're going to go again this fall when we get a break from school." Colleen glowed as she told Maggie about their journey on the Skyway trail.

"Well, if you decide to go again, just let me know and you can start from my cabin if you'd like. It's a pretty good starting place; all you have to do is show up and pitch a tent. Max and I would love to have you come for a visit."

"Thanks, Maggie that would be great! We'd like that a lot." Josh smiled as he snuggled a little closer to Colleen.

After they exchanged addresses, Maggie decided it was time to find something to eat. She said her goodbyes and moved on through the crowd. Many people walked around the square and visited the craft booths. Some visitors stopped to purchase food items made by local cooks. A woman dressed as a clown sat under one of the shade trees and made balloon animals while her partner painted funny faces on children as parents watched their children have fun.

Maggie watched the teams of country square dancers as they prepared for their performances. Pairs of couples in matching outfits practiced their twists and turns behind the eaves of the merchant's tents. Men with checked shirts, cowboy boots and hats matched women who wore gathered, ruffled skirts that flounced out with many layers of organza and lace underneath to make the dresses bounce and swirl with the slightest movement. They all danced in patterns called by the announcer while musicians played.

Teams of four couples lined up together to form a square as the jaunty music flowed over the air. The Caller began his rhythmic singsong chant as he beseeched the dancers to "Bow to your partner" then, "Do-si-do". The dancers hooked elbows with their partners and swung them around the square as they kept time with the music while they danced. Their feet clicked and tapped in time as they moved across the dance floor and formed a beautiful kaleidoscope of color.

Maggie watched for a few moments before she moved on to a section where several of the old timers sat in their overalls. They chewed tobacco and tapped their feet to the music. A lively debate seemed to be going on among the trio. She scanned the crowd for Digger when one of them noticed her and waived her over.

"Howdy, Maggie, come on over here 'n hep us out fer a minute. Pull ye up a chair 'n set fer a while." George waived her over to the group and offered her a rickety, worn lawn chair to use.

"Hey, guys, what's going on?" She smiled as she joined them.

"Neil here's been tellin' us a big one," George continued. "He sez if'n we wuz ta set here ta'day on this here street korner, sum purty lady would come by 'n pick us up." George hitched up his overalls and spat a long stream of tobacco juice onto the ground as he continued. "Well, ah've been settin' rite here all afternoon 'n ain't nary a one tried to come git me yet!"

Maggie laughed, "That could be a good thing, George. It can always be worse; I hear they have women attendants working on the ambulances these days. I'd hate for you to need an ambulance to get picked up by a woman."

Neil and Bob laughed as George waived off Maggie's teasing. Maggie watched Bob toss a fake twenty dollar bill tied to a piece of fishing wire into the path. He left it there and carefully avoided looking at the bill until some passerby noticed it. Then, carefully, just as the person started to pick it up, he yanked it just out of their reach. Maggie laughed at the expressions on the faces of people when they realized the old men tricked them.

"Got your mouth harp today, Neil?" she asked, as she looked his direction. Neil always carried one of his harmonicas in his pocket and waited for someone to ask him to play a tune.

"Thought ye might be asking," he answered with a twinkle in his eyes. He winked as he pulled out the harmonica and played his own version of Amazing Grace and Church in the Valley pausing, often to catch his breath.

Maggie smiled when he finished. "That was beautiful, Neil!"

"Bout got kicked outta church last time ah played that song," he winked with a sly grin.

"Whatever for?" Maggie asked, curious.

"Thought ah was playin' Church in the Valley, but ah fergot 'n started ta' play 'Dance Hall Gals Won't Cha Come Out Tonight," he said with a grin.

George and Bob started to laugh and slap their thighs. When she realized Neil had caught her off guard and she was pulled in by their prank, Maggie shook her head and laughed.

"You guys are nuts!" She shook her head and laughed with them. "I don't know what we're going to do with you guys."

"You could try to pick us up," Bob teased. George and Neil laughed and nudged each other.

"Anybody crazy enough to pick you guys up needs to have their head examined!" She laughed.

Just then, an older woman in a bright, loud print moo-moo style dress and pink sandals with large plastic daisies on top rushed up to the group and started to click pictures of the men in their overalls. "Hurry up, honey!" She gushed as she moved closer to the trio.

Her husband followed close behind her and burst out in a loud obnoxious guffaw. "You mean you guys really wear that stuff! How much do they pay you to sit here dressed up like that?" He laughed as his wife continued to click away with the camera.

George spat a long stream of tobacco juice that splattered on the ground just short of the woman's foot. She wrinkled her nose and carefully avoided stepping on the brown stain.

"Oh, look honey, they even have a harmonica! Isn't that cute. Won't you play it for me, sweetie. I'll take your picture," she cooed in a syrupy sweet voice when she noticed the mouthpiece Neil kept in his pocket.

"Ain't tuned it yet today," Neil said stiffly then avoided looking in her direction.

"Ohhh, well -" she started, not knowing what else to say.

Maggie could barely hold back a chuckle. She rolled her eyes and slipped a sideways glance towards Neil.

"Ask and ye shall receive," she whispered under her breath as she got up to leave. "I'm going to go for now." She laughed as the obnoxious couple continued to walk their way through the crowd. "Hope you guys have fun today. Oh, and try to avoid getting picked up by any strange women."

"Don't worry yer head about that!" George called after her. "We only want the beee-uuu-tiful ones. Ye kin take that last 'un and keep 'er." Maggie smiled and shook her head. She left the mischievous trio to their pranks and continued to walk through the festival.

About midway through the town square, the voice of a loud, obnoxious speaker blared over the loudspeaker. She stepped up to one of the street corners filled with several onlookers who intently listened to something the man was saying. Curious, she moved closer into the crowd until she realized the man speaking to the crowd was none other than, Mr. Hubert T. Brown!

"Ohh, mann! What a bummer! I was having such a good time, too," Maggie blurted out as she walked closer. *I really didn't want to get into something that was going to get me all riled up today, I'm having too much fun even though I'd sure like to know what he's saying that's captivated everyone's interest so much,* she told herself as she moved in close enough to hear.

"- is the only way we are going to be able to lower taxes, folks. Trust me, we are going to all have to stick together on this and use this land to our own benefit. New industry will bring in more jobs for you and help you get all those things you want for your family. I'm telling you," he started to speak louder. "We're going to have to sell the protected lands so we can profit. Who needs a million trees in the wilderness when your family needs something to eat and something to wear?" Mr. Brown seemed to puff up and strut around the crowd as several people nodded and cheered him on with his speech. "That's right folks, listen to me - we don't need all this wilderness area when there are so many companies who would love to have it and can make some use of it. We need to be the ones to profit from it."

"Darn! Here we go again," Maggie said loud enough for others to hear when she listened to all she could stand. She could hold her temper no more. She began to fire away questions.

"Excuse me, Mr. Hubert T. Brown, but can you tell us exactly who is going to profit from the sale of our protected land? And, when you talk about job opportunities, isn't it a policy with big companies that they bring in workers from other areas who are already trained in their company to run those companies when a new site is bought to develop, often ignoring local people who are just as qualified?"

His face turned beet red and he began to look as though he was going to blow a gasket or two. He searched through the crowds to find the source of the person who disrupted his speech.

*Ummm, maybe this is going to be more fun than I thought at first,* she thought as she paused and waited for him to locate her. Maggie smiled and waited for him to find her.

"Can you guarantee jobs for local people and if you can - for how long?" she called from the crowd. She stood up higher on a curb when he seemed to have trouble locating her voice.

He desperately scanned the crowd to see who was interrupting his speech. When their eyes locked, she saw his face turn blood red. Even though Maggie felt as though someone flipped a switch inside her when she first heard the politician's speech, a cool calm now enveloped her as she continued. She realized she was getting under his skin. She was beyond stopping herself now.

"Isn't it practical to think the city is going to have to improve roads then the city water and sewer systems before any of those companies will ever sign an agreement to build in this area?" She watched his reaction to her comments as she relentlessly continued to fire away questions. "Those improvements are going to have to be made and paid for by the people who already live here. How do you plan to pay for those improvements? Do you plan to raise the taxes again, or can we look forward to some type of a new tax?"

"Now, listen here -" he began. His face turned several shades of a deeper red as he tried to clear his throat.

"What are the people who have been in this area for their entire lives supposed to do when these big industries come in and rape all of the natural resources from the land and then leave us high and dry while they head off for other places? When those companies use up the resources of the protected forests and the animals are gone, what will we have left? Is there a plan for that?"

Maggie asked as the crowd began to mumble and talk among themselves about her questions. Now, enormously amused with the obnoxious politician's intense discomfort, a peaceful, calm seemed to come over her. Amused, she watched him squirm under the intense, expectant looks of the crowd.

"Let me tell you a thing or two, little missie," he started to yell as the vein on his forehead began to pump and he began to sweat. Several other crowd members interrupted him and began to ask him similar questions. One woman asked him about his plan to improve the school system, another person asked about the need for a small emergency hospital in the area.

As he tried to regain control of the crowd again, he made a futile attempt to turn on his southern charm with the crowd after several women joined in the discussion.

"Now, let's just calm down here a little bit, you ladies need to leave the worry to us men folks," he retorted tensely which raised the eyebrows of men and women alike. He realized his mistake and desperately looked for a way out of the corner he painted for himself as several of the men in the group quietly stepped back in an attempt to place a little distance between themselves and his bandstand.

Maggie giggled. *Mission accomplished! Guess I stirred up a hornet's nest now, when all I really wanted to do was to show him for the side-winding, snake in the grass he is,* she told herself. She quietly slipped away from the crowd and left him to answer questions on his own.

As she continued her journey through the crowd, she kept her eyes open for some sign of Digger. The smells drifting up from the food in the vender's booths were tantalizing as Maggie walked among the tents. Hot dogs, chili, popcorn, and cotton candy all increased the gnawing sensation in her stomach. She quickly passed through the booths and looked for something to eat. The smells, music and happy noises from the crowd gave a thrilling carnival-like atmosphere to the area. It was pleasant and uplifting. Maggie smiled as and spoke to people she knew as she walked through the crowd and enjoyed the excitement.

She turned to a side street when she heard a roar of laughter from the crowd near the dunking booth. She walked over to see what the commotion might be. Several men were busy pouring bags of ice into a large vat of cold water that had a small plank hovering over the center. The crowd cheered as workers poured each bag of ice to the vat. Eager anticipation spread through the crowd when the superintendent of schools came forward to the microphone and began to speak.

"Ok, folks, here we go. This is what you have been waiting for all day long. Kids, line up now! Your chance to take a shot at dunking the principal of your school is almost here."

Just at that moment, the principal of the local school came out from behind a makeshift curtain. He wore enormous red and white polka dot swim trunks, purple flippers on his feet and a green snorkel on his head. He even had an inflatable child's float around his waist. The crowd roared with delight.

"Let me remind you," the speaker continued as the principal awkwardly climbed on the plank and scooted out to the end until he dangled precariously over the icy water. "All proceeds go toward the purchase of new baseball uniforms for the school team, so bring your change folks. Come one, come all! Let's see who can dunk the principal for fifty cents a shot!"

Several of the parents in the crowd began to tease the principal and egged on the competition a little bit more. An old baseball buddy stepped up to the marked spot and threw the first softball. His first attempt missed. On his second try, he hit the plate, but the system malfunctioned and did not dunk the principal after all. The crowd was in an uproar. Excitement continued to build as one after another of students and parents lined up to try and dunk the principal.

Eager anticipation swept through the crowd when the school's baseball star stepped up to the plate and threw his first attempt. It was a clear miss.

His second and third ball both hit the area around the place where the metal trigger switch hung, although his throws did not set the trigger off and only brought boos and hisses from the watchers. The principal grinned and taunted the crowd with each miss. By now, the crowd had grown even larger than before. Everyone wanted to see the principal dunked.

"Come on now, folks, lets keep this show on the road, who's next?" The speaker tried to keep the crowd's emotions building in a positive way and ignore some of the troublemakers who became unruly. Suddenly, a quiet hush fell over the crowd when one tiny figure among the adult's legs slipped forward and dropped two quarters into the donation jar.

"That looks like Jonah!" Maggie said excitedly. She worked her way closer to the dunking booth for a better view. Everyone watched the small child walk up to the spot marked with a bright red bear paw that represented the Tellico Plains Bears. It was set just a little bit closer to the mark for smaller contestants.

"Ok, folks, we've got a hot one here now. Let's see if he can compete with the big boys!" the superintendent spoke loudly into the microphone.

Jonah squinted his eyes and he looked toward the principal. Then, he reached down, picked up a handful of dust and rubbed it between his palms. He shuffled his feet and blinked his eyes. He slowly worked the softball in his small hands covering it with dust from the ground. Not a whisper could be heard in the crowd. He cranked his arm around his head three times then released the ball and threw it directly towards the metal trigger plate.

"DING!" The metal plate rang loud and clear! The principal's eyes popped open wide in disbelief when he immediately plunged into the icy water snorkel, fins and all! The crowd roared! Cheers and applause rose from everyone there as the shivering principal slowly climbed out of the icy tank and awkwardly flopped his way over to where Jonah stood.

Once in front of Jonah, the principal shoved the snorkel to the top of his head. He reached his dripping arm forward and firmly shook Jonah's hand, then cheered and lifted Jonah's arm in victory. "Good job, young man."

The crowd clapped and whistled again. Jonah tucked his bottom lip inside his mouth and looked down at the ground. A bashful half smile crept around the corners of his mouth and a rosy glow covered his face. He grinned and shuffled his boots in the dust.

"Folks we've got us a winner!" blared the voice on the loudspeaker.

Maggie watched Ranger Stratton lift Jonah to his shoulders as Zack jumped up and down beside them. Rena stood nearby and held the baby, her face filled with pride and excitement.

"Way to go Jonah!" Maggie called as she waved and clapped with the rest of the spectators. Stratton carried Jonah off through the crowd. Everyone patted him on the back as they walked past. Maggie was thrilled for him because he won almost as much as she was thrilled to see the little family forming in front of her.

Maggie worked her way to one of the food booths and purchased a large lemonade to go with a plate of nachos, salsa, cheese and hot peppers to eat while she watched some of the other competitions. Thoroughly enjoying herself, she stayed until almost sundown when the crowd started to disperse. Slowly, while she made her way back to the jeep, Maggie noticed the politician and the crowd around him seemed to have dispersed.

*At least he is not still up there trying to fill everyone's heads with lies and nonsense. I don,t care if it does make him mad. I just want people to make their own decisions about what they want based on truths, not lies and dishonesty. I hope some of the people that heard him today will at least start to think and question his motives before they wholeheartedly trust someone just because they say you should trust them,* Maggie thought to herself. As she walked, it dawned on her she had not seen Digger at the festival. She kept a look out for him on her way back to the jeep. *It isn't like him to miss a big festival like this. I wonder where he is,* she thought to herself as she climbed into the jeep, cranked it up and headed towards home.

"I'll look him up tomorrow. I'm too tired to look anymore tonight. He is always off on some big new adventure that can't seem to wait. One of these days he's going to realize he needs to tell folks where he's going and what he's up to before he disappears like that."

Maggie smiled when she realized she often did the same thing and disappeared without warning. She knew friends tried to protect her when they cared about her and wanted to keep her from dangers she did not see.

"Well, I'm not going to worry about him anymore tonight he's a big boy and can certainly take care of himself. He doesn't need me to watch over his shoulder all the time."

A light drizzle began to fall as she headed the jeep back up the mountain to her little cabin. *Umm, good thing it's raining, we've really been needing it,* she thought as she drove home, exhausted from the day's activities.

# Hasty Mistakes

Digger paused as he neared the entrance of the cave. He stood perfectly still, looked over his shoulder and carefully scanned the ridge top that surrounded the secluded valley. He allowed his eyes to work their way down the slope and over each tree within view of his stance. He carefully watched for any movement, any sign he was being followed or observed.

The fine mist that moved into the area as he began his hike was now a steady spring rain. The gentle sound of raindrops on the leaves drowned out the normal sounds of the forest and left him unable to distinguish noises or smells that were out of place. Carefully, he searched each section of the terrain and found nothing. Yet, the odd, uncomfortable feeling that something was not right still nagged at him. Digger stood still for a few more moments before he continued his treacherous journey.

He hesitated when he arrived near the creek where the opening to the mine hid behind the brush. He looked upstream into the dark, deep woods above the area where the steam flowed around the stone near the entrance of the cave. Something did not feel right. He could not quite put his finger on it yet, but something was not the way it should be.

He paused. Anger stirred within him when he saw unusual footsteps in the sand near the entrance of the cave. It looked like the prints of someone heavy perhaps, or worse. He looked carefully around the small sandy area as he searched for some sign that would tell him something about the person who belonged to the footprints left behind until he finally found the evidence he needed.

There, under the shrubs, more footprints lay in the sand. Only, these footprints barely left an imprint. They were not deeply embedded in the sand as the ones he had just seen were. Beside the lighter footprints, he saw the indentation of a pack, a large, heavy pack that leaned against the stone until the person lifted the heavy pack and placed it on their back causing their shoes to leave deeper tracks in the sand.

He looked up toward the opening of the mine and carefully searched the entrance bit by bit. Finally, he saw a place where someone had pulled a pack or something large out of the cave dragging leaves and sand along with it. He panicked. Then, leaving all caution behind, Digger carelessly rushed into the cave, as he feared the worst.

Silently, the dark figure moved from behind the wall of brush and shrubs that lined the stream near the opening of the cave. In the fading light of day, he laid his pack to the side of the entrance and quietly followed Digger inside the cave as the steady spring rain increased and began to fall harder.

# Perilous Journey

Max ran down to greet her as Maggie pulled into the driveway. She reached her arm out to pet him as he jumped up, put his paws on the door of the jeep and stuck his head through the window. "Hey there, Max. What have you been up to today?" She rubbed behind his ears before she gently pushed him aside so she could open the door and get out.

Max ran back and forth in front of her and barked continually as she tried to walk up the path to the cabin. She was unable to pass him. When she finally stopped, frustrated because she could not walk around him, he ran to the shade tree where Digger parked his truck and began to pace back and forth in front of his truck.

"Oh, Wow! Digger's here! No wonder you are so excited!" She placed her purse and packages on the porch steps and followed Max over to the truck. Max started to jump excitedly as she neared. "Where is he Big Guy?" she asked as she approached the truck. "Did Digger stop by to see us?"

Seeing no one in or around the truck, she slowly walked around it looking for a direction he might have taken. She placed her hand on the hood of the truck as she walked around it.

"Looks, like he's been here for a while, the engine of the truck feels cool and he made footprints before the rain started."

She looked at the ground and checked for prints. Slowly and carefully, she walked back toward the cabin. Max barked and almost knocked Maggie down when he bumped her harshly with his head and shoulders and ran past her. He paused at the head of the trail and continued to bark and wag his tail from there.

"Oh, Max, don't tell me Digger's gone down the trail!" Maggie's heart dropped as she walked over to the place where Max continued to bark. She looked quickly at the trail. There, she saw the telltale sign of footprints, which indicated Digger started across the trail that eventually led to Whipperwill Mine.

"Oh, no. He must have come up here looking for me to go with him." She stood looking at the trail, undecided about what she should do. "It's raining, and it's almost dark. There's no way I could make it there safely tonight," she thought as she contemplated the situation.

"Come on, Max, let's go up to the cabin for a minute," she said urgently as she turned and walked quickly up the path to the cabin. When she reached the front door, she noticed the scrap of paper that hung on the nail and took it inside so she could see it well enough to read. The note, scribbled in Digger's halting scrawl simply said:

"Maggie ned yure hep com quik ye no whur"

"Ohh, geeze, now why did he have to go and leave without waiting for me to get home," she mumbled as she methodically began to pack her small lightweight pack. She tried to push the fear and panic out of her chest as she quickly worked. There was no question about whether or not she would follow him down the trail. "I don't like to hike at night, but if Digger was that anxious to leave, then something big is going on and he needs me to be there with him."

She quickly packed her backpack and securely fastened it on her back, then slipped a large green poncho over her head and pack to keep them dry on her trek down the mountain. She grabbed her largest, most powerful flashlight and a smaller one to use in case the large one gave out. As an afterthought, she quickly scrawled a note on a pad of paper and placed it on the nail beside the front door of the cabin along with Digger's note where it would be easy to see.

*Just in case something happens*, she thought as she gave one last glance around the room and headed out the door.

Silently, the dark figure slipped out of the cave into the hidden area behind the bushes and shrubs where he hid just before Digger's arrival in the secluded valley. Once again, he strapped the heavy knapsack on his back and worked his way across the valley floor. Cautiously, he crossed the flooded stream that usually flowed peacefully along the edge of the meadow and now was a raging torrent of treacherous water as it leaped and bounded over its banks.

Slowly, he began to climb the hazardous switchback trail that led up the side of the mountain to the safety of the plateau above. He took his time as he carefully crossed a tree that lay across the path.

Occasionally, he slipped in the mud as he slowly worked his way closer to the crest of the mountain where the power of the storm intensified.

Lightening began to strike the rocks and trees around him and torrents of rain pummeled him and made travel life threatening; yet he continued his journey. He struggled with his footing as he neared the large oak tree on the crest of the ridge.

Hiking became increasingly more difficult as Maggie worked her way over the treacherous trail. The steady rain that started as she began her journey turned into a downpour at times making every step hazardous. Slowly, Maggie worked her way to the top of the ridge. She slipped and slid on the muddy, washed out path. Suddenly, just as she reached the crest of the ridge, the whole area lit up as a bolt of lightening streaked though the sky and struck the ground nearby. A deafening crack of thunder followed as the storm continued to rumble and pour a deluge of rain over the area where Maggie stood.

Fearing the destructive force of the lightening more than the treacherous trail, Maggie quickly looked for shelter along the ridge top. She found the slight overhang of a stone shelf and called Max, who remained in the middle of the trail, huddled and drenched by the onslaught of rain. Maggie motioned for Max to move up against the stone ledge as she moved in beside him and spread the end of her poncho over them in an attempt to block the brunt of the storm.

The acidic smell of ozone that followed the strike of lightening permeated the air as one bolt after another struck the ridge around them. The ground shook and the sky lit up as if it was mid-afternoon when one tremendous bolt of lightening struck a large oak tree that stood precariously at the edge of the trail. A momentary silence preceded the deafening crack as the ancient tree began to split in half and leaned precariously toward the valley basin below the cliff.

Chills ran through her when she recognized something familiar about the tree. At first, she thought she saw the image of a man standing in front of the tree, but she could not be sure. She blinked her eyes and tried to wipe some of the rain from them as she looked in the direction of the tree and waited for the next bolt of lightening to light up the sky enough for her to see the tree once more.

With the next bolt of lightening, she recognized the tree as the same one she stood beside to look over the valley the day she first hiked the trail with Digger. Within the roll of thunder, she thought she heard someone call out her name from some distant far away place, but she could not be sure.

*I must be hallucinating*, she thought. *First, I think I see a man by the tree and now I hear someone call out my name in the storm.* She shuddered when she heard a distant crash when a portion of the tree struck the floor of the valley below the ridge.

She moved a little closer to Max and waited for the next bolt of lightening to strike. Maggie began to shiver uncontrollably in the damp night air as she huddled under the eave of the stone ledge. She could not tell if she was shaking because she was cold and wet, or because she was so afraid. Storms like this were extremely dangerous and difficult to protect oneself from when on such a high ridge top.

Her mind began to whirl as she speculated about where Digger might be. Fear for him gripped her as the image of Digger ran through her mind. The image of him as he hiked on the trail alone or trapped in the cave during the storm now raged ran through her mind. His chilling words to her the last time they camped in the valley rang in her ears.

"Don't NEVER come here alone," he said, and, "Don't NEVER go in to the cave when it rains!" She knew he was the world's worst person to follow his own advice, no matter how good the advice was.

"Please don't let him be in the mine," she breathed, as fears of him lying harmed or injured inside the mine during the storm gripped her with fear and forced all rational thoughts aside. She urgently wanted to rush down the mountain as quickly as possible.

"Let him be somewhere outside where he can climb up the ridge to safety to get away from the stream if it starts to flood. At least that way he will have a chance of survival. If he's inside the cave he's going to be in real trouble," she prayed fervently for his safety.

The intensity of the storm continued to increase when the whole ridge top lit up with the blinding white light of a tremendous bolt of lightening as it seared across the sky and struck the ground nearby. Maggie's ears rang with the deafening sound that followed the bolt of lightening when a loud crack of thunder shook the ground and filled the air with a sound so loud it felt as thought the whole earth would open up and swallow them.

Just at that moment, as the lightening flashed and lit up the sky, Maggie looked up to see the image of Frank looming over her in the torrents of rain. His eyes were wild and filled with rage. Water ran off his clothing and long stringy hair. He held a large stone over his head and let out a blood curdling yell.

He thrust the stone down toward Maggie and attempted to strike her in the head. She instinctively lifted her arm to shield the blow of the rock and rolled her body away from the thrust of the stone. She tried to defend herself with the flashlight and smashed it against his head as Frank lunged toward her again.

In a flash as quick as a streak of lightning, Max lunged from beneath the shelter of the ledge and thrust all his weight against the attacker. His front paws struck the man in the center of the chest and knocked him down. Angrily, the man leaped from the ground and tried to grab the dog around the throat. The weight of his knapsack made his movements awkward and off balance as he clumsily tried to fight off the raging beast and strike back at Maggie again.

Max was in a frenzy now. His white fangs glistened as he knocked Frank down again and grasped the man's arm in his teeth, ripping and tearing at the sleeve. The man screamed and cursed as he tried to fight Max off. He reached beside him, grabbed a stick and struck Max on the head in an effort to keep him away.

Frank finally stood up at the edge of the trail. His body swayed as he tried to regain his balance. The weight of his knapsack seemed to make him teeter and sway as he stood near the rim of the ledge. A large bolt of lightening lit up the sky as part of the trail where Frank stood began to give away. The weight of the knapsack began to pull Frank downward when the rim of the trail broke away and caused him to slip and fall backward.

Desperately, he grasped the ground in search of a handhold. He tried to find something to keep from falling any further down the steep bank. The weight of his pack continued to drag him slowly down. Maggie leaped from beneath the ledge to look for something to throw to Frank and help pull him to safety. Again, Maggie thought she heard the voice of someone calling from somewhere behind her on the trail. She turned to see Chris run up the trail behind her.

"Maggie! Maggie! Where are you?" he called as he reached the top of the ridge.

"Chris, hurry," she shouted as she desperately looked for a branch to use to pull Frank to safety. "It's Frank, he's about to fall. I need something to pull him onto safer ground," she said as another desperate, blood-curdling scream erupted from Frank's mouth.

"Be careful, Chris, the trail's breaking away," Maggie warned.

Chris quickly lay flat on his stomach and scooted out toward the rim to offer Frank his hand and pull him into safety. Frank frantically grasped Chris' arm, his eyes wild with fear and desperation as he reached and clawed for a more secure grasp. The weight of Frank's body and heavy pack began to pull Chris forward along the soft, muddy trail along with him, dragging them both down towards the sheer cliff and into the dark valley below.

"Let go of the pack, Frank!" Chris shouted desperately as they slid closer to the edge. "It's pulling you back."

The knapsack on Frank's back began to slip and slide off his shoulders even as the overwhelming weight of the pack pulled him down. Desperately, Chris tried to dig his feet into the ground to get some traction and halt their bodies from sliding further onto the perilous, crumbling rim of the cliff.

Quickly, Maggie wrapped her arms around Chris' waist when he began to lose traction and slide closer to the edge. Their combined weight slowed them down enough for Chris to dig his toes into the ground and wrap one arm around a small tree near the rim.

"Let go of the pack, Frank," he yelled through the sounds of the storm, "It's pulling us in, it's not worth it, Frank."

The muscles in Chris' arms began to tremble and quake as he supported the sheer weight of Frank and the pack as they dangled precariously over the rim into mid air. Frank looked at him with wild, desperate eyes. Terror and furry erupted across his face when the pack began to slide off his back and fall into the darkness below. He twisted and turned as he struggled to maintain his hold on the pack.

"Frank! Frank! Let go of the pack, NOW!" Chris yelled. He desperately continued to struggle with the writhing man in his grasp.

Max paced nearby and continued to bark and charge in a wild frenzied attack while Frank dangled precariously over the edge of the cliff. Maggie called to Max and tried to calm him down while she frantically held on to Chris' waist. She tried everything in her power to slow their slide.

Suddenly, the pack slipped off Frank's shoulders. He twisted and turned in an attempt to grab it one last time and almost caused Chris to lose hold of his wrist. When the pack finally fell into the valley below, Frank abruptly began to frantically climb and claw his way back up the cliff digging his fingernails into Chris' wrist and arm on his way to the top and safety.

Finally making it to solid ground, Frank flopped on the trail and writhed in the mud momentarily, before he leapt to his feet again. In an instant, Frank began to act like a madman again. His eyes were wild and manic. Suddenly, he began to scream and curse at Chris and Maggie in a frantic rage and ran recklessly down the path toward the Skyway Trail in a frantic effort to get away from the pair. .

With the weight of Frank and the heavy pack released from his arm, Chris rolled over and moaned. He gasped for air and tried to regain his strength. Maggie and Chris struggled to regain their footing in the mud as Frank ran past them. Chris reached for him and tried to grab his arm. Frank jerked out of Chris' grasp and slid chaotically down the trail. Chris rose quickly to follow him but Maggie quickly reached up, put her hand on his arm and stopped him. Maggie shouted as loudly as she could so Chris could hear her over the storm.

"Wait, Chris, let him go. We can deal with him, later. Digger needs us more. I think he may be in serious trouble."

Max came over and stood beside them as Chris turned and quickly held Maggie in his arms. "I was so worried about you."

"How did you know I was here?" she asked when she noticed the bloody scratches on Chris' arm where Frank clawed him during the rescue attempt when Frank almost fell over the cliff.

"The Rangers stopped by my cabin looking for you tonight. They thought you might be there," he said as they briefly moved into the protection of a small grove of trees to treat the wounds on Chris' arm. The brunt of the storm seemed to have passed although a steady rain continued to fall. Maggie took a fresh bandana out of her pack and wrapped it around Chris' bloody arm.

"What did they want?" she asked. She securely tied the ends of the bandana around his arm and began to hurry down the trail.

"Be careful, Maggie, the trail is extremely dangerous right now," Chris cautioned her as he held on to the trunk of a tree in order to get around a washed-out area of the trail. "Sam said those kids you met on the Skyway trail went back to their campsite after the festival today and stumbled onto a new meth lab operation," Chris continued.

"Evidently, when the last meth lab was discovered, Frank and Wes moved sites to another place on the mountain and the kids just happened to chose the same site to set up their camp," he continued. They quickly worked their way down the treacherous mountain trail and avoided the areas of the trail washed away by the storm.

"You should have heard Sam and Fred talk about it! These kids hiked into the campground and ran right into Wes actually making the stuff. He was higher than a kite and tried to attack them when they showed up. One of the girls hit him with a skillet; then they tied him up with their tent ropes while one of the boys went for help," Chris laughed. "Fred said when the Rangers arrived at the campsite, the man was hogtied to a tree with both of the girls standing over him until the Calvary showed up."

Maggie giggled softly at the comical image of Wes hog-tied to a tree with two girls holding frying pans as they stood over him. She wondered if he managed to preserve his Elvis hairstyle while the girls had him tied up like that.

"Anyway," Chris continued, "When they got Wes into custody, he started to spill the beans about their drug operation. He said he and Frank split up over some drug and money issues. He told them Frank planed to kill you. He was the one who left the snake on your porch although there's some indication another person may be involved, we just can't prove it."

Maggie stopped and looked at him as she heard his chilling words. She shook her head in disbelief; then continued to hike.

"Wes told the Rangers Frank stalked you for some time. He was bragging about a secret he knew and said he was coming into a 'jackpot' soon."

"Digger's mine!" Maggie exclaimed. She became alarmed when she realized that Frank most likely came up from Digger's mine when she encountered him near the crest of the mountain just now. "We've got to hurry, Chris! Frank was coming from this area when I ran into him on the trail! Hurry, he may have done something to Digger!" she said as she called Max and urgently continued down the long, steep path down the ridge, again.

"The first thing I thought of was Digger's mine, too," Chris said as he followed and worked his way as quickly as possible along the trail behind Maggie.

A slight rain continued as they came to the end of the trail and neared the bottom of the ridge. The sound of rushing water soon intensified when they came to the opening of the valley. In the early darkness before dawn, their feeble flashlights could barely penetrate the devastation in the small valley basin caused by torrents of water.

Water from the high mountain ridges surrounding the once peaceful little valley tumbled in torrents down the sides of the ridges and rushed into the small stream that flowed along the side of the valley. It now was a raging torrent of wild, angry water. The entire field before them appeared to be a small lake instead of the spring field she remembered. It now was completely flooded and covered with rushing water.

They stood in awe of the power and force of the water as it raged through the little valley. Frantically, they searched for a way across the field and tried to decide what to do next. Exhausted, Max sat on a grassy spot on the small knoll where the golden yellow jonquils that had been so brilliant only a few weeks before, were now soggy and bent over to the ground from the force of the heavy rains. Everywhere Maggie looked water, mud and debris from the mountain ridges washed through the valley floor.

*Even though it seems like we have to go through the bowels of hell and back to save him - whatever it takes, that is what we will have to do,* she thought to herself as she viewed the destruction and massive amounts of debris they would have to climb over to save Digger from the cave. *We'll save him If he's still there, and IF he's still alive!*

The brunt of the storm seemed to have subsided enough for them to talk without having to shout at each other through the noise of the storm. They paused long enough to gather their thoughts and make a decision about the best route to take them to Digger's cave.

# Daring Rescue

Chris grabbed Maggie's wrist with his hand, "Here, hold my wrist as tightly as you can, it will give us a stronger hold when we walk across the field together," Chris said. He tentatively stepped out into the floodwaters that covered the small field.

As Maggie looked across the dark field, she was barely able to see the outline of the ancient oak tree that stood on a small rise in the center of the clearing. She tapped Chris' shoulder and pointed to it, urging him to head in that direction. Chris waded toward the old tree and held tightly to Maggie's wrist as they struggled through the soggy, flooded field. They worked their way across the dark field carefully, often slipped and slid as the treacherous cold waters rushed around them.

"The waters through this part of the valley only seem to be six inches deep in most places, so I don't think we have much to worry about until we reach the stream," he called over his shoulder.

Max trotted along beside them in most places. In some places, he leaped or jumped through the water when it became too high for him to walk. The water was never deep enough in the field for him to have to swim. When they reached the small rise in the field where the oak tree stood, Maggie stopped and leaned against the tree.

"Wait just a minute," she gasped and tried to catch her breath from struggling through the floodwaters.

"Which way is the mine, Maggie?" Chris asked. They tried to get their bearings and determine which would be the best direction to take to get to the mine and help Digger.

"It's over there." She pointed towards the base of the ridge in front of them as she wiped rainwater from her face. "There's a large stone in the river right in front of the entrance to the cave. We'll have to hurry. The stream hasn't come to a crest yet and when it does, there's a danger the cave might fill up with water," she said as she headed toward the cave.

"Maybe we should wait until after the water crests, then," Chris said with concern in his voice. He looked across the valley to the raging stream that already seemed to be sweeping everything out of its path. Crossing the stream seemed almost impossible.

"We can't, Chris. We have to go now!" Maggie responded firmly, determination in her voice. "If Digger's hurt and inside the cave when it floods, he won't make it out alive. We have to go now!"

Chris looked into her eyes and realized the determination and urgency in her voice. "Let's go now, then, before it's too late." He firmly grasped her wrist and plunged into the flooded field again.

"Max, you stay here," she ordered sternly, then followed Chris into the water and struggled to keep up. Carefully they headed for the stream bank on the other side of the flooded stream.

Max hesitated by the lone oak tree and wagged his tail, unsure if he wanted to obey Maggie or not. The waters became deeper and stronger as he watched Maggie and Chris struggle to make their way to the edge of the stream bank. Their efforts to wade through the now, knee-deep water in the field were even more difficult, partially due to the low visibility in the valley. The sun was not up yet, and although the worst part of the storm subsided, the skies were not clear enough to offer any light from the moon or stars.

At the edge of the stream, Maggie and Chris were able to climb on top of one of the large rocks and catch their breath. Maggie began to remove her pack and tie it to one of the small trees beside the rock where she stood.

"I don't need anything to drag me down when we cross the stream," she told Chris while she removed her poncho and wrapped it around one of the branches.

"Good idea. If anyone looks for us they will see our packs and know we are nearby," he said as he tied his poncho to the tree also. "Where do we need to go from here?"

"Ok, we need to cross the stream and go up that bank just a little bit." She pointed to the Rhododendron bush beside the boulder that shielded the cave entrance. "I'm not sure where would be the best place to cross the stream; it looks like it's going to be difficult no matter where we start."

"I agree," Chris said while he looked at the stream thoughtfully. "Sometimes, during a flood, a stream is more turbulent and forceful after it turns a bend, but it may be deeper on the front end of the bend."

"Let's take the front side then, I can swim if I have to," Maggie said as she began to head into the stream.

"Wait a second, I'll go first if you want me to. I'm taller and heavier than you are and may be able to get a little better traction than you can. That way, I can pull you across if you can't get your footing," Chris cautioned her. He paused long enough to pick up a couple of long branches from a tree that were broken off and fallen along the side of the stream.

"Here, hold this in your free hand to help balance you in the stream. He then took a step into the raging waters and reached back for Maggie's wrist.

She held on tightly to his arm as they slowly worked their way across the stream, which now was more than doubled its usual size. The force of the water against her legs often pushed them out from under her and caused her to teeter and nearly loose her balance. She tried to keep her feet firmly planted on the streambed and scooted her feet along the bottom of the stream as she moved across to the other side. She wedged the stick Chris gave her into the streambed to keep from slipping.

Slowly, they made their way across the stream to the bank on the other side. They climbed up high enough to be clear of the rising, dangerous floodwaters as the stream continued to swell with waters from the rains. Maggie urgently called for Digger in hopes that he was camped somewhere outside the cave safe and sound.

"Digger! Digger! Where are you?" she called over and over again. The thunderous sound of the water as it rushed past them made hearing a return call from Digger almost impossible. Maggie rushed to the opening of the cave and peered inside.

"Digger! Digger, are you in here?" She called. She stuck her head inside and tried to hear some answer from within. She quickly began to crawl inside the entrance of the cave.

"Whoa! Wait a minute! Are you sure that's safe?" Chris reached for her leg and pulled her back out before she crawled completely inside the cave.

"Of, course it's not safe! However, I don't have any other choice. I have to get him out if he is in there. He doesn't have a chance if I don't," Maggie answered quickly. "I didn't come this far to wait for him outside the cave."

"We don't even know if he's in there, Maggie," Chris tried to reason with her as she moved toward the cave entrance again.

"And we don't know that he's not either." She looked at Chris urgently, eager to go. "I'm the one that has to go down the shaft. It will be easier for me to fit into this section of the cave. One of us needs to stay on the outside to help pull Digger out if something has happened to him. I can't do it by myself."

He paused briefly and looked at her. His face filled with fear for her safety. Concern flooded his eyes.

"Ok, get going then, but hurry! No - take your time. No - be careful, but go as fast as you can. I want you to come back to me."

She smiled and kissed him before she lay on her stomach and began to crawl through the entrance of the cave. "You'd better be right there when I come back," she shouted over her shoulder as she turned on her flashlight and moved deeper into the cave.

"I'm not moving!" Chris called into the cave. His voice became fainter as Maggie moved along the passage deeper into the belly of the mountain. "Please, hurry."

Maggie's light shown along the bend in the tunnel. Fear gripped her and her heart began to beat furiously when she noticed a small amount of water begin to run through the tunnel from somewhere deep inside the cavern.

"Oh, please be ok, Digger," she whispered. She urgently began to call his name again. "Digger! Digger! Where are you?" she called again and again. She crawled even more quickly to reach the main chamber of the mine. Her belly now covered in mud, was only inches above the water as she frantically moved along.

"Digger! We've come to take you home. Digger!" Her voice began to echo around her when she reached the innermost chamber of the cavern. Still, she could hear no response to her calls, only the soft sound of running water as she moved along.

She reached the area where the cave opened into the larger chamber and noticed the steady stream of water seemed to flow through the room at an alarming rate. She crawled out of the tunnel and stood up, then realized several inches of water now covered the entire floor of the main room. It seemed to be rising and flowing from the back of the cave to the entrance tunnel. Fear gnawed at her stomach when she stood on the floor of the chamber and saw her feet and ankles now completely covered with water.

A faint sound came from the back of the room. She held her breath and stood very still. Holding her flashlight over her head, she slowly moved it section by section along the wall of the chamber, looking for any sign of Digger. There, along the back section of the cave where the wall was crumbling and falling down, Digger lay partially covered by mud and debris. A large rock had fallen and pinned his legs. He barely lifted one of his arms in an attempt to halt Maggie from coming any closer.

"Don' com 'inny further, girl, she's 'bout ta go. The whole dang wall's givin' in on me," he said in a horse, feeble whisper. "Hurry up now, git outta 'ere," he said more sternly. He tried to waive her back when she did not heed his protests.

"You're crazy if you think I'm going to leave you in here, you old coot!" Maggie exclaimed. She quickly waded to his side through the water. "Tell me what happened, Digger, do you hurt anywhere?" she demanded as she gently checked out his arms and legs to see if any bones were broken.

"Ah com in 'ere cuz ah thought sumbody wuz in the cave. As soon as ah com in, sumbody hit me on the haid, 'n that's whin the wall started comin' down 'n trapped mah laigs."

Maggie only halfway listened to him. She moved quickly. She desperately looked around the cave for something to pry the large rock off his legs, frantic to get him out as quickly as possible.

"Digger, where's your pick?" she demanded.

"Over yonder 'side mah pack," he pointed in the direction of the opposite wall. "Ah dropped it thar whin sumbody hit mah haid."

Maggie held her flashlight in the direction he pointed and was instantly alarmed to see the water had risen even higher than before. She could not see his pack anywhere. Pure fear rose within her when she realized several feet of water now covered the entire floor of the cavern. Digger's pack was now submerged. She gulped and tried to swallow down the panic that rose within her.

"Ok, Digger," she said urgently. She tried to make her voice sound calm. "We've got to hurry. I am going to push the big rock off you with my legs. You just be very still."

She climbed onto the soft muddy wall and tried to push the stone off. She strained and groaned with the effort yet was unable to budge it even an inch. Desperate, Maggie realized she needed some help very quickly. She quickly splashed through the water toward the tunnel that led out of the cave.

"Chris! Chris! Can you hear me? Chris, I need you. Digger's trapped!" she yelled. She thought she saw the faint glow of a flashlight in the tunnel as she continued to call his name. "Chris, are you out there? Can you hear me?"

Faintly, in the distance, she heard him answer. "I'm here, I'm already headed your way, Maggie. I couldn't wait outside any longer."

She almost broke down into tears of relief when she saw the glow of his flashlight come through the tunnel. It was the most welcome site she had ever seen. Maggie saw the light of Chris' flashlight shine a little brighter as he neared the opening of the chamber where Digger lay trapped. A rush of relief and hope filled her when she finally could see his shape and he entered the chamber of the now flooded room.

"Hurry, Chris. He's under a big rock and I can't budge it," she said as she headed back to Digger. "You're almost here, Chris. As soon as you can see my light, you'll be able to stand up."

Chris entered the cavern as Maggie slipped her hands under Digger's head to keep it from dipping underneath the water that filled the cave. Chris immediately waded across the room, using his stick to balance himself in the swelling water. He rushed to the wall where Digger was pinned precariously under the large stone. He then shoved the stick behind the stone. Using the weight of his body for leverage, he began to push on the stick and loosen the stone. In a few moments, the stone rolled off and tumbled away.

Maggie frantically began to dig the rest of the mud away from Digger's legs. "Are you ok? What do your legs feel like, do they hurt anywhere?" She asked as she tried to check the bones for breaks.

"Can't feel a thang in 'em Maggie. That's why ah'm a'tellin' ye ta git outta here 'afore the whole place fills up wi' water! Ah ain't gonner be much use ta ya on the way out." Digger grasped her arm as she frantically continued to dig away debris from his legs.

"Save yersef, Maggie, "Do it fer me," he begged. "Both of ye. Now git outta here, ah mean it!" He began to cough violently.

"I AM doing this for you, Digger! I can't save myself without saving you, too. I won't do that again," she said as the memory of little Timmy flashed through her mind. "I won't ever leave anyone behind again, Digger! I can't!" she cried desperately as she helped Chris scrape the last of the muck and rocks away from Digger's legs. "Now, darnit quit being in such an all-fired hurry to give up and help us out here a little bit!"

Chris moved to Digger's shoulders, reached underneath his arms and tugged as Maggie slowly pulled his legs away from the rest of the debris. A rumbling sound sent chills down her spine when a section of the cave tumbled and fell into the rising water.

"We've got to go NOW, Maggie!" Chris said urgently. He started to drag Digger toward the entrance tunnel of the cave.

Maggie lifted Digger's legs and trudged through the water after Chris and tried to help as much as she could. The cave continued to rumble and groan. Frantically, Maggie urged them forward when she realized the water was now as high as her hips.

"Digger, how much can you use your arms right now?" Chris asked as they neared the tunnel.

"Ah gots mah arms, Doc," Digger said, "Jest git me in th' tunnel 'n ah'll take it frum thar," as he began to violently cough again.

"You'd better crawl fast, old man, 'cause I'm gonna kick you where the sun don't shine, if you don't move out of here faster than you ever have before," Maggie said with a grin. She smiled and gave Chris the thumbs up sign.

"You'd better be right behind me, Maggie," Chris said with a worried look. He crawled into the tunnel and led the way out of the cave. "Digger, if you get too tired trying to use your arms, just hold on to one of my legs and I'll pull you along with me," Chris instructed as he moved along the tunnel, now filled with rushing water.

The waters in the tunnel were moving swiftly now, leaving only a few inches of headspace to breathe. Strange rumbling sounds echoed through the cave as they maneuvered their way down the tunnel. Digger moved slowly, often slipped and dipped completely underwater, gasping for air when his head popped up again. He often had to stop, overcome by coughing spells.

Maggie tried to urge him forward. "Digger, hold on to Chris! He can pull you through," Maggie shouted as the force of the water often pushed them against the walls of the cave and made travel difficult.

Maggie dug her fingers into the sides of the tunnel and tried to get enough traction to propel her along the shaft. A frightening groan from the back of the cave forced a violent surge of water through the channel and filled it completely with water for a few moments. Maggie felt the force of water as it crammed her body against the side of the cave and made it impossible for her to move. She held her breath and tried to regain her bearings as the force of the water pressed against her and shoved her into Digger. Suddenly, the water forced her head against the wall and slammed it against a rock. She began to see stars.

Disoriented and confused, she feebly tried to grope her way along the shaft of the cave. Her lungs began to burn and feel as though they were going to burst. She ached for air. She pressed her hand along the top of the shaft, searching for a pocket of air, but could find none. The pitch-blackness of the water surrounded her as her flashlight began to flicker and fade. The power and strength of the waters propelled her forward. She was unable to resist the tremendous force. The force knocked and banged her like a rag doll in a raging stream. Her body looked like a lifeless form as it tossed and tumbled in the water...

.....she felt something tug violently on her leg - something behind her that tried to pull her down into the water again so she would drown. Vaguely, the image of Frank came toward her through the water. Frank - wearing a minister's stiff black suit - Frank, the Evil One, was coming to get her. He held her ankle as he tried to pull her down into a watery grave. Terrified, Maggie tried to escape, but was unable to free herself from the grasp of the Evil One. Then, out of the depths of the waters came a mystical snake with emerald green eyes that sparkled and shone through the darkness. It wrapped its body around the Evil One and pulled him away from her as he screamed and struggled into the depths below.

Slowly, Maggie felt the remaining air in her lungs begin to escape one bubble at a time. They each floated up through the dark waters and drift away. Her need for air ceased as all consciousness slowly began to slip away - she began to float on one of the tiny bubbles as it drifted through the dark waters in the cavern, then, fly through the dark night sky as a million tiny stars sparkled and beckoned her to come their way. She wore a long white gown with a train as long as a comet's tail that glistened and sparkled as bright as the Milky Way as she soared through the midnight sky. The night suddenly filled with a blinding white light all around her...

A loud rumbling sound filled the air and the ground violently shook as two strong arms grasped Maggie's wrists and pulled her out of the cave. She gasped for air, then fell on top of the unconscious bodies of Chris and Digger and almost tumbled into the stream in front of the cave. Maggie curled on her side as she heaved in deep gulps of air. She coughed and wheezed with the effort. Her lungs felt as though they were gong to burst. She began to cough up water from her lungs as she tried to breathe.

Maggie moaned and rolled over on her back when a loud, sharp barking sound rang in her ear. Slowly she began to regain consciousness as the rough feel of Max's tongue swept across her face and helped revive her. She weakly brushed away his attempts to lick her as he eagerly continued to stroke her face again and again. Frantically, Max barked louder, right in her face when she didn't get up from the ground. He grasped her arm in his mouth and tried to pull her away from the entrance of the mine. Slowly, Maggie sat up and groaned.

"Uhhh, Max," she mumbled, still confused. Max barked loudly again, then bit her sharply on the arm. "OUCH!" she said angrily, now, fully awake. "Why did you do that?" she asked as she rubbed her arm.

Max barked again even louder and ran toward the opposite side of the stream then back again. He looked fiercely at Maggie, then growled with his fangs bared and continued to bark; his body in a tense, defensive stance, tail pointed straight up in the air.

Alarmed, Maggie realized Max was trying to get her to move away from the mine. Fear gripped her as she quickly looked around for Digger and Chris. They were lying nearby. Digger seemed to be unconscious. Chris laid moaning and groaning on his side. She quickly crawled to Chris' side and shook him.

"Chris, Chris, wake up! Come on Doc, we've got to move!" She patted his cheeks with her hands in an effort to bring him around to consciousness. "Hurry, Chris, I need you." Slowly, he began to flutter his eyes and wake up. He moaned as he moved his head from side to side and struggled to sit up. Maggie helped him sit up then rushed to Digger's side, quickly checking his pulse to make sure he was alive.

Again, the rumbling sounds from the cave began to shake the ground where they lay. Rising as quickly as he could, Chris tried to help Digger to his feet by slipping his shoulder under Digger's armpit and wrapping Digger's arm around his shoulder. Maggie slipped under his arm on the other side.

Cautiously, they waded through the swollen stream, often slipping on slick stones. Just as they reached the other side of the stream; they heard a deafening roar as a spew of water and muck erupted from the cave and caused them to lose their balance and fall. They covered their heads with their hands as the ground began to tremble and shake before it sent a mountain of mud and rocks crashing down and forever closing the entrance of the cave.

"She's gone, Maggie," Digger mumbled. "The mountain claimed 'er fer its own, jest like ah tole ye she wud," he said as he drifted in and out of consciousness, waking only when the violent coughing spasms jarred his body awake.

"It's ok, Digger," Maggie smiled. "Remember what you've always told me, 'When one vein plays out, there's always another mountain to mine.'"

They sat huddled together on the opposite bank and waited for the air to clear. Each one in shock and a little numb from the shock of witnessing the collapse of the mountain and their brush with near death. Max laid his head on Maggie's lap and licked her arm where he bit her. She scratched him behind the ear.

"It's ok, buddy, thank you for saving us." He woefully rolled his eyes up at her as if to beg forgiveness for biting her on the arm. "It's ok, Max, you did the only thing you knew to do, good boy." Maggie smiled and hugged him tightly then looked over at Chris and Digger.

"Are you guys ready to move on to the middle of the field?"

Wearily, Chris smiled at her. "We're ready whenever you are, Maggie." Digger's head rolled over on his shoulder as he slipped out of consciousness again. "We need to get Digger on a little higher ground if we can, so I can check him out." Together, they both moved under Digger's arms again and began the struggle to the middle of the field.

# Bright Horizons

The morning sun was raising high in the sky as they made their way to the small rise in the field where the old oak tree stood. The sky was a brilliant, crystal blue without a cloud anywhere in sight. The waters began to recede from the fields leaving bright emerald green grass behind. Max ran ahead of the trio as they worked their way through the soggy field.

When they reached the drier knoll by the oak tree, they eased Digger to the ground and tried to make him as comfortable as possible. Chris instantly transformed into "Doc" again. He thoroughly examined Digger from head to toe for injuries. Maggie anxiously waited by his side to hear what Doc had to say.

"He's going to be ok, Maggie," Chris said with concern in his voice. "He may have a concussion and a possible broken rib or two. We can't be sure until we get him to an ER and take some X-rays. My biggest concern is preventing him from developing pneumonia, if he does not already have it. He has a terrible cough, probably from being wet and down in the cave for so long."

Max suddenly jumped up and began to bark and run toward the path that led up the mountain when suddenly, several forest rangers and one of the town deputies walked out of the woods and into the clearing. Maggie jumped up and began to call them and motion them in the direction of the knoll.

"We're here! We're over here!" she called as she jumped up and down to get their attention. She ran over to hug them as they neared the tree. "Hurry, Digger's hurt!"

Sam and Stratton ran over to talk to Chris and get an update on Digger's medical condition while Deputy Campbell called headquarters to order a Medic helicopter to fly into the area and rush Digger to a hospital. They all worked quickly to make sure help was on the way.

"How did you find us?" Maggie asked while they opened their packs and brought out bottles of water and fresh bandages to place on Digger's cuts and scratches. They worked quickly and skillfully as they told Maggie and Chris about the most recent events.

"I'm sure Doc here has already told you we ended up arresting Wes yesterday for operating a drug lab in one of the campgrounds," Stratton began. "He spilled the beans and told us about Frank's plan to find Digger's fortune and then get rid of you for uncovering their first drug operation on the Skyway Trail."

Maggie nodded and watched them work on Digger as exhaustion and shock began to seep into every fiber of her being. Numbly, she listened as Sam continued to tell her about the events that led them to Digger's little valley.

"Wes wasn't sure what kind of fortune Digger had and wasn't much for hiking into the backwoods to find it. I think he was afraid he might get dirty," he said as they laughed. "So, he stuck with the drug operation. But evidently, Frank had some previous experience as a miner and knew enough about the mountains and geology to follow Digger and know what to look for when he saw it," he continued as they washed and bandaged Digger's wounds.

"How did he find this mine?" Maggie asked.

"He must have followed Digger for some time. He was waiting for the right opportunity to pilfer from the mine," Sam commented. "His biggest downfall was he just seemed to have a drug addiction and ended up using drugs every time he was with Wes. I think that was how Wes controlled him for as long as he did. Wes just kept Frank supplied with drugs."

"What happened to Frank?" Maggie asked as she gently slipped Stratton's pack under Digger's head when he began to heave and rack with another violent coughing spasm. "He tried to kill Digger in the mine yesterday and attacked me on the trail during the storm."

"We stopped by your cabin to warn you that Frank was going to try to get rid of you," Sam said with a smile. "Your cabin looks like a used car parking lot right now, by the way. With your jeep, Digger's truck, Doc's vehicle and several forest service vehicles, you could go into business. We saw the notes you left on the cabin door and headed this way as soon as we got a couple of deputies together so we could make an arrest when we found him," he continued as he looked at Maggie and Doc.

"We ran into him on the trail and arrested him there. He was higher than a kite, kept talking about some crazy people that just appeared out of nowhere and chased him across the mountain during the storm," Stratton chuckled. Maggie and Chris looked at each other and grinned. "He had some wild kind of story about a golden palace and a dog as big as a grizzly bear."

"The chopper is on its way, boys," Deputy Campbell said as he walked up to the group, "Should be here in about fifteen minutes."

Doc nodded his head and checked Digger's pulse then left him to the care of Sam and Stratton so he could talk to Maggie.

"It looks like I'm going to need to ride on the chopper with Digger to the hospital in case he needs me," he said as he gently touched her cheek. "He's going to be ok, but I just want to go along with them to make sure he gets the best possible treatment. I thought he might feel a little more comfortable on the trip if he had someone he knew ride along with him."

"Yes! You need to go with him. I would feel so much better if you did! He needs you more than I do right now. I'll be fine, don't worry about me," Maggie assured him as she urged him to go.

"Will you be ok getting back to the cabin?" he asked, concerned.

"Of, course I will. I'll walk back with the Rangers so don't worry, besides, I have Max." She smiled. "I'm just so glad this is all about over," she sighed. She looked at Chris; then shook her head. "So much for Digger's secret gold mine, guess it won't be a secret much longer. After today, everyone will know about it."

Chris chuckled, "Everyone already knows Digger has mines. He buys and sells them all the time. He probably has mines all over the mountains around here."

"Did you know about THIS mine?" Maggie asked alarmed.

"Not really, but it would be a simple matter for anyone to check in the county records and see where he owns property if they really wanted to find the exact locations." Chris shrugged his shoulders. "I always thought it was his own business, if he wanted me to know, he'd tell me. I knew he was working on a special vein in a secret mine, I just didn't know which one it was."

"It's common knowledge that Digger is usually looking for gold or trying to sell some piece of property where he's found a new vein. After all, Digger is the oldest gold miner on the mountain. It's what he's famous for in these parts." Chris smiled at her. "In fact, he sold me the mine I have."

Suddenly, something he said began to make a little sense in her numb brain, she asked, "What do you mean your mine?" She was a little confused when she realized he said he owned some kind of a mine.

"You know how much I love gemstones. When I decided to retire, I started to look for a place where I could work on gemstones whenever I had the time or the urge. Digger sold me a place that has a gemstone mine on the back of the property. I go down in it several times a week and find quartz, blue star sapphires and a crystalline sapphire now and then."

She stopped and looked at him incredulously, "The miner's hat!"

"Yes." He looked at her, puzzled, "I keep one hanging on the outside wall of my shed so it's easy to grab on my way down to the mine. It's too risky to go into a mine without one."

"I thought it was you!" she cried as she rushed to his arms and surprised him with her burst of affection. Maggie felt as though a dam broke inside her chest and released her from the sudden doubts and fears she harbored of Chris. She sobbed and burst into tears.

"When I had dinner at your cabin I saw the miner's hat on the wall of your shed and immediately thought you were the person I saw in the woods outside my cabin! It really frightened me. I kept seeing a man with a miner's hat."

"That must have been Frank, Maggie. Remember, Wes told the Rangers Frank followed Digger around for quite some time when he was trying to find his special mine," Chris said as he searched her face. "All he had to do was follow Digger through the woods long enough, and he would be able to find the mine."

"Yes, that makes sense," she answered thoughtfully. "I thought Digger was the only person who knew about the trail from my cabin to the Skyway because he was the one who helped me build it. He used it all the time on his treks and sometimes stopped by the cabin when he was out on the trails before going to one of his mines."

"Frank must have followed him from your place then," Chris said as he placed his arm around her shoulder. "It must have been pretty simple to follow him, or watch what you were up to once they found out where you live. Everyone knows Digger is like a father to you and spends a lot of time with you and Max."

Chris held her in his arms and tenderly kissed her on the lips. "I wish I knew before now what was worrying you. I knew there was something that was holding you back," he said sincerely. "I'd never do anything to hurt you, Maggie. If I only knew what those two characters were up to, I could have done something to help. I would do anything to protect you, Maggie, if you would only let me. I think you know how much I care for you."

"Well, I couldn't exactly tell you what I was thinking about if I suspected you of something." She smiled as a feeling of relief rushed over her. "Oh

Chris, I had such confused feelings, especially when I thought you were the one lurking in the woods near my house." She held him tightly, "Can you ever forgive me for misjudging you?"

"There's nothing to forgive," Chris answered sincerely. "It's all very understandable. Now, it's easy for me to see why you were so reluctant to get involved with me. I must have seemed like a real shady character at times!" he said with a wry smile. "So, where do we go from here? I'd really like to get to know you, Maggie."

"I'd like that very much, Doc," she said with a smile.

"Chris," he said as he kissed her passionately on the lips.

Maggie felt as though her heart was going to pound right out of her chest as he held her in a warm embrace. She grasped his arm to keep from falling down when her legs began to sway. The experience of true love almost took her breath away. She felt as though something broke away inside her chest as a warm feeling flooded through her. She smiled and she cleared her throat then brushed a loose curl hair away from her face.

"It may take some time for me to get used to this, though. We will have to take it slow, one day at a time. I'm used to being on my own, I'm pretty independent," Maggie said feeling flustered.

"We'll take it as slow as you want, Maggie." Chris smiled.

"Chris, I've dealt with some difficult situations in my own life and then, in my career, I worked with people in crisis who didn't always show me the good side of humanity. It was enough to make me want to get away from most people entirely." She slipped her hand in his and gazed into his eyes. "I guess it was always easier to protect myself by not trying to have a relationship with anyone than risk getting hurt. I think I'm finally going to be able to start sorting things out, though."

"What happened to help you change your mind, Maggie?"

She smiled and thoughtfully said, "I had a few guides along the way." A sudden tingling feeling came over her as she remembered the prophetic story told my old Ms. Cates. "Things are happening the way they were meant to happen." She shook her head in wonder. As they began to walk back toward Digger and the Rangers, Maggie mentally started putting more and more of the story together.

"It's a wonder you ever found me on the mountain in that terrible storm. It's not every day guys dash out into a powerful electrical storm to find someone who avoided them for a long time and continually tried to run away from them."

"I drove to your cabin to tell you about Wes being caught and warn you of Frank's threat. When I got there and saw Digger's truck and your jeep in the driveway, I was concerned. Then, I noticed the notes you left on the door, he explained. "That was pretty smart thinking. Just count your blessings I was able to read your map on how to get to Whipperwhill mine." He grinned as he wiped the mud from her face; then tenderly kissed her on the lips.

The sound of the helicopter began to grow louder as it neared the small valley where they waited. As soon as it appeared over the ridge and landed, they began to prepare Digger for his flight to the hospital. Chris gave instructions to the emergency personnel as they packed Digger into a gurney and loaded him into the chopper. Maggie leaned into the chopper and kissed Digger on the cheek.

"No pinching the nurses while you're at the hospital!" she teased as she waived and grinned. Digger weakly smiled before he began violently coughing again. Maggie stopped Chris as he started to climb aboard the helicopter and leave.

"I never did get a chance to thank you for saving me from drowning in the mine shaft," she shouted over the roar of the engines as she smiled and gazed into his eyes.

"Thank me? There is no need for you to thank me. I didn't do anything. You saved yourself," he said as he wrapped his arms around her waist.

"I mean, when you pulled me out of the cave," Maggie repeated, a little more loudly over the sound of the chopper engine.

"What are you talking about? I didn't pull you out of the cave, Maggie," Chris said emphatically. "I have no idea what you're talking about, seriously."

"You know, Chris, remember? When we were crawling through the tunnel of the cave, trying to get to the entrance - something happened in the back of the mine. I think it must have started to collapse, or something," Maggie said with a puzzled look. "The water surged forward and knocked me against the side of the cave. It knocked my head on a rock or something, because I was seeing stars! I think I may have even been unconscious for a little bit," Maggie continued feeling flustered and confused.

Chris looked as though he did not understand a word she said.

"I was so confused I didn't know where I was or how to get out. Then, just as I thought my lungs were going to burst from lack of air, when I thought I wasn't going to make it out of the cave, someone with really strong arms reached in and pulled me out." She leaned back to look into his eyes.

"Maggie," Chris hesitated. "I was unconscious - remember?"

Maggie shivered as the hair stood up on the back of her neck and a million tiny Goosebumps popped up on her arms.

"When I got to the opening of the cave Digger was right behind me holding on to one of my legs, so I pulled him out with me." Chris placed his arm across her shoulders while he prepared to climb into the helicopter; then continued.

"You were no where to be found! I panicked! I jumped up and tried to get back inside the cave to find you, but the force of the water knocked me down. That's all I remember until you woke me up," he said sincerely. "It wasn't me," Chris repeated. "I'm not the one who pulled you out," he said as the engine on the helicopter revved up and the propellers began to whirl.

"Then, who could it have been?" she exclaimed as Chris climbed into the helicopter to be by Digger's side. "Who could have pulled me out of the cave?"

Just as the doors began to shut and hold them securely inside, Digger slowly turned his head. He grinned his silly, crooked grin and hoarsely whispered,

"Dynamite Dan!" he exclaimed as he winked his eye.

Maggie's mouth flew open. She gasped in disbelief as the door closed and the helicopter lifted off and whirled away into the sky.

# HOMECOMING

Maggie placed a Mason jar filled with field daisies on the table and checked on the homemade bread baking in the oven as she glanced around the room one more time. Everything seemed to be in place and ready for the celebration to begin. Quickly, she glanced in the mirror, fluffed up her hair and straightened her soft cotton dress before going back outside to join the guests that gathered in the yard by her cabin.

Today was a special day, a homecoming - a day to remember. Today, Chris was bringing Digger home from the hospital and almost everyone came to her cabin to help them celebrate. Digger recovered from his brush with near death and was finally able to return home. Chris was bringing him there. Soon, Chris would be in her arms again. Her heart began to beat with anticipation and excitement.

Maggie glanced around the yard as it continued to fill with well-wishers. So many people came from town bringing gifts and food for the celebration. There were picnic tables coved with bright red checked table cloths, trays and plates filled with food and many quilts on the ground where people sat and talked to each other. Children played with Max in the creek. So much happiness and excitement was all around as the crowd waited for the arrival of the honored guest, it was easy to see a big celebration was about to begin.

Maggie watched Sam and his wife talk to Stratton and Rena as Zack and Jonah played stickball with Sam's girls on one side of the field. The three old timers found a comfortable place on the bench under the oak tree and began to whittle. A group of fiddlers played bluegrass music on the porch while several of the young people found a level place in the yard to dance. Maggie laughed when she saw Colleen even convinced Josh to try the two-step with Justin and Amy as they led the festivities.

She looked up when something scampered quickly around the corner of her cabin and realized someone even stopped by to bring Old Lady Cates. The hunched little woman looked right at home as she scurried around the yard and talked to herself while she checked out the herbs and plants, she gave Maggie to plant in her yard.

Everywhere Maggie looked, she saw friends and neighbors who seemed to be happy and at peace. Calm settled over the mountain and troubles were a million miles away. A sense of relief and peace washed over Maggie when the local deputies informed her that the county relocated Wes to the county jail. There, he would await his trial for participation in making illegal drugs on national park land. The judge ordered Frank placed in an intensive treatment program at a long-term mental health institution until he was capable of standing trial. His increased drug use appeared to leave him in such a psychotic state he was now unable to distinguish reality from the monsters he saw in his head.

Authorities were still looking for Hubert T. Brown to question him about Wes' allegations he was behind the illegal drug operation and the attempt on Maggie and Digger's lives. Brown seemed to have disappeared after the May Day celebration and no one heard from him since. Voters vetoed the petitions he tried to pass in the elections immediately when some local reporters investigated them and discovered a company that would bring more harm to the area than benefits backed his campaign.

Suddenly, Max started to bark and leap into the air when Chris pulled his white truck into the yard. The crowd began to cheer and gather around the door as they quickly ushered Digger out of the truck and into the yard. Digger looked as though he could not wait to get into the heart of a new tale with everyone gathered around him. Maggie could hear the beginning of a tall one as he started to tell of his adventure in the mine and brush with near death.

Maggie's heart began to pound in her chest as she walked slowly into the shade of the trees to meet Chris. He walked toward her and gathered her into his arms. Maggie could hear the fiddlers begin a lively tune while someone on the porch called out to the crowd, "Let the party begin!"

Printed in the United States
63622LVS00006B/1-150